I0615449

Monier Williams

Indian Epic Poetry

Monier Williams

Indian Epic Poetry

ISBN/EAN: 9783741127106

Manufactured in Europe, USA, Canada, Australia, Japa

Cover: Foto ©Andreas Hilbeck / pixelio.de

Manufactured and distributed by brebook publishing software
(www.brebook.com)

Monier Williams

Indian Epic Poetry

INDIAN EPIC POETRY;

BEING

THE SUBSTANCE OF

LECTURES

RECENTLY GIVEN AT OXFORD:

WITH

A FULL ANALYSIS OF THE RÁMÁYAṆA

AND OF THE

LEADING STORY OF THE MAHÁ-BHÁRATA.

BY MONIER WILLIAMS, M.A.

OF UNIVERSITY COLLEGE, OXFORD,

BODEN PROFESSOR OF SANSKRIT, &C.

WILLIAMS AND NORGATE,

14, HENRIETTA STREET, COVENT GARDEN, LONDON;

AND

20, SOUTH FREDERICK STREET, EDINBURGH.

MDCCCLXIII.

OXFORD:

PRINTED BY T. COMBE, E. PICKARD HALL, AND H. LATHAM,

PRINTERS TO THE UNIVERSITY.

PREFACE.

THE following pages contain the substance of a public lecture delivered by me at Oxford on the 9th of May, 1862. They also embody much of the information on the subject of Indian Epic Poetry, which I have conveyed to my classes in a more familiar manner during the past year.

The Rámáyaṇa and Mahá-bhárata, unlike the Iliad and the Odyssey, are closely connected with the present religious faith of millions; and these millions, be it remembered, acknowledge British sway, and have a right to expect the British public to take an interest in works which are the time-honoured repository of their legendary history and mythology, of their ancient customs and observances, as well as of their most cherished gems of poetry. It needs no argument to show that some knowledge of the two great Indian Epics ought to be required of all who hold office in India, whether in the Civil Service, or in any other capacity. Nor is it right, or even possible, for Englishmen generally to remain any longer wholly ignorant of the nature and contents of these poems. British India is now brought so close to us by steam and electricity, and the present condition of the Hindú community, social, political, and religious, forces itself so peremptorily on our attention, that the duty of studying the past history of our Eastern empire, so far as it can be collected from ancient Sanskṛit literature, can no longer be evaded by educated men. Hitherto the Indian Epics, which, in the absence of all real history, are the only guides to the early condition of our Hindú fellow-subjects, have been sealed books to the majority of Englishmen. Continuous translations of works, so tediously spun out, have never been accomplished: no reliable summaries have been printed of either poem *;

* A short outline of the story of the Mahá-bhárata, written by Prof. Wilson, has been prefixed to Prof. Johnson's useful edition of Selections from the text of that work. It is, however, but a bare sketch; and the absence of references makes it impossible to verify some of the statements. For instance, Páṇḍu is described as incapable of succession to the throne; whereas it will be seen from my Summary (p. 95) that he not only reigned,

and such metrical versions of the more beautiful episodes as have from time to time appeared are so scattered about in reviews and ephemeral publications, as to be practically inaccessible.

I trust, then, that the present volume may do something towards supplying a manifest want. Its object is to exhibit, in a popular manner, the general features of Indian Epic Poetry, to indicate the points of contact and divergence between that poetry and the Greek epos, and to furnish the Sanskṛit scholar with a full analysis of the Rámáyaṇa and of the leading story of the Mahá-bhárata. In justice to myself I should state that the size of the book does not represent the amount of labour employed on its composition. To produce a few insignificant pages, I have had to work my way through volumes of Sanskṛit; but I shall not regret the time I have devoted to the task, if any useful purpose be thereby served.

I should also state that, in writing the following lectures, I have had occasion constantly to refer to the various excellent reviews and anonymous critiques

---

but extended his empire in all directions. Again, Yudhishṭhira is said to be vanquished at dice by Duryodhana; whereas he does not play at all with Duryodhana, but with S'akuni (Saubala), who appears to have been a form of Dwápara; see my Summary, p. 103, and p. 123, note; and compare Udyoga-parva 10, Swargárohaṇika-parva 167.

on Sanskṛit literature which have appeared from time to time in India and Europe, and to which I acknowledge my obligations. I have, moreover, derived great benefit from the valuable 'Sanskṛit Texts' of Dr. John Muir, to whom also I am indebted for many pertinent criticisms on my statements as they passed through the press.

M. W.

OXFORD, May 1863.

CONTENTS.

LECTURES ON INDIAN EPIC POETRY.

ANALYSIS OF THE RÁMÁYAṆA.

SUMMARY OF THE LEADING STORY OF THE MAHÁ-BHÁRATA.

ERRATUM.

Page 31, line 7, *for* Vaitariṇí *read* Vaitaraní.

INDIAN EPIC POETRY.

IN India, literature, like the whole face of nature, is on a gigantic scale. Poetry, born amid the majestic scenery of the Himálayas, and fostered in a climate which inflamed the imaginative powers, developed itself with Oriental luxuriance. Although the Hindús, like the Greeks, have only two great epic poems, namely, the Rámáyaṇa and Mahá-bhárata *, yet to compare these with the Iliad and the Odyssey, is to compare the Indus and the Ganges, rising in the snows of the world's most colossal ranges, swollen by numerous tributaries, spreading into vast shallows or branching into deep divergent channels, with the streams of Attica or the mountain-torrents of Thessaly. There is, in fact, an immensity of bulk about this, as about every other department of Sanskṛit literature, which to a European mind, accustomed to a more limited horizon, is absolutely bewildering.

Nevertheless, a sketch, however imperfect, of the two Indian epics can scarcely fail to interest the admirers of Homer; for all true poetry,

* I am here speaking of that form of epic poetry which may be called natural and spontaneous as distinguished from artificial. Whether the Indian epics (Itihásas) or even the Iliad can be said to answer Aristotle's strict definition of Epos, is another question. Specimens of the more artificial epic poetry (kávyas) are not wanting in Sanskṛit; ex. gr. the Raghu-vanśa by Kálidása, on the same subject as the Rámáyaṇa; the Śiśupála-badha of Mágha, on a subject taken from the 7th chapter of the 2d book (or Sabhá-parva) of the Mahá-bhárata; the Kirátárjuníya of Bháravi, on a subject taken from the 4th chapter of the 3d book (or Vana-parva) of the Mahá-bhárata; the Nalodaya, said to be by Kálidása, and the Naishadha by Śrí Harsha, on the same subject as the Nala. These are all artificial poems written when men began to be learned and critical rather than poetical. The story of Ráma and many of the episodes of the Mahá-bhárata are stock-subjects, which appear over and over again in the later literature.

whether European or Asiatic, must have features of resemblance; and no poems could have achieved celebrity in the East as these have done, had they not addressed themselves to feelings and affections common to human nature, and belonging alike to Englishmen and Hindús.

I propose therefore, before commencing a dry analysis of the Rámáyaṇa and Mahá-bhárata, to give a brief general idea of their character and contents, comparing them in some important particulars with each other, and pointing out the most obvious features of similarity or difference, which must strike every classical scholar who contrasts them with the Iliad and the Odyssey.

To begin with the *Rámáyaṇa*, said to have been composed by the poet *Válmíki*, and so called from two Sanskṛit words *Ráma* and *ayana*, meaning 'the adventures of Ráma' (who as an incarnation of Vishṇu, the Preserver *, is still a favourite deity in parts of India, especially in districts of Oude and Bahár where Kṛishṇa has not supplanted him). This is the more ancient of the two Indian epics. For centuries its existence was probably only oral, and we know from the 4th chapter of the 1st book that it had its minstrels and reciters like the Greek *ῥαψῳδοί*.

To fix the period of the composition of the work as we now possess it with absolute certainty is as impossible as to settle the date of any other portion of Sanskṛit literature. We can only make conjectures from such chronological data as are furnished by internal evidence.

Songs in celebration of great heroes were doubtless current in India quite as early as the Homeric poems in Greece, and perhaps earlier.

---

* There are three Rámas in Hindú mythology (Paraśu-Ráma, Ráma-chandra, and Bala-Ráma), all three regarded as avatárs of Vishṇu. The last is the Hindú Hercules, and, as the elder brother of Kṛishṇa, appears frequently in the Mahá-bhárata. Paraśu-Ráma, as the son of the sage Jamadagni, is the type of Bráhmanism arrayed in opposition to the military caste. He is introduced once into the Rámáyaṇa, but only to exhibit his inferiority to the real hero Ráma-chandra, who, as the son of Daśaratha, a prince of the solar dynasty, typifies the conquering Kshatriyas, advancing towards the south and subjugating the barbarous aborigines, represented by the demon Rávaṇa and his followers.

No mention is indeed made of Ráma in the Veda, but he may be regarded as the first real (Kshatriya) hero of the post-Vedic age; and looking to the great simplicity of the style of the Rámáyaṇa, the absence in the purer version of any reliable allusion to Buddhism as an established fact *, and to practices ascertained to have prevailed in India as early as the fourth century before Christ; observing at the same time the evidence it affords of that independent spirit among the military tribes of the north †, and of that tendency to sceptical inquiry even among Bráhmans, which, working its way southwards, led to the great Buddhist reformation ‡, we cannot be far wrong in asserting that a great portion of the Rámáyaṇa, if not the entire Rámáyaṇa now before us, must have been current in India as early as the fifth century B.C.

It is, of course, a principal characteristic of epic poetry, as distinguished from lyrical, that it should concern itself more with external action than internal feelings. It is this which makes epos the natural expression of early national life. When centuries of trial have turned the popular mind inwards, and men begin to speculate, to reason, to elaborate language and cultivate science, there may be no lack of refined poetry, but the spontaneous production of epic song is as impossible as for an octogenarian to delight in the giants and giant-killers of his childhood. The Rámáyaṇa then, as reflecting the Hindú character in ancient times, may be expected to abound in stirring incidents of exaggerated heroic action.

The main story of the poem, although often interrupted by long episodes which have little bearing on the plot, flows in a more continuous and traceable course than in the Mahá-bhárata. It may be divided into three principal parts or periods, corresponding to the three

* In the 12th chapter of the 1st book of the Bengálí recension, Śramaṇas or Buddhist mendicants are mentioned, and some verses in a more modern metre have been added to chapter 109, book II, in which Buddha is named, but these passages are evidently later interpolations.

† See the episode of Viśwámitra.

‡ The speech of the Bráhman Jáváli (Ram. II. 108) contains infidel doctrines.

chief epochs in the life of Ráma. I. The account of his youthful days; his education and residence at the court of his father Daśaratha, king of Ayodhyá; his happy marriage to Sítá, and his inauguration as heir-apparent or crown-prince. II. The circumstances that led to his banishment; the description of his exile and residence in the forests of central India. III. His war with the giants or demons of the south for the recovery of his wife Sítá, who had been carried off by their chief Rávaṇa; his conquest and destruction of Rávaṇa, and his restoration to the throne of his father.

In the first two portions of the poem there is little extravagance of fiction, but in the third the Indian poet mars the beauty of his descriptions by the wildest exaggeration and hyperbole.

At the commencement we are introduced to the Hindú Olympus, where the gods are met in solemn conclave, dismayed at the insolence of the ten-headed demon-monarch, Rávaṇa, who from his island-throne in Ceylon menaced earth and heaven with destruction. The secret of his power lay in a long course of penance*, which according to the Hindú conception gained for him who practised it, however evil his designs, superiority to the gods themselves, and enabled Rávaṇa to extort from the god Brahmá this remarkable boon—that neither gods, genii, demons, nor giants should be able to vanquish him. As, however, in his pride, he scorned to ask security from man also, he remained vulnerable from this one quarter, if any mortal could be found capable of coping with him. At the request of the gods†,

* According to the Hindú theory, the performance of penances was like making deposits in the bank of heaven. By degrees an enormous credit was accumulated, which enabled the depositor to draw to the amount of his savings, without fear of his drafts being refused payment. The power gained in this manner by weak mortals was so enormous, that gods as well as men were equally at the mercy of these all but omnipotent ascetics; and it is remarkable, that even the gods are described as engaging in penance and austerities, in order, it may be presumed, not to be outdone by human beings. Śiva was so engaged when the god of love shot an arrow at him.

† The address of the alarmed gods to Vishṇu is nobly given in the 10th chapter of the Raghu-vanśa (Kálidása's epitomized version of the Rámáyaṇa). There is a trans-

Vishṇu consents to become mortal for this purpose, and four sons are born to Daśaratha, king of Ayodhyá (Oude), from his three wives; the eldest, Ráma-chandra, possessing half the nature of Vishṇu; the second (Bharata) a fourth part; and the other two (Lakshmaṇa and Śatrughna) sharing the remaining quarter between them. While yet a stripling, Ráma and his brothers are taken to the court of Janaka, king of Mithilá*. He had a wonderful bow, once the property of Śiva, and had given out, that the man who could bend it should win his beautiful daughter Sítá. On the arrival of Ráma and his brothers the bow is brought on an eight-wheeled platform, drawn by no less than 5000 men. Ráma not only bends the bow, but snaps it asunder with a concussion so terrible that the whole assembly is thrown to the ground, and the earth quivers as if a mountain were rent in twain.

---

lation in the Calcutta Review (XLV) which, though incomplete, gives a fair representation of the original. The gods thus commence their address:

"O thou, whom threefold might and splendour veil,
Maker, Preserver, and Destroyer—hail!
Thy gaze surveys this world from clime to clime,
Thyself immeasurable in space or time:
To no corrupt desires, no passions prone:
Unconquered Conqueror—Infinite—Unknown:
Though in one form Thou veil'st Thy might divine,
Still at Thy pleasure every form is Thine:
Pure crystals thus prismatic hues assume,
As varying lights, and varying tints illume:
Men think Thee absent—Thou art ever near:
Pitying those sorrows which Thou ne'er canst fear:
Unsordid penance Thou alone canst pay:
Unchanged—unchanging—old without decay:—
Thou knowest all things:—who Thy praise can state?
Createdst all things, Thyself uncreate."

* It is evident that Mithilá, situated quite towards the east, was an Áryan country at this time, for Janaka is described (Rám. I. 12) as conversant with all the Śástras and Vedas.

Sítá thus becomes the wife of Ráma. On his return to his father's capital preparations are made for his inauguration, as successor to the throne, when the mother of one of his brothers (Bharata), jealous of the preference shewn to Ráma, demands of the king the fulfilment of a promise, made to her in former years, that he would grant her any two boons she asked. A promise of this kind in eastern countries is quite inviolable; and the king being required to banish his favourite son Ráma and instal Bharata, is forced to comply.

Ráma, therefore, with his wife Sítá and his brother Lakshmaṇa are banished; and the heart-broken king pines away in inconsolable anguish. Here occurs a touching episode (Ram. II. 63). The king, in the midst of his despondency, confesses that his present bereavement is a punishment for a deed of blood committed by himself accidentally in his youthful days. Thus it happened *:

One day when rains refreshed the earth, and caused my heart to swell with joy,
When, after scorching with his rays the parchèd ground, the summer sun
Had passed towards the south; when cooling breezes chased away the heat,
And grateful clouds arose; when frogs and pea-fowl sported, and the deer
Seemed drunk with glee, and all the wingèd creation, dripping as if drowned,
Plumed their dank feathers on the tops of wind-rocked-trees, and falling showers
Covered the mountains till they looked like watery heaps, and torrents poured
Down from their sides, filled with loose stones and red as dawn with mineral earth,
Winding like serpents in their course; then at that charming season I,
Longing to breathe the air, went forth, with bow and arrow in my hand,
To seek for game, if haply by the river-side a buffalo
Or elephant or other animal might cross, at eve, my path,
Coming to drink. Then in the dusk I heard the sound of gurgling water:
Quickly I took my bow, and aiming toward the sound, shot off the dart.
A cry of mortal agony came from the spot,—a human voice
Was heard, and a poor hermit's son fell pierced and bleeding in the stream.
"Ah! wherefore then, he cried, am I a harmless hermit's son struck down?
Hither to this lone brook I came at eve to fill my water-jar.

* I translate as nearly as I can word for word, in a metre resembling the sixteen-syllable heroic verse of the original.

By whom have I been smitten? whom have I offended? Oh! I grieve
Not for myself or my own fate, but for my parents, old and blind,
Who perish in my death. Ah! what will be the end of that loved pair,
Long guided and supported by my hand? this barbèd dart has pierced
Both me and them." Hearing that piteous voice, I Dasaratha,
Who meant no harm to any human creature, young or old, became
Palsied with fear; my bow and arrows dropped from my senseless hands;
And I approached the place in horror; there with dismay I saw,
Stretched on the bank, an innocent hermit-boy, writhing in pain and smeared
With dust and blood, his knotted hair dishevelled, and a broken jar
Lying beside him. I stood petrified and speechless—he on me
Fixed full his eyes, and then, as if to burn my inmost soul, he said,
"How have I wronged thee, monarch? that thy cruel hand has smitten me—
Me a poor hermit's son, born in the forest: father, mother, child
Hast thou transfixed with this one arrow: they, my parents, sit at home
Expecting my return, and long will cherish hope—a prey to thirst
And agonizing fears. Go to my father—tell him of my fate,
Lest his dread curse consume thee, as the flame devours the withered wood.
But first in pity draw thou forth the shaft that pierces to my heart,
And checks the gushing life-blood, as the bank obstructs the bounding stream."
He ceased, and as he rolled his eyes in agony, and quivering writhed
Upon the ground, I slowly drew the arrow from the poor boy's side.
Then with a piteous look, his features set in terror, he expired.
Distracted at the grievous crime, wrought by my hand unwittingly;
Sadly I thought within myself, how best I might repair the wrong.
Then took the way he had directed me towards the hermitage.
There I beheld his parents, old and blind; like two clipped wingless birds
Sitting forlorn, without their guide, awaiting his arrival anxiously,
And, to beguile their weariness, conversing of him tenderly.
Quickly they caught the sound of footsteps, and I heard the old man say,
With chiding voice, "Why hast thou lingered, child? Quick give us both to drink
A little water. Long forgetful of us, in the cooling stream
Hast thou disported; come in—for thy mother yearneth for her son.
If she or I in ought have caused thee pain, or spoken hasty words,
Think on thy hermit's duty of forgiveness; bear them not in mind.
Thou art the refuge of us refugeless—the eyes of thy blind sire.
Why art thou silent? Speak! Bound up in thee are both thy parents' lives."
He ceased, and I stood paralysed—till by an effort resolutely
Collecting all my powers of utterance, with faltering voice I said,

"Pious and noble hermit; I am not thy son—I am the king:
Wandering with bow and arrow by a stream, seeking for game, I pierced
Unknowingly thy child. The rest I need not tell. Be gracious to me."
Hearing my pitiless words, announcing his bereavement, he remained
Senseless awhile; then drawing a deep sigh, his face all bathed in tears,
He spake to me as I approached him suppliantly, and slowly said,
"Hadst thou not come thyself, to tell the awful tale, its load of guilt
Had crushed thy head into ten thousand fragments. This ill-fated deed
Was wrought by thee unwittingly, O king, else hadst thou not been spared,
And all the race of Rághavas had perished. Lead us to the place:
All bloody though he be, and lifeless, we must look upon* our son
For the last time, and clasp him in our arms." Then weeping bitterly
The pair, led by my hand, came to the spot and fell upon their son.
Thrilled by the touch, the father cried, "My child, hast thou no greeting for us?
No word of recognition? wherefore liest thou here upon the ground?
Art thou offended? or am I no longer loved by thee my son?
See here thy mother. Thou wert ever dutiful towards us both.
Why wilt thou not embrace me? speak one tender word. Whom shall I hear
Reading again the sacred śástra in the early morning hours?
Who now will bring me roots and fruits to feed me like a cherished guest?
How, weak and blind, can I support thy aged mother, pining for her son?
Stay! Go not yet to Death's abode—stay with thy parents yet one day,
To-morrow we will both go with thee on the dreary way. Forlorn
And sad, deserted by our child, without protector in the wood,
Soon shall we both depart toward the mansions of the King of death."
Thus bitterly lamenting, he performed the funeral rites; then turning
Towards me thus addressed me, standing reverently near—"I had
But this one child, and thou hast made me childless. Now strike down
The father: I shall feel no pain in death. But thy requital be
That sorrow for a child shall one day bring thee also to the grave."

After narrating this affecting incident of his early life, king Daśaratha, struck with remorse and sorrow, sickens and dies†. The banished Ráma establishes himself with Sítá and his brother Laksh-

* This is literally translated. It is well known that blind people commonly talk of themselves as able to see.

† His body is burnt with much pomp; and we may note, as a proof of the antiquity of the poem, that his widows are not burnt with him.

maṇa in the Daṇḍaka forest near the Godávarí*. There Sítá is carried off by Rávaṇa, the demon-king of Ceylon. Upon this, Ráma makes an alliance with Sugríva, king of the monkeys, or foresters, and assisted by them and by Vibhíshaṇa, the brother of Rávaṇa†, invades the capital of the ravisher, slays Rávaṇa himself, and after recovering Sítá returns to Ayodhyá, of which he assumes the sovereignty.

Such is a brief sketch of the story of the Rámáyaṇa; which, notwithstanding its wild exaggerations, rests, in all probability, on a foundation of historical truth. It is certainly likely that at some remote period, probably not long after the settlement of the Áryan races in the plains of the Ganges, a body of invaders, headed by a bold leader, and aided by the barbarous hill-tribes, may have attempted to force their way into the peninsula of India as far as Ceylon. The heroic exploits of the chief would naturally become the theme of songs and ballads, the hero himself would be deified‡, the wild mountaineers and foresters of the Vindhya and neighbouring hills, who assisted him, would be poetically converted into monkeys§, and the powerful but savage aborigines of the south into many-headed ogres and blood-lapping demons (called Rákshasas). These songs would at first be

* The Daṇḍaka forest is described as beginning south of the Jumná and extending to the Godávarí. The whole of that country was a wilderness, inhabited by savage tribes (who are spoken of as Rákshasas) and infested by wild beasts.

† Vibhíshaṇa is described by his sister Súrpaṇakhá as having forsaken the practices of the Rákshasas. Dr. Muir thinks that he may represent a southern tribe which had been converted to Bráhmanism, or had adopted Bráhmanical usages. Vibhíshaṇas cha dharmátmá Rákshasáchára-varjitah. Rám. III. 23. He was evidently a great contrast to his brother Rávaṇa; see also Mahá-bhár. III. 15913—18.

‡ Heroism, undaunted bravery, and personal strength will always find worshippers in India. It is recorded that a number of Hindús commenced worshipping the late John Nicolson, one of the bravest and noblest of men, under the name of Nikkil Seyn. He endeavoured to put a stop to the absurdity by having some of them punished, but they persisted in their worship notwithstanding.

§ It would be natural to call them monkeys out of mere contempt. The Rákshasas, who represented the savage and ferocious aborigines of India (and are some-the property of the Kshatriya or fighting caste, whose deeds they celebrated; but the ambitious Bráhmans, who aimed at religious and intellectual supremacy, would soon see the policy of collecting the rude ballads which they could not suppress, and moulding them to their own purposes *.

This task was committed to a poet writing under their influence. Those ballads which described too plainly the independence of the military caste, and their successful opposition to the sacerdotal, were modified, obscured by allegory, or rendered improbable by monstrous

---

times called *anárya*, 'base-born,' in opposition to *árya*), had been gradually driven southwards by the Áryans, but it is clear that they made great resistance in the north at the time the Ṛig-veda was composed. They are there spoken of (under the name of Dasyus, Yátudhánas, &c.) as monstrous in form, godless, haters of Bráhmans, disturbers of sacred rites, inhuman, eaters of human and horse-flesh. See Muir, Sanskṛit texts, II. p. 435. In the Rámáyaṇa (III. i. 15) they are described as black, with woolly hair and thick lips (Muir II. pp. 426. 437). The following description is taken from Rám. III. i. 22: "Men-devouring Rákshasas of various shapes and wild-beasts dwell in this vast forest. They harass the devotees in the settlements. These shapeless and ill-looking monsters testify their abominable character by various cruel and terrific displays. These base-born wretches (anárya) perpetrate the greatest outrages. Changing their shapes and hiding in the thickets they delight in terrifying the devotees. They cast away the sacrificial ladles and vessels (śrug-bháṇḍam), pollute the cooked oblations, and defile the offerings with blood. They utter frightful sounds in the ears of the faithful." Virádha, a Rákshasa, is said (Rám. III. vii. 5; Muir II. 427) to be "like a mountain-peak, with long legs, a huge body, a crooked nose, hideous eyes, a long face, pendent belly, &c., like Death with an open mouth." The Nishádas of the Puráṇas, though described as dwarfish, have similar features, and no doubt intended for the same race. In the same way, in describing races unknown to the Greeks, such as the Cyclopes, Lærstrygones, Centauri, &c., Homer and other Grecian writers are given to exaggeration, and relate the most absurd fables.

* At the very outset of the poem there is clear evidence that however the original songs of the Rámáyaṇa may have belonged to the Kshatriya caste, the poem was moulded into its present form under direct sacerdotal influence. King Daśaratha at the seat of his empire is described as surrounded by wise Bráhmans, who, as his ministers, direct all the affairs of his government. (I. vii. 2, &c.)

mythological embellishments. Any circumstances which appeared to militate against the Bráhmanical system were speciously explained away, glossed over, or mystified. Thus when Daśaratha kills the boy in the wood, the dying youth is made to explain that, although a hermit's son, he is no Bráhman, thereby relieving the king from the guilt of Bráhmanicide, which according to Manu was unpardonable either in this world or the next (Manu VIII. 381. XII. 55). Again, the account of Ráma-chandra's victory over Paraśu-Ráma—the mythical champion of the sacerdotal caste*—is slurred over and surrounded with a haze of mystic uncertainty; while the interesting episode which relates at full Viśwámitra's quarrel with the great saint Vaśishṭha, and the success of the former, though a Kshatriya, in elevating himself to a Bráhman's rank, introduces the wildest hyperbole, with the manifest object of investing the position of a Bráhman with unapproachable grandeur, and deterring others from attempts in the same direction †.

* In the later mythology Paraśu-Ráma is always represented as a previous incarnation of Vishṇu, though his divinity does not appear to be clearly recognised in the Rámáyaṇa. At any rate, before he challenged Ráma-chandra, that is, before one incarnation challenged another, we must suppose that the divine essence had left the first. Paraśu-Ráma, the ex-incarnation, is compelled to acknowledge the superiority of Ráma-chandra, but there is no very intelligible account of the victory over the Bráhmanical champion. In the Mahá-bhárata, on the other hand, which has less uniformly the stamp of Bráhmanism, Ráma is described as shooting arrows at Paraśu-Ráma, and striking him senseless. See Wilson's Uttara-Ráma-charitra, p. 299, note.

† Viśwámitra, son of Gádhi, was a prince of the lunar race, sovereign of Kanoj, and the district of Magadha (or Patna). He had a tremendous conflict with the bráhman Vaśishṭha for the possession of the cow of plenty (Káma-dhenu, also called Śavalá), which no doubt typified the earth (go) or India. At the command of Vaśishṭha, the cow created hordes of barbarians, such as Pahlavas or Persians, Śakas or Scythians, Yavanas or Greeks, Kambojas, &c., by whose aid Vaśishṭha conquered Viśwámitra. The latter, convinced of the superior power inherent in Bráhmanism, determined to raise himself to that dignity; and the Rámáyaṇa records how, in order to effect this object, he increased the rigour of his austerities for thousands of years. See Rám. I. 51—65. The gods, who had a hard struggle to hold their own against over-zealous ascetics, did what they could to interrupt him, and partially succeeded. Viśwámitra

Notwithstanding these and other even greater drawbacks, such as that of extreme diffuseness, there is not in the whole range of Sanskṛit literature a more charming poem than the Rámáyaṇa. The classical purity, clearness, and simplicity of its style, the exquisite touches of true poetic feeling with which it abounds, its graphic descriptions of heroic incidents and nature's grandest scenes, the deep acquaintance it displays with the conflicting workings and most refined emotions of the human heart, all entitle it to rank among the most beautiful compositions that have appeared at any period or in any country. It is like a spacious and delightful garden; here and there allowed to run wild, but teeming with fruits and flowers, watered by perennial streams, and even its most tangled jungle intersected with delightful pathways. The character of Ráma is nobly pourtrayed. It is only too consistently unselfish to be human. We must in fact bear in mind that he is half a god. Yet though occasionally dazzled by flashes from his superhuman nature, we are not often blinded or bewildered by it. At least in the earlier portion of the poem he is not generally represented as more than a heroic, nobleminded, pious, and virtuous man, whose bravery, unselfish generosity, filial obedience, tender attachment to his wife, love for his brothers, and freedom from all resentful feelings, we can appreciate and admire *. When he falls a victim to the spite of his father's second wife, he cherishes no sense of wrong. When his father decides on banishing him, not a murmur escapes his lips. In noble

yielded for a time to the seductions of the nymph Menaká, sent by them to call back his thoughts to sensual objects. A daughter (S'akuntalá) was the result of this temporary backsliding. However, in the end, the obstinate old ascetic was too much for the whole troop of deities. He obtained complete power over his passions, and when the gods still refused to brahmanize him, he began creating new heavens and new gods, and had already manufactured a few stars, when the celestial host thought it prudent to give in, and make him a Bráhman.

* When identified with the deity, he seems himself unconscious of his true character. (See Yuddha-káṇḍa, 119.) It is even possible that the passages which make him an incarnation of Vishṇu may be later interpolations.

language he expresses his resolution to sacrifice himself rather than allow his parent to break his pledged word*. As to Sítá, she is a paragon of domestic virtues. Her pleadings for permission to accompany her husband into banishment breathe such noble devotion to her lord and master, that it may be worth while to subjoin a few extracts†.

A wife must share her husband's fate. My duty is to follow thee
Where'er thou goest. Apart from thee, I would not dwell in heaven itself.
Deserted by her lord, a wife is like a miserable corpse.
Close as thy shadow would I cleave to thee in this life and hereafter.
Thou art my king, my guide, my only refuge, my divinity.
It is my fixed resolve to follow thee. If thou must wander forth
Through thorny trackless forests, I will go before thee, treading down
The prickly brambles to make smooth thy path. Walking before thee, I
Shall feel no weariness: the forest-thorns will seem like silken robes;
The bed of leaves a couch of down. To me the shelter of thy presence
Is better far than stately palaces, and paradise itself.
Protected by thy arm, gods, demons, men shall have no power to harm me.
With thee I'll live contentedly on roots and fruits. Sweet or not sweet,
If given by thy hand, they will to me be like the food of life.
Roaming with thee in desert wastes, a thousand years will be a day;
Dwelling with thee, e'en hell itself would be to me a heaven of bliss.

Time would fail, if we were to attempt even the briefest epitome of all the episodes of the Rámáyaṇa. One has been already noticed. Another curious legend is the story of the Ganges (Rám. I. 36–44).

---

* He persists in this resolution, notwithstanding the entreaties of his mother Kauśalyá, the taunting remarks of his fiery brother Lakshmaṇa, and his own anxious fear for the safety of his wife Sítá, who determines on accompanying him. Again, after the death of his father, when Bharata makes an expedition into the forest to urge Ráma to return to Ayodhyá and accept the government, and when all the citizens add their entreaties, and the atheistical Jáváli his sophistical arguments, Ráma replies, "There is nothing greater than truth; and truth should be esteemed the most sacred of all things. The Vedas have their sole foundation in truth. Devoted by promise to my father's commands, I will neither, through covetousness nor forgetfulness nor blind ignorance, break down the barrier of truth." II. cix. 17.

† I have translated these nearly literally, but not consecutively. The substance of them will be found in Gorresio's Rámáyaṇa, vol. II. p. 74 et seq.

Gangá, the personified Ganges, was the eldest daughter of Himavat, lord of mountains, her younger sister being Umá. Sagara, a king of Ayodhyá, of the solar race, had 60,000 sons, who were directed by their father to look for a horse which had been stolen by a Rákshasa at an Aśwa-medha or horse-sacrifice. Having first without success searched the earth, they proceeded to dig up the ground towards the infernal regions. Meeting with the sage Kapila, they accused him of the theft, which enraged him to such a degree, that without more ado he reduced them all to ashes. Sagara's grandson sometime afterwards found the ashes, and commenced performing the funeral obsequies of his relatives with water, but was told that only Gangá could do this with her sacred stream. Neither Sagara, however, nor his grandson could devise any means for effecting the descent of the heavenly river. It was reserved for his great-grandson, Bhagíratha, by his austerities to bring down the sacred stream from heaven. In her descent she fell first with great fury on the head of Śiva, who had promised to break her fall, thinking to sweep him down to the infernal regions. Śiva, however, quelled the pride of the goddess, and compelled her to wander for many years in the tresses of his hair. Then, by further austerities, Bhagíratha forced her to flow over the earth, and to follow him thence to the ocean (therefore called Ságara), and thence to the infernal regions (Pátála), where she watered the ashes of Sagara's sons, and became the means of conveying their souls to heaven. Hence a common name for the Ganges is Bhágírathí. This river is also called Jáhnaví, because in its course it inundated the sacrificial ground of the sage Jahnu, who thereupon without any ceremony drank up its waters, but consented to discharge them again from his ears. Notwithstanding all this wild fiction, the description of the descent of the river and its rushing course is highly poetical *.

Perhaps, however, the most noticeable episode is that of Viśwámitra, before referred to, which contains many remarkable legends. Before

* The beautiful translation of Dean Milman is well known. The story is also told in the Mahá-bhárata, Vana-parva 9920, &c.

passing to the Mahá-bhárata, it may be well to state that the Rámáyaṇa (exclusive of the Uttara-káṇḍa) consists of about 50,000 lines, or 24,000 verses. The great flexibility of Sanskṛit, and the easy unfettered flow of its common heroic metre *, offered great facilities for interpolations, alterations, and additions. Hence there are two distinct recensions or versions of the poem; one belonging to Benares and the north-west, which is probably the nearest extant approach to the primitive text; the other, which is less pure and more 'spun out,' to Calcutta and Bengal proper †. It is probable that the entire last book, or Uttara-káṇḍa, of the Rámáyaṇa, in which Ráma receives adoration as a god, and is even identified with the Supreme ‡, and the introductory chapters, giving

* The metre in which the greater part of the Rámáyaṇa and Mahá-bhárata is written is the common śloka (see my Sanskṛit Grammar, 935), in which only four syllables out of sixteen in each line are really fixed. The others may be either long or short. The Indra-vajrá variety of Trishṭubh is however frequently used in the Mahá-bhárata, and in the Rámáyaṇa, at the end of the chapters, we have often the Jagatí (Gram. 937. 941). The former of these has eleven syllables to the half-line, the latter twelve; and the quantity of every syllable being fixed generally interferes with the simplicity and freedom of the style.

† With regard to the Bengal (Gauḍa) recension, it may be observed that in Bengal, where there is little demand for MSS., learned men have been their own scribes, and have always tampered more freely with original texts than the unlearned copyists of the north. In 1806 and 1810 Carey and Marshman published the text and translation of two books out of the seven which complete this recension; but here and there they have followed the northern. Twenty years afterwards Augustus William Schlegel published the text of two books of the northern version, with a Latin translation of the first; and after another interval of twenty years Signor Gorresio, a native of Sardinia, published, at the expense of Charles Albert, a very handsome edition of all the Bengal recension, except the 7th book, or Uttara-káṇḍa, with an Italian translation; but the greater portion of the older and purer recension of Benares, the editing of which was commenced by Schlegel, remained in MSS. till quite recently. A copy of the whole of this recension, with a commentary, has now reached the Bodleian from Calcutta, printed, I am sorry to say, in imitation of a MS. It has also been printed very lately at Bombay, I presume in a similar style.

‡ See Uttara-káṇḍa, ch. 123. He is also so identified in the 6th book, or Yuddha-káṇḍa, ch. 119, but this chapter may be an interpolation.

a summary of the plot, are comparatively modern appendages. These interpolations, 'spinnings out,' and variations do not impair the sacred character of the poem in the eyes of the natives. Some idea of the veneration in which it is held may be formed from the verses at the end of the introductory chapter, which declare that "he who reads and repeats this holy life-giving Rámáyaṇa is liberated from all his sins, and exalted with all his posterity to the highest heaven *."

I come now to the Mahá-bhárata or Great Bharateid, that is, the great poem which describes the achievements, mutual rivalries, and contests of the descendants of Bharata †. This huge epic, which is in all probability later in date than the Rámáyaṇa ‡, and consists of about

* Brahmá also in the 2d chapter is made to utter the following prophecy in the presence of the poet Válmíki: Yávat stháyanti girayah saritaścha mahítale Távad Rámáyaṇa-kathá lokeshu pracharishyati; 'As long as the mountains and rivers shall continue on the surface of the earth, so long shall the story of the Rámáyaṇa be current in the world.'

† The title of the poem is Mahá-bháratam, a compound word in the neuter gender, the first member of which, *mahá* (for *mahat*), means 'great,' and the second, *bhárata*, 'a descendant of Bharata.' It is not uncommon in Sanskrit to put the title of a book in the neuter gender, some word like *kávyam*, 'a poem,' being understood. Here the word with which Mahá-bháratam agrees may be either *ákhyánam*, 'a historical poem,' or *yuddham*, 'war.'

It is curious that in the *Sangraha-parva*, or introductory summary (I. 264), the word Mahá-bhárata is said to be derived from *mahá-bhára*, 'having great weight,' because the poem is described as outweighing all the four Vedas and mystical writings together. Here is the passage (which I do not pretend to explain grammatically)—Ekataś chaturo vedán Bháratam chaitad ekatah Purá kila suraih sarvaih sametya tulayá dhṛitam, Chaturbhyah Sarahasyebhyo vedebhyo hy adhikam yadá, Tadá prabhṛiti loke 'smin Mahá-bháratam uchyate.

‡ That at least a portion is later than the Rámáyaṇa can hardly be doubted, as the story of Ráma in the 3d book (15913) appears to be an analysis made from the Rámáyaṇa itself; and that the greater part is later than Alexander's invasion may be conjectured from the frequent references to the Yavanas or Greeks (i. e. Ionians, a term afterwards applied to the Muhammedans), who must have come into contact with the frontier of India, and penetrated here and there into the interior at a period prior to the principal events of the poem. It is also noticeable that in the Rámáyaṇa the

220,000 long lines, is rather a cyclopædia of Hindú mythology, legendary history, and philosophy, than a poem with a single subject. It is divided into eighteen books, nearly every one of which would form a large volume, and the whole is a vast thesaurus of national legends, said to have been collected and arranged by Vyása (the Hindú Pisistratus or supposed compiler of the Vedas and Puráṇas *), a name derived from a Sanskṛit verb meaning 'to fit together' or 'arrange †;' just as the name *Homer* is alleged by some to come from ὁμοῦ and ἄρω.

Many of the legends are Vedic, and of great antiquity—quite as old as any in the Rámáyaṇa, or even older; while others, again, are much more modern, probably interpolated during the first centuries of the Christian era. In fact, the entire work may be compared to a confused congeries of geological strata. The principal story, which occupies

---

wives of Daśaratha do not burn themselves with their husband, whereas in the Mahá-bhárata, Mádrí, the most dearly loved of the two wives of Páṇḍu, really makes herself a Satí. (I. 4896.)

* It may seem strange that the compilation of such very different works as the Vedas, Puráṇas, and Mahá-bhárata should be attributed to the same person. To illustrate the relation supposed by learned natives to subsist between these productions, I here give an extract from the Vedártha-prakáśa of Mádhava Áchárya (who lived in the 14th century) on the Taittiríya Yajur-veda (p. 1. Bibliotheca Indica), translated by Dr. Muir in his Sanskṛit texts, vol. III. p. 47. "It may be said that all persons whatever, including women and Śúdras, must be competent students of the Veda, since the aspiration after good (ishṭam me syád iti) and the deprecation of evil are common to all mankind. But it is not so. For though the expedient exists, and women and Śúdras are desirous to know it, they are debarred by another cause from being competent students of the Veda. The scripture (śástra) which declares that those persons only who have been invested with the sacrificial cord are competent to read the Veda, intimates thereby that the same study would be a cause of unhappiness to women and Śúdras (who are not so invested). How then are these two classes of persons to discover the means of future happiness? We answer, from the Puráṇas and other such works. Hence it has been said, 'Since the triple Veda may not be heard by women, Śúdras, and degraded twice-born men, the Mahá-bhárata was, in his benevolence, composed by the Muni.'"

† Vivyása vedán yasmát sa tasmád vyása iti smṛitah. Mahá-bhár. I. 2417.

little more than a fifth of the whole, forms the lowest layer *; but this has been so completely overlaid by successive incrustations, and the mass so compacted together, that the original substratum is not always clearly traceable. If the successive layers can ever be critically analysed and separated, the more ancient from the later additions, and the historical element from the purely fabulous, it may be expected that light will be thrown on a subject still veiled in great obscurity †—I mean, of course, the early history of India, both religious and political.

The following is a brief outline of the leading story of the Mahábhárata, which, like that of the Rámáyaṇa, is probably founded on fact; the rival families representing different branches of a warlike tribe of Sanskṛit-speaking settlers called *Kurus*, who may have entered India together, and would naturally come into collision at their first halting-place on the Ganges, their jealousies ending in an internecine civil war.

If the legendary history of India may be trusted, two dynasties were originally dominant in the north, called *Solar* and *Lunar*, under whom numerous petty princes held authority, and to whom they acknowledged fealty. The most celebrated of the solar line, which commenced in Ikshwáku and reigned in Oude, was the Ráma of the Rámáyaṇa. Under this dynasty the Bráhmanical system gained ascendancy more rapidly and completely than under the lunar kings in the more northern districts, where fresh arrivals of martial tribes preserved an independent spirit among the population already settled in that district ‡. The most famous of the lunar race who reigned in the neighbourhood of Hasti-

* Although the Mahá-bhárata is so much longer than the Rámáyaṇa as to preclude the idea of its being, like that poem, the work of one or even a few authors, yet it is the number of the episodes which, after all, causes the disparity. Separated from these, the main story of the Mahá-bhárata is not longer than the other epic.

† Notwithstanding the valuable researches of Prof. Lassen of Bonn.

‡ Weber (Ind. Stud. I. 220) remarks, "The north-western tribes retained their ancient customs, which those who migrated to the east had at one time shared. The former kept themselves free from the influences of the hierarchy and caste, which arose among the latter as a consequence of their residence among the aborigines."

nápur or ancient Delhi, was Bharata, whose authority is said to have extended over a great part of India, and from whom India is to this day called by the natives, Bhárata-varsha.

This Bharata, then, was an ancestor of Kuru, the twenty-third in descent from whom was Vyása (the supposed author of the Mahábhárata), who had two sons, Dhritaráshtra and Páṇḍu. The former, though blind, consented to assume the government when resigned by his younger brother Páṇḍu, and undertook to educate with his own hundred sons the five reputed sons of his brother. These five sons were, 1st, Yudhishthira (i. e. 'firm in battle'); 2d, Bhíma (i. e. 'the awful one'); 3d, Arjuna*. All these three were born from Páṇḍu's wife, Prithá or Kuntí, but were really her children by three gods, Dharma, Váyu, and Indra respectively. 4th and 5th, Nakula and Sahadeva, born from his wife Mádrí, but really her children by the Aświní-kumáras.

The characters of the five Páṇḍavas are drawn with much artistic delicacy of touch, and maintained consistently throughout the poem. The eldest, Yudhishthira, is the Hindú ideal of excellence—a pattern of justice, integrity, calm passionless composure, chivalrous honour, and cold heroism †. Bhíma is a type of brute courage and strength: he is of gigantic stature, impetuous, irascible, somewhat vindictive, and cruel even to the verge of ferocity, making him, as his name implies, 'terrible ‡.' But he has the capacity for warm unselfish love, and is devoted in his affection for his mother and brothers. Arjuna rises more to the European standard of perfection. He may be regarded

* I think it probable that the name 'Arjuna' may come from the root *ṛij*, 'to be straight, steadfast, upright,' although I am aware that others explain it differently.

† Yudhishthira was probably of commanding stature and imposing presence. He is described as Mahá-sinha-gati, 'having a majestic lion-like gait,' with a Wellington-like profile (Pralambojjwalachâru ghoṇa) and long lotus-eyes (kamaláyatáksha).

‡ It would appear that his great strength had to be kept up by plenty of food; as his name Vrikodara, 'wolf-stomached,' indicated a voracious appetite; and we are told that at the daily meals of the five brothers, half of the whole dish had to be given to Bhíma. (Ádi-parva, 7161.)

as the hero of the Mahá-bhárata*, of undaunted bravery, generous, modest†, with refined and delicate sensibilities, tender-hearted, forgiving, and affectionate as a woman, yet of superhuman strength, and matchless in arms and athletic exercises. Nakula and Sahadeva are both amiable, noble-minded, and spirited. All five are as unlike as possible to the hundred sons of Dhṛitaráshṭra, commonly called the *Kuru* princes, or *Kauravas*‡, who are represented as mean, spiteful, dishonourable, and vicious.

So bad indeed are these hundred brothers, and so uniformly without redeeming points, that their characters present few distinctive features. The most conspicuous is the eldest, Duryodhana, or 'the unfair fighter'‖, sometimes by euphemism called Suyodhana, who, as the representative of the others, is painted in the darkest colours, and embodies all their bad qualities. Many Hindús regard him as a visible type of Vice, or the evil principle in human nature§, for ever doing battle with Virtue, or the good and divine principle, symbolised by the five sons of Páṇḍu.

The cousins, though so uncongenial in character, were educated together at Hastinápur, the city of Dhṛitaráshṭra, by a Bráhman named Droṇa¶, who found in the Páṇḍu princes apt pupils. From him they

* Strictly, however, as in the Iliad, there is no real hero kept always in view.

† Perhaps it may be objected that some of Arjuna's acts were inconsistent with this character. Thus he carried off Subhadrá, the sister of Kṛishṇa, by force. It must be borne in mind, however, that Kṛishṇa himself encourages him to this act, and says, *Prasahya haraṇam Kshatriyáṇám prasasyate*. Mahá-bhár. I. 7927.

‡ This name, however, is occasionally applied to the Páṇḍavas, as they and the sons of Dhṛitaráshṭra were equally descendants of Kuru.

‖ Rendered by some, 'difficult to conquer.' The names of all are given in the Ádi-parva, l. 4541. Duhśásana is the most conspicuous next to Duryodhana.

§ There are certainly many points in his character, as well as in that of Rávaṇa, which may be compared to Milton's conception of Satan. Dr. Muir suggests that the intimacy with the Asura Chárváka ascribed to Duryodhana may be intended to mark him out as a type of heresy and infidelity, as well as of every other bad quality.

¶ Droṇa appears to have kept a kind of school, to which all the young princes of the neighbouring countries resorted. (Ádi-parva, 5220.)

acquired 'intelligence and learning, lofty aims, religious earnestness, and love of truth.' All the cousins were equally instructed in war and arms; and Arjuna distinguishes himself in every exercise, 'submissive ever to his teacher's will, contented, modest, affable, and mild.'

Their education finished, a grand tournament is held, at which all the youthful cousins display their skill in archery, in the management of chariots (Ratha-charyá), horses, and elephants, in sword, spear, and club exercises, and wrestling. The scene is graphically described (I. 5324). An immense concourse of spectators cheer the combatants. The agitation of the crowd is compared to the roar of a mighty ocean. Arjuna, after exhibiting prodigies of strength, shoots five separate arrows simultaneously into the jaws of a revolving iron boar, and twenty-one arrows into the hollow of a cow's horn suspended by a string. Suddenly there is a pause. The crowd turns as one man towards a point in the arena, where a murmur gradually rising to a clamour, which rent the sky like a thunder-clap, announces the entrance of another combatant. This proves to be a warrior named *Karṇa*, who enters the lists in full armour, and after accomplishing the same feats in archery, challenges Arjuna to single combat. But each champion is required to tell his name and pedigree; and Karṇa's parentage being doubtful (he was really the illegitimate child of Pṛithá by the sun, and therefore half-brother of Arjuna), he is obliged to retire, "hanging his head with shame like a drooping lily."

Karṇa, thus publicly humiliated, becomes afterwards a conspicuous and valuable ally of the Kurus against his own half-brothers. His character is well imagined. Feeling keenly the stain on his birth, his nature is chastened by the trial. He exhibits in a high degree fortitude, chivalrous honour, self-sacrifice, and devotion. Especially remarkable for a liberal and generous disposition *, he never stoops to ignoble practices like his friends the Kurus, who are intrinsically bad men.

The superior skill of the Páṇḍavas, displayed at this public contest,

* He is often to this day cited as a model of liberality. See his name, Vasu-sheṇa.

excited all the malevolence of their cousins, and they endeavoured to destroy them by setting fire to their house; but the Páṇḍavas, warned of their intention, escaped by an underground passage to the woods. Whilst living there disguised as mendicant Bráhmans, they were induced to join a number of other Bráhmans on their way to a *Swayamvara*, or public choice of a husband by a beautiful maiden named Draupadí, daughter of Drupada, king of Panchála. An immense concourse of princely suitors, with their retainers, came to the ceremony; and king Drupada (who was an old schoolfellow of the Bráhman, Droṇa, but had offended him by repudiating his friendship in later years) eagerly looked for Arjuna amongst them, that, strengthened by that hero's alliance, he might defy Droṇa's anger. He therefore prepared an enormous bow, which he was persuaded none but Arjuna could bend, and proposed a trial of strength, promising to give his daughter to any one who could by means of this bow shoot five arrows simultaneously through a revolving ring into a target beyond. An amphitheatre was erected outside the town, surrounded by tiers of lofty seats and raised platforms, with variegated awnings. Magnificent palaces, crowded with eager spectators, overlooked the scene. Actors, conjurors, athletes, and dancers exhibited their skill before the multitude. Strains of exquisite music floated in the air. Drums and trumpets sounded. When expectation was at its height, Draupadí in gorgeous apparel entered the arena, and the bow was brought. The hundred sons of Dhṛitaráshṭra strain every nerve to bend the ponderous weapon, but without effect. Its recoil dashes them breathless to the ground, and makes them the laughing-stock of the crowd. Arjuna now advances, disguised as a Bráhman. (Ádi-parva, 7049.)

A moment motionless he stood and scanned
The bow, collecting all his energy.
Next walking round in homage, breathed a prayer
To the Supreme bestower of good gifts;
Then fixing all his mind on Draupadí . .
He grasped the ponderous weapon in his hand,

And with one vigorous effort braced the string.
Quickly the shafts were aimed; they flew—
The mark fell pierced; a shout of victory
Rang through the vast arena; from the sky
Garlands of flowers crowned the hero's head,
Ten thousand fluttering scarfs waved in the air,
And drum and trumpet sounded forth his triumph.

I need not suggest the parallel which will at once be drawn by the classical scholar, between this trial of archery and a similar scene in the Odyssey.

When the suitors find themselves outdone by a mere stripling in the coarse dress of a mendicant Bráhman, their rage knows no bounds. A real battle ensues. The Páṇḍu princes protect Drupada, and enact prodigies. Bhíma tears up a tree, and uses it as a club. Karṇa at last meets Arjuna in single combat, rushing on him like a young elephant. They overwhelm each other with showers of arrows, which darken the air. But not even Karṇa can withstand the irresistible onset of the godlike Arjuna, and he and the other suitors retire vanquished from the field*, leaving Draupadí as the bride of Arjuna.

The Páṇḍu princes, thus strengthened by Drupada's alliance, throw off their disguise, and the king, Dhṛitaráshṭra, is induced to settle all differences by dividing his kingdom between them and his own sons.

Soon afterwards, at a great assembly, the artful Kuru princes propose a game at dice. No Hindú is proof against the love of gambling. Yudhishṭhira, excellent as he is in other respects, has this one fault. By degrees he stakes every thing, and, after losing his territory and possessions, pledges himself that he and his brothers shall live for twelve years in the woods, and shall pass the thirteenth concealed under assumed names in various disguises. Their term of banishment ended, they prepare to make war on their cousins, and recover their kingdom. We have then the preparations on both sides described. Each party seeks

* They console themselves by declaring that they are defeated, not by physical force, but by the divine power of the sacerdotal caste. (I. 7123.)

alliances. Kṛishṇa, king of Dwáraka (worshipped in the present day as the most popular incarnation of Vishṇu), takes the side of his cousins, the Páṇḍavas, and condescends to serve as the charioteer of Arjuna.

The rival armies meet on a vast plain, north-west of the modern Delhi, called 'the field of the Kurus.' Duryodhana entrusts the command of his troops to his ablest generals, and first to his grand-uncle Bhíshma, the oldest warrior present. The Páṇḍavas, on the other side, are led on in the first engagement by Bhíma.

And now as the hosts advanced a tumult filled the sky; the earth shook—"Chafed by wild winds, the sands upcurled to heaven, and spread a veil before the sun." Showers of blood fell*. Shrill kites, vultures, and howling jackalls hung about the rear of the marching armies. Thunder roared, lightnings flashed, blazing meteors shot across the darkened sky; yet the chiefs, regardless of these portents, "pressed on to mutual slaughter, and the peal of shouting hosts commingling, shook the world."

There is to a European a ponderous and unwieldy character about Oriental warfare, which he finds it difficult to realize; yet the battle-scenes, though exaggerated, are vividly described, and carry the imagination into the midst of the conflict. Monstrous elephants career over the field, trampling on men and horses, and dealing destruction with their huge tusks; enormous clubs and iron maces clash together with the noise of thunder; rattling chariots dash against each other; thousands of arrows hurtle in the air, darkening the sky; trumpets, kettle-drums, and horns add to the uproar; confusion, carnage, and death are every where. The individual deeds of prowess and single-combats between the heroes are sometimes graphically narrated. Each chief has a conch-shell (śankha) for a trumpet, which, as well as his principal weapon, has a name, as if personified†. Thus we read:

* So Jupiter rains blood twice in the Iliad, XI. 53. and XVI. 459.

† Trumpets do not appear to have been used by Homer's heroes. Whence the value of a Stentorian voice. But there is express allusion in Il. XVIII. 219. to the use of trumpets at sieges.

Arjuna blew his shell called 'God-given' (Deva-datta), and carried a bow called Gáṇḍíva. Kṛishṇa sounded Pánchajanya (a shell made of the bones of the demon Panchajana). Bhíma blew a great trumpet called Pauṇḍra, and Yudhishṭhira sounded his, called 'Eternal victory' (Ananta-vijaya). Here is a description of a single-combat between Bhíma and Salya, the king of Madra (taken from the Salya-parva, 594), which I have translated nearly literally. It will give an idea of the redundance of similes in the original.

Soon as he saw his charioteer struck down,
Straightway the Madra monarch grasped his mace,
And like a mountain firm and motionless
Awaited the attack. The warrior's form
Was awful as the world-consuming fire,
Or as the noose-armed god of death, or as
The peaked Kailása, or the Thunderer
Himself, or as the trident-bearing god,
Or as a maddened forest elephant.
Him to defy did Bhíma hastily
Advance, wielding aloft his massive club.
A thousand conchs and trumpets and a shout,
Firing each champion's ardour, rent the air.
From either host, spectators of the fight,
Burst forth applauding cheers: "The Madra king
Alone," they cried, "can bear the rush of Bhíma;
None but heroic Bhíma can sustain
The force of Salya." Now like two fierce bulls
Sprang they towards each other, mace in hand.
And first as cautiously they circled round,
Whirling their weapons as in sport, the pair
Seemed matched in equal combat. Salya's club,
Set with red fillets, glittered as with flame,
While that of Bhíma gleamed like flashing lightning.
Anon the clashing iron met, and scattered round
A fiery shower; then fierce as elephants
Or butting bulls they battered each the other.
Thick fell the blows, and soon each stalwart frame,
Spattered with gore, glowed like the Kinsuka,

Bedecked with scarlet blossoms; yet beneath
The rain of strokes, unshaken as a rock
Bhíma sustained the mace of S'alya, he
With equal firmness bore the other's blows.
Now like the roar of crashing thunder-clouds
Sounded the clashing iron; then, their clubs
Brandished aloft, eight paces they retired,
And swift again advancing to the fight,
Met in the midst like two huge mountain-crags
Hurled into contact. Nor could either bear
The other's shock; together down they rolled,
Mangled and crushed, like two tall standards fallen.

The following description, from the Droṇa-parva (544), is less literal.

High on a stately car
Swift borne by generous coursers to the fight,
The vaunting son of Puru proudly drove,
Secure of conquest o'er Subhadrá's son.
The youthful champion shrank not from the conflict.
Fierce on the boastful chief he sprang, as bounds
The lion's cub upon the ox; and now
The Puru chief had perished, but his dart
Shivered with timely aim the upraised bow
Of Abhimanyu *. From his tingling hand
The youthful warrior cast the fragments off,
And drew his sword, and grasped his iron-bound shield;
Upon the car of Paurava he leapt
And seized the chief—his charioteer he slew,
And dragged the monarch senseless o'er the plain †.

In all this there is nothing extravagant; but when Arjuna is described as killing five hundred warriors simultaneously, covering the whole plain with dead and filling rivers with blood; Yudhishṭhira as slaughtering a hundred men 'in a mere twinkle' (*nimesha-mátreṇa*);

* The name of Arjuna's son by Subhadrá.

† In this extract I have partly followed a spirited though too free translation in the Oriental Magazine.

Bhíma as annihilating a monstrous elephant, including all mounted upon it, and fourteen foot-soldiers besides, with one blow of his club; Nakula and Sahadeva, fighting from their chariots, as cutting off heads by the thousand, and sowing them like seed upon the ground; when, moreover, the principal heroes make use of mystical weapons, given to them by the gods, possessed of supernatural powers, and supposed to be themselves celestial beings *; we at once perceive that there is an unreality about such scenes, which mars the beauty of the description. Still it must be borne in mind that the heroes of the Indian epics have semi-divine natures, and that what would be incredible in a mere mortal is not only possible but appropriate in a demigod †. It would be impossible of course to detail all the events of the great battle, which was protracted, with various successes on either side, for many days. Several times, like "clouds before the gale," the Páṇḍavas were driven back by the veteran Droṇa (their former tutor); but the day is generally

* About a hundred of these weapons are enumerated in the Rámáyaṇa (I. xxix), and constant allusion is made to them in battle-scenes both in the Rámáyaṇa and Mahá-bhárata. Arjuna, in the latter, undergoes a long course of austerities to obtain celestial weapons from Śiva. It is by the terrific *brahmástra* that Vaśishṭha conquers Viśwámitra, and Ráma kills Rávaṇa. Sometimes they appear to be mystical powers exercised by meditation, rather than weapons, and are supposed to assume animate forms, and possess names and faculties like the genii in the Arabian Nights. Thus in Rámáyaṇa I. xxix. they address Ráma: 'Behold us here present, O Ráma, as your servants;' and Ráma, taking them by the hand, replies, 'Be present to me, when called to mind.' Certain distinct spells, charms, or prayers had to be learnt for the due using (*prayoga*) and restraining (*sanhára*) of these weapons or powers. See Rám. I. xxx, and Raghu-vanśa V. 57. (Sammohanam náma astram ádhatswa prayoga-sanhára-vibhakta-mantram.) When once let loose, he only who knew the secret spell for recalling them, could bring them back; but the *brahmástra* returned to its possessor's quiver of its own accord.

† Aristotle says that the epic poet should prefer impossibilities which appear probable to such things as though possible appear improbable. (Poetica III. 6.) But previously, in comparing epic poetry with tragedy, he observes, "the surprising is necessary in tragedy, but the epic poem goes further, and admits even the improbable and incredible, from which the highest degree of the surprising results." (III. 4.)

restored by Arjuna, and one after another the leaders of the Kuru party are slain.

At last a fearful combat takes place between Bhíma and Duryodhana, in which the latter receives a mortal blow. He falls like a huge forest-tree felled to the ground, causing the earth to vibrate. Various prodigies succeed. A whirlwind rises, showers of dust fall, trees are uprooted, mountains quiver, meteors stream in the sky, the clouds rain blood, demons and evil spirits fill the air with their hideous yells *.

After the fall of their chief an attempt is made by some of the surviving Kuru princes to retrieve their shattered fortunes in a night attack on the camp of the sleeping Páṇḍavas. The description of this incident, told in the Sauptika-parva (or 10th book), resembles very strikingly Homer's narrative of the night-adventures of Diomed and Ulysses in the camp of the Trojans. (Iliad, book X.)

The battle having terminated in favour of the Páṇḍavas, they recover their possessions, and the eldest brother is elevated to the throne; and here a European poet would have brought the story to an end. The Sanskṛit poet has a deeper knowledge of human nature, or at least of Hindú nature.

In the most popular of Indian dramas (the S'akuntalá) there occurs this sentiment (see my translation of this play, p. 124):

> 'Tis a vain thought that to attain the end
> And object of ambition is to rest.
> Success doth only mitigate the fever
> Of anxious expectation: soon the fear
> Of losing what we have, the constant care
> Of guarding it doth weary.

If then the great national epic was to respond truly to the deeper emotions of the Hindú mind, it could not leave the Páṇḍavas in the

* This description favours the idea expressed at p. 20, note §. Showers of blood are a common prodigy in the Indian epics. A similar portent occurs, as we have seen (p. 24, note), twice in the Iliad. The following parallel from Hesiod, Scut. Herc. 384, may be added: Κὰδ δ' ἄρ' ἀπ' οὐρανόθεν ψιάδας βάλεν αἱματοέσσας.

contented enjoyment of their kingdom. It had to instil a more sublime moral—a lesson which even the disciples of a divine philosophy are slow to learn—namely, that all who desire rest must set their faces heavenwards. Hence we are brought in the concluding chapters to the fine description of the renunciation of their kingdom by the five brothers, and their journey towards Indra's heaven in mount Meru. Part of this (see Mahá-prasthánika-parva, 24) I will now translate, as nearly as I can, word for word *.

When the four brothers knew the high resolve of king Yudhishṭhira,
Forthwith with Draupadí they issued forth, and after them a dog
Followed: the king himself went out the seventh from the royal city,
And all the citizens and women of the palace walked behind;
But none could find it in their heart to say unto the king, 'Return.'
And so at length the train of citizens went back, bidding adieu.
Then the high-minded sons of Páṇḍu and the noble Draupadí
Roamed onwards, fasting, with their faces towards the east; their hearts
Yearning for union with the Infinite; bent on abandonment
Of worldly things. They wandered on to many countries, many a sea
And river. Yudhishṭhira walked in front, and next to him came Bhíma,
And Arjuna came after him, and then, in order, the twin brothers.
And last of all came Draupadí, with her dark skin and lotus-eyes—
The faithful Draupadí, loveliest of women, best of wives—
Behind them walked the only living thing that shared their pilgrimage,
The dog—And by degrees they reached the briny sea. There Arjuna
Cast in the waves his bow and quivers †. Then with souls well-disciplined
They reached the northern region, and beheld with heaven-aspiring hearts
The mighty mountain Himavat. Beyond its lofty peak they passed
Towards the sea of sand, and saw at last the rocky Meru, king
Of mountains. As with eager steps they hastened on, their souls intent
On union with the Eternal, Draupadí lost hold of her high hope,
And faltering fell upon the earth.

* Since the above was written I have received from Paris M. Foucaux's translation into French of eleven episodes of the Mahá-bhárata, including a French version of this passage.

† Arjuna had two celebrated quivers, besides the bow named Gáṇḍíva, given to him by the god Agni.

One by one the others also drop, till only Bhíma, Yudhishṭhira, and the dog are left. Still Yudhishṭhira walks steadily in front, calm and unmoved, looking neither to the right hand nor to the left, and gathering up his soul in inflexible resolution. Bhíma, shocked at the fall of his companions, and unable to understand how beings so apparently guileless should be struck down by fate, appeals to his brother, who without looking back explains that death is the consequence of sinful thoughts and too great attachment to worldly objects; and that Draupadí's fall was owing to her excessive affection for Arjuna; Sahadeva's (who is supposed to be the most humble-minded of the five brothers) to his pride in his own knowledge; Nakula's (who is very handsome) to feelings of personal vanity; and Arjuna's to a boastful confidence in his power to destroy his foes. Bhíma then feels himself falling, and is told that he suffers death for his selfishness, pride, and too great love of enjoyment. The sole survivor is now Yudhishṭhira, who still walks steadily forward, followed only by the dog.

When with a sudden sound that rang through earth and heaven came the god
Towards him in a chariot, and he cried, "Ascend, O resolute prince."
Then did the king look back upon his fallen brothers, and address'd
These words unto the Thousand-eyed, in anguish—"Let my brothers here
Come with me. Without them, O god of gods, I would not wish to enter
E'en heaven; and yonder tender princess Draupadí, the faithful wife,
Worthy of happiness, let her too come. In mercy hear my prayer."

Upon this, Indra informs him that the spirits of Draupadí and his brothers are already in heaven, and that he alone is permitted to ascend there in bodily form. Yudhishṭhira now stipulates that his dog shall be admitted with him. Indra says sternly, "Heaven has no place for those who are accompanied by dogs (śwavatám);" but Yudhishṭhira is unshaken in his resolution, and declines abandoning the faithful animal. Indra remonstrates—"You have abandoned your brothers and Draupadí; why not forsake the dog?" To this Yudhishṭhira haughtily replies, "I had no power to bring them back to life: how can there be abandonment of those who no longer live?"

The dog, it appears, was his own father Dharma in disguise (Mahá-prasthánika-parva, 88*). Reassuming now his proper form he praises Yudhishthira for his constancy, and they enter heaven together. There, to his surprise, he finds Duryodhana and his cousins, but not his brothers or Draupadí. Hereupon he declines remaining in heaven without them. An angel is then sent to conduct him across the Indian Styx (Vaitaraṇí) to the hell where they are supposed to be. The scene which now follows may be compared to the Necyomanteia in the eleventh book of the Odyssey, or to parts of Dante.

The particular hell to which Yudhishthira is taken is a dense wood, whose leaves are sharp swords, and its ground paved with razors†. The way to it is strewed with foul and mutilated corpses. Hideous shapes flit across the air and hover over him. Here there is a horror of palpable darkness. There the wicked are burning in flames of blazing fire. Suddenly he hears the voices of his brothers and companions imploring him to assuage their torments, and not desert them. His resolution is taken. Deeply affected, he bids the angel leave him to share their miseries. This is his last trial. The whole scene now vanishes. It was a mere illusion, to test his constancy to the utmost. He is now directed to bathe in the heavenly Ganges; and having plunged into the sacred stream, he enters the real heaven, where at length, in company with Draupadí and his brothers, he finds that rest and happiness which were unattainable on earth.

I proceed to give one or two specimens from the most celebrated episodes of the Mahá-bhárata. The 'Story of Nala' is so well known

---

* So I infer from the original, which, however, is somewhat obscure. The expression is *dharma-swarúpí bhagaván*. At any rate, the dog was a mere phantom created to try Yudhishthira, as it is evident that a real dog is not admitted with Yudhishthira to heaven.

† I. e. Asi-patra-vana. The Hindús exaggerate the horrors of their infernal regions, as they do every thing else; nor does one place of punishment satisfy them. In Manu (IV. 88) twenty-one hells are enumerated, and in the Puráṇas various others are added, comprising every species of possible torment.

through various editions of the text, and especially that published by this University *, that I need not refer to it here.

A still more celebrated episode is the Bhagavad-Gítá or Divine song, (a philosophical poem, introduced into the Mahá-bhárata subsequently to the Christian era.) This combines the Pantheism of the Vedánta with the more modern principle of *bhakti*, or devotion to Kṛishṇa as the supreme Being †; and teaches that renunciation of the world ought not to involve the avoidance of action or the neglect of professional duties. These doctrines are propounded in a discourse supposed to take place between Kṛishṇa, acting as Arjuna's charioteer, and Arjuna himself, in the chariot stationed between the rival armies just before the commencement of the battle. Arjuna, seeing his relatives drawn up in battle array, is suddenly struck with compunction at the idea of fighting his way to a kingdom through the blood of his kindred. He confides his misgivings to Kṛishṇa in the following words: "Beholding my kindred about to engage in killing one another, my limbs give way, my face dries up, my body trembles; I will not fight, O Kṛishṇa. I seek not victory nor a kingdom. What shall we do with a kingdom? What with enjoyments or with life itself, when we have slain these relations?" Kṛishṇa replies in a long metaphysical dialogue, full of fine passages, the moral of which is that as Arjuna belongs to the military caste his duty is to fight. He is urged not to hesitate about slaughtering his relations by an argument drawn from the eternal existence of the soul, which I will now translate ‡—

The wise grieve not for the departed, nor for those who yet survive.
Ne'er was the time when I was not, nor thou, nor yonder chiefs; and ne'er
Shall be the time when all of us shall be not; as the unbodied soul

* Which has the advantage of Dean Milman's translation synoptically exhibited.

† It also combines a strong tinge of the Sánkhya philosophy.

‡ I do not pretend to have translated this passage as poetically as Dean Milman, although I am indebted to him for some expressions. My only reason for retranslating is that I may give a more literal version.

In this corporeal frame moves swiftly on through boyhood, youth, and age,
So will it pass through other forms hereafter—be not grieved thereat.
The man whom pain and pleasure, heat and cold affect not, he is fit
For immortality: that which is not cannot be—and that which is
Can never cease to be. Know this;—the Being that spread this universe
Is indestructible; who can destroy the Indestructible?
These bodies that enclose the everlasting soul, inscrutable,
Immortal, have an end—but he who thinks the soul can be destroyed,
And he who deems it a destroyer, are alike mistaken: it
Kills not, and is not killed; it is not born, nor doth it ever die;
It has no past nor future—unproduced, unchanging, infinite: he
Who knows it fixed, unborn, imperishable, indissoluble,
How can that man destroy another, or extinguish aught below?
As men abandon old and threadbare clothes to put on others new,
So casts the embodied soul its worn out frame to enter other forms.
No dart can pierce it; flame cannot consume it, water wet it not,
Nor scorching breezes dry it: indestructible, incapable
Of heat or moisture or aridity—eternal, all-pervading,
Steadfast, immoveable; perpetual, yet imperceptible,
Incomprehensible, unfading, deathless, unimaginable.

There is a touching episode, full of true poetic feeling, in the first book of the Mahá-bhárata (Ádi-parva, 6104), usually known as 'the Bráhman's lament,' but called in the original *Baka-badha* *. The story is briefly as follows. In the neighbourhood of Ekachakrá, a town in which the Páṇḍavas had taken refuge after the treacherous attempt of their cousins to destroy them by setting fire to their dwelling, resided a fierce giant, named Baka, who forced the citizens to send him every day a dish of food by a man, whom he always devoured as his daintiest morsel at the end of the repast. The turn had come to a poor Bráhman to provide the Rákshasa with his meal. He determines to go himself, but laments bitterly the hardness of his fate. Upon this, his wife and daughter address him in language full of the deepest pathos, each in turn insisting on sacrificing herself for the good of the family.

* This episode, as well as that noticed next, has been printed by Bopp, and translated by Milman; I therefore confine myself to a brief outline.

Lastly, the little son, too young to speak distinctly, with beaming eyes and smiling face, runs to his parents, and with prattling voice says, 'Weep not, father, sigh not, mother.' Then breaking off and brandishing a pointed spike of grass, he adds in childish accents, 'With this spike will I slay the fierce man-eating giant.' (I. 6202.) His parents (so proceeds the story), hearing this innocent prattle of their child, in the midst of their heart-rending anguish felt a thrill of exquisite delight. The end of it is that Bhíma, who overhears the whole conversation, undertakes to convey the meal to the monster, and, of course, speedily despatches him.

The next episode I select is one (from the Vana-parva) illustrating in a striking manner the wide diffusion of the tradition of the Deluge. Manu, the Noah of the Hindús (not the grandson of Brahmá, and reputed author of the Code, but the seventh Manu, or Manu of the present period, called Vaivaswata, and regarded as one of the progenitors of the human race; see Manu I. 61, 62), is represented as conciliating the favour of the Supreme by his penances in an age of universal depravity. The earliest account of him is in the Śatapatha Bráhmaṇa (attached to the Vájasaneyí Sanhitá of the Yajur-veda, Adhy. I. viii. 1. 1). It is so interesting to compare the simple narrative of this ancient work (which represents the tradition of the flood as it existed in India many centuries B.C., perhaps not much later than the time of David) with the poetical embellishments of the epic version, that I commence by translating an extract from the Bráhmaṇa, as literally as I can.

"It happened one morning that they brought water to Manu, as usual, for washing his hands. As he was washing, a fish came into his hands. It spake to him thus: 'Take care of me, and I will preserve thee.' Manu asked, 'From what wilt thou preserve me?' The fish answered, 'A flood will carry away all living beings; I will save thee from that.' He said, 'How is thy preservation to be accomplished?' The fish replied, 'While we are small, we are liable to constant destruction, and even one fish devours another: thou must first preserve me in an earthen vessel; when I grow too large for that, dig a trench, and keep me in that. When I grow too large for that, thou must convey me to the ocean; I shall then be beyond the risk of destruction.' So saying, it rapidly became a great fish, and still grew larger and larger. Then it said, 'After so many years, the deluge will take place; then construct a ship, and pay me homage, and when the waters rise, go into the ship, and I will rescue thee.' Manu therefore, after preserving the fish as he was directed, bore it to the ocean; and at the very time the fish had declared he built a ship, and did homage to the fish. When the flood rose he embarked in the ship, and the fish swam towards him, and he fastened the ship's cable to its horn. By its means he passed beyond this northern mountain. The fish then said, 'I have preserved thee: now do thou fasten the ship to a tree. But let not the water sink from under thee while thou art on the mountain. As fast as it sinks, so fast do thou go down with it.' He therefore so descended; and this was the manner of Manu's descent from the northern mountain. The flood had carried away all living creatures. Manu alone was left. Wishing for offspring, he diligently performed a sacrifice. In a year's time a female was produced *. She came to Manu. He said to her, 'Who art thou?' She answered, 'Thy daughter.' He asked, 'How, lady, art thou my daughter?' She replied, 'The oblations which thou didst offer in the waters, viz. clarified butter, thick milk, whey and curds; from these hast thou begotten me. I can confer blessings.' With her he laboriously performed another sacrifice, desirous of children. By her he had offspring, called the offspring of Manu; and whatever blessings he prayed for were all granted to him †."

In the Mahá-bhárata account (Vana-parva, 12746—12804) the fish, which is an incarnation of Brahmá, appears to Manu whilst engaged in penance on the margin of a river, and accosting him craves his protection from the larger fish. Manu complies, and places him in a glass

* I omit a portion here.

† After making my own translation I have consulted those made by Dr. Muir in his Sanskrit Texts, and Prof. Max Müller in his History of Ancient Sanskrit Literature.

vessel, which he soon outgrows, and requests to be taken to a more roomy receptacle. Manu then places him in a lake. Still the fish grew, till the lake, though three leagues long, could not contain him. He next asks to be taken to the Ganges; but even the Ganges was soon too small, and the fish is finally transferred to the ocean. There the monster continues to expand, till at last, addressing Manu, he warns him of the coming deluge.

Manu, however, is to be preserved by the help of the fish, who commands him to build a ship and go on board, not with his own wife and children, but with the seven Rishis or patriarchs; and not with pairs of animals, but with the seeds of all existing things. The flood comes; Manu goes on board, and fastens the ship, as he is directed, to a horn in the head of the fish. He is then drawn along *—

Along the ocean in that stately ship was borne the lord of men, and through
Its dancing, tumbling billows, and its roaring waters; and the bark,
Tossed to and fro by violent winds, reeled on the surface of the deep,
Staggering and trembling like a drunken woman: land was seen no more,
Nor far horizon, nor the space between; for every where around
Spread the wild waste of waters, reeking atmosphere, and boundless sky.
And now when all the world was deluged, nought appeared above the waves
But Manu and the seven sages, and the fish that drew the bark.
Unwearied thus for years on years that fish propelled the ship across
The heaped-up waters, till at length it bore the vessel to the peak
Of Himaván; then softly smiling thus the fish addressed the sage:
"Haste now to bind thy ship to this high crag. Know me the lord of all,
The great creator Brahmá, mightier than all might—omnipotent.
By me in fish-like shape have you been saved in dire emergency.
From Manu all creation, gods, asuras, men, must be produced;
By him the world must be created, that which moves and moveth not."

I now leave this interesting episode with the remark that there is still a later account of the deluge in the Bhágavata-Puráṇa, where the fish is represented as an incarnation of Vishṇu.

---

* I have preferred to translate this in metre. Dr. Muir (II. p. 331) gives a still more literal prose version, and some valuable remarks on the whole subject.

The only other specimen I propose giving is a brief epitome of the story of Sávitrí and Satyaván (from the Vana-parva, l. 16619, &c.), which, for true poetic feeling and pathos, is not excelled by that of Admetus and Alcestis.

Sávitrí, the lovely daughter of a king Aśwapati, loves Satyaván, the son of an old hermit, but is warned by a seer to overcome her attachment, as Satyaván is a doomed man, having only one year to live. But Sávitrí replies *—

> Whether his years be few or many, be he gifted with all grace
> Or graceless, him my heart hath chosen, and it chooseth not again.

The king's daughter and the hermit's son are therefore married, and the bride strives to forget the ominous prophecy; but as the last day of the year approaches her anxiety becomes irrepressible. She exhausts herself in prayers and penances, hoping to stay the hand of the destroyer; yet all the while dares not reveal the fatal secret to her husband. At last the dreaded day arrives, and Satyaván sets out to cut wood in the forest. His wife asks leave to accompany him, and walks behind her husband smiling, but with a heavy heart. Satyaván soon makes the wood resound with his hatchet, when suddenly through his temples shoots a thrill of agony, and feeling himself falling he calls out to his wife to support him.

> Then she received her fainting husband in her arms, and sate herself
> On the cold ground, and gently laid his drooping head upon her lap;
> Sorrowing, she call'd to mind the sage's prophecy, and reckoned up
> The days and hours. All in an instant she beheld an awful shape
> Standing before her, dressed in blood-red garments, with a glittering crown
> Upon his head: his form, though glowing like the sun, was yet obscure,
> And eyes he had like flames, a noose depended from his hand; and he
> Was terrible to look upon, as by her husband's side he stood
> And gazed upon him with a fiery glance. Shuddering she started up
> And laid her dying Satyaván upon the ground, and with her hands

* I translate as closely as I can to the original. This and other select specimens of Indian poetry have been more freely translated in rhyme by Mr. Griffiths, and I therefore limit myself to a brief outline.

Joined reverently, she thus with beating heart addressed the Shape:
Surely thou art a god, such form as thine must more than mortal be.
Tell me, thou godlike being, who thou art, and wherefore art thou here?

The figure replies that he is Yama, king of death; that her husband's time is come, and that he must bind and take his spirit.

Then from her husband's body forced he out and firmly with his cord
Bound and detained the spirit, like in size and length to a man's thumb *.
Forthwith the body, reft of vital being and deprived of breath,
Lost all its grace and beauty, and became ghastly and motionless.

After binding the spirit, Yama proceeds with it towards his own quarter, the south. The faithful wife follows him closely. Yama bids her go home and prepare her husband's funeral rites; but she persists in following, till Yama, pleased with her devotion, grants her any boon she pleases, *except* the life of her husband. She chooses that her husband's father, who is blind, may recover his sight. Yama consents, and bids her now return home. Still she persists in following. Two other boons are granted in the same way, and still Sávitrí follows closely on the heels of the king of death. At last, overcome by her

* According to Carey, the Hindús believe that the spirit after death (preta) remains floating about in the atmosphere in the form of air, without support, until ten śráddhas or funeral ceremonies are performed; when it obtains the preta-śaríra (also called *ativáhika*), or misery-enduring body, which is a receptacle about the size of a thumb. The present rule is that the body be burnt on the day of death; after which for ten days, during the daśa-piṇḍa-śráddha, the relations are supposed to be mourning and in a state of aśaucha or impurity, so that no one can communicate with them, the soul of the deceased being daily fed with libations of water (tarpaṇa) and cakes (piṇḍa) of rice mixed with milk, &c. On the eleventh day the ekádaśí is performed, when the period of uncleanness ceases. These śráddhas are repeated once a month for a year; and on the anniversary of death the *sapiṇḍana* is performed, when the soul enters the divya-śaríra or bhoga-deha, that is, the vehicle in which it enjoys or suffers the reward of its actions. If a person die at Gayá, or other holy place, the soul departs to bliss without the discipline of the preta-śaríra. When the soul has entered the divya-śaríra it is considered a pitṛi; the deceased is then associated with his progenitors, and all future offerings are called pitṛi-kṛiyá. See Carey's Rámáyaṇa, vol. III. p. 72.

constancy, Yama grants a boon without exception. The delighted Sávitrí exclaims—

"Nought, mighty king, this time hast thou excepted: let my husband live;
Without him I desire not happiness, nor even heaven itself;
Without him I must die." "So be it! faithful wife," replied the king of death;
"Thus I release him;" and with that he loosed the cord that bound his soul.

The whole story, of which I have merely given the briefest outline, will, if read in the original, well repay the reader for the labour of his Sanskṛit studies.

I have already stated that the episodes of the Mahá-bhárata occupy more than three-fourths of the whole poem. It is in fact not one poem, but a compilation of many poems; not a *Kávya* by one author, but an *Itihása* by many authors. This is one great distinctive feature in comparing it with the Rámáyaṇa. In both epics there is a leading story, about which are collected a multitude of other stories; but in the Mahá-bhárata the main narrative only acts as a slender thread to connect a vast mass of independent legends together; while in the Rámáyaṇa the episodes, though numerous, never break the solid chain of one principal and paramount subject, which is ever kept in view.

It should be remembered that the two epics belong to different periods and different localities. Not only was the Mahá-bhárata composed later than the Rámáyaṇa, parts of it being comparatively modern, but the places which gave birth to the two poems are distinct. It is well known that in India different customs and opinions frequently prevail in districts almost adjacent; and it is certain that Bráhmanism never gained the ascendancy in the more martial north which it acquired in the neighbourhood of Oude. Each poem therefore, though often running parallel to the other, has yet a distinct point of departure; and the Mahá-bhárata, as it became current in various localities, diverged more widely from the straight course than its elder sister. In fact, the Mahá-bhárata presents a complete circle of post-Vedic mythology, including many myths which have their germ in the Veda, and continually enlarging its circumference to embrace the later phases of Hindúism, with its whole train of confused and conflicting legends*. From this storehouse are drawn all the Puráṇas, and many of the more recent heroic poems and dramas. Here we have repeated many of the legends of the Rámáyaṇa, and even the history of Ráma himself†. Here also are most of the narratives of the incarnation of Vishṇu, numberless stories connected with the worship of S'iva, and various details of the life of Kṛishṇa. Those which especially bear on the modern worship of Kṛishṇa are contained in the supplement called Hari-vanśa, which is itself a long poem, longer than the Iliad and Odyssey combined‡. Hence the religious system of the Mahá-bhárata is far more popular, liberal, and comprehensive than that of the Rámáyaṇa. It is true that the god Vishṇu is connected with Kṛishṇa in the Mahá-bhárata, as he is with Ráma in the Rámáyaṇa, but in the latter Ráma is every thing; whereas in the Mahá-bhárata, Kṛishṇa is by no means the centre of the system. His divinity is even occasionally disputed ||. The five Páṇḍavas have also partially divine natures, and

* It should be noted, that not only is the germ of many of the legends of Hindú epic poetry to be found in the Rig-veda, but that epic poetry itself is there adumbrated in hymns and songs laudatory of Indra and other gods who were supposed to protect the Árya races from the Anáryas. It should also be observed that the same legend is sometimes repeated in different parts of the Mahá-bhárata, with considerable variations; as, for example, the story of the combat of Indra, the god of air and thunder, with the demon Vṛitra, who represents 'enveloping clouds and vapour.' See Vana-parva, 8690 et seq.; and compare with S'ánti-parva, 10124 et seq. Compare also the story of the 'Hawk and Pigeon,' Vana-parva, 10558, with Anuśásana-parva, 2046.

† Rámopákhyána, book III. (15913); and again alluded to in Droṇa-parva (2224). The story of Ráma is one of those stock-subjects of Indian literature, which, from its sacredness, is so dear to popular reminiscences, that Sanskṛit poets are never tired of repeating it. Bhavabhúti has dramatized it in the Víra-charitra and Uttara-Ráma-charitra: and other dramatists have done the same, just as Greek poets dramatized the Homeric narratives. The story is still acted every year in districts near the modern Oude.

‡ The Hari-vanśa bears to the Mahá-bhárata a relation very similar to that which the Uttara-káṇḍa, or last book of the Rámáyaṇa, bears to the preceding books of that poem. The Iliad and Odyssey together contain about 30,000 lines.

|| As by S'iśupála and others. See Muir's Sanskṛit Texts, vol. IV. p. 151.

by turns become prominent. Sometimes Arjuna, sometimes Yudhishṭhira, at others Bhíma, appears to be the principal orb round which the plot moves*. Moreover in various passages S'iva is described as supreme, and receives worship from Kṛishṇa. In others, Kṛishṇa is exalted above all, and receives honour from S'iva †. In fact, while the Rámáyaṇa generally represents one-sided and exclusive Bráhmanism ‡, the Mahá-bhárata reflects the multilateral character of Hindúism; its monotheism and polytheism, its spirituality and materialism, its strictness and laxity, its priestcraft and anti-priestcraft, its hierarchical intolerance and free-thinking philosophy, combined. Not that there was any intentional variety in the original design of the work, but that almost every shade of opinion found expression in a compilation formed by gradual accretion through a long period.

In unison with its more secular, popular, and *human* character, the Mahá-bhárata has less of mere mythical allegory, and more of historical probability in its narratives than the Rámáyaṇa. Hence also it contains many more illustrations of domestic and social life and manners than the more ancient epic. Its diction again is more varied than that of the Rámáyaṇa. The bulk of the latter poem (notwithstanding interpolations and additions) being by one author, is written with uniform simplicity; and the antiquity of the greater part is proved by the absence of studied elaboration, and the use of occasional irregular forms of grammar. The Mahá-bhárata, on the other hand, though generally simple and natural in its language, and free from the conceits and artificial constructions of later writers, comprehends a greater diversity of composition, rising sometimes (especially when the Indravajrá metre is

* In this respect the Mahá-bhárata resembles the Iliad. Achilles can scarcely be regarded as its hero. Other warriors too much divide the interest with him.

† In the Bhagavad-gítá Kṛishṇa is not merely an incarnation of Vishṇu; he is identified with Brahma, the supreme spirit. It is well known that in Homer the supremacy of one god (Jove), and due subordination of the other deities, is maintained.

‡ Some free thought, however, has found its way into the Rámáyaṇa; see II. cviii (Schl.); VI. lxii. 15 (Gorr.); VI. lxxxiii. 14 (Calc. edit.).

employed) to the higher style, and using not only loose and irregular, but also studiously complex grammatical forms *.

In contrasting the two Indian poems with the Iliad and the Odyssey, we may observe many points of similarity. Some parallel passages have been already pointed out, and others will be noted in the analysis at the end of this book. We must of course expect to find the distinctive genius of two very different people in widely distant localities, colouring their epic poetry very differently, notwithstanding general features of resemblance. Though the Rámáyaṇa and Mahá-bhárata are no less wonderful than the Homeric poems as monuments of the human mind, and no less interesting as pictures of human life and manners in ancient times, they bear in a remarkable degree that peculiar impress ever stamped on the productions of Asiatic nations, and separating them from European. On the side of art and harmony of proportion, they can no more compete with the Iliad and the Odyssey than the unnatural outline of the ten-headed and twenty-armed Rávaṇa can bear comparison with the symmetry of a Grecian statue. While the one commends itself to the most refined classical taste, the other by its exaggerations only excites the wonder of the Asiatic mind, or if attractive to the European, can only please an imagination nursed in an Oriental school.

Thus, in the Iliad, time, space, and action are all restricted within the narrowest limits. In the Odyssey they are allowed a wider though not too wide a cycle; but in the Rámáyaṇa and Mahá-bhárata their range is almost unbounded. The Rámáyaṇa, as it traces the life of a single individual with tolerable continuity, is in this respect more like the Odyssey than the Iliad. In other points, especially in its plot, the greater simplicity of its style, and its comparative freedom from irrelevant episodes, it more resembles the Iliad. There are many graphic passages in both the Rámáyaṇa and Mahá-bhárata which, for beauty of description, cannot be surpassed by any thing in Homer. It

* The use of irregular grammatical forms is sometimes due to the exigency of the metre: thus, *pariṇayámása* for *pariṇáyayámása*, *má bhaiḥ* for *má bhaishíḥ*: but not always; thus *vyavasishyámi* is used where the metre would admit of *vyavasásyámi*.

should be observed, however, that the diction of the Indian epics is more polished, regular, and cultivated, and the language altogether in a more advanced stage of development * than that of Homer. This, of course, tells to the disadvantage of the style on the side of nervous force and vigour; and it must be admitted that in the Sanskṛit poems there is a great redundance of epithets, too liberal a use of metaphor, simile, and hyperbole, and far too much repetition, amplification, and prolixity.

Let the reader of these poems, however, bear in mind, that Oriental compositions must not be judged from an exclusively European point of view. In the eyes of a Hindú, quality is nothing without quantity; and even quantity does not commend itself to the taste, unless seasoned with exaggeration. The reader's appreciation of many passages will depend upon his familiarity with Indian mythology, as well as with Oriental customs, scenery, and even the habits and appearances of the animal creation in the East. Most of the similes in Hindú epic poetry are taken from the motions of Asiatic animals, such as elephants and tigers †, or from peculiarities in the aspect of Indian plants and natural objects. Then, as to the description of scenery, in which Hindú poets are certainly more graphic and picturesque than either Greek or Latin ‡,

---

* An interval of many centuries must have separated the language of the Indian epics from that of the Ṛig-veda. A comparison of diction would, I think, lead us to place the Rámáyaṇa very close to Manu, if not to make these works nearly contemporaneous.

† Thus any eminent or courageous person would be spoken of as 'a tiger of a man.' Other favourite animals in similes are the lion (*sinha*), the ruddy goose (*chakraváka* or *rathánga*), the buffalo (*mahisha*), the boar (*varáha*), the koïl or Indian cuckoo (*kokila*), the heron (*krauncha*), the ox (*gavaya*, i.e. *bos gavæus*), &c. &c. It should be noted, however, that similes in the Indian epics, though far too frequent (see p. 25 of this book), are generally confined to a few words, and not, as in Homer, drawn out for three or four lines.

‡ The descriptions of scenery and natural objects in Homer are too short and general to be really picturesque. They want more colouring and minuteness of detail. Twining accounts for this by observing that the Greek poets were not accustomed to look upon nature with a painter's eye. (Poetics, p. 43.)

the whole appearance of external nature in the East, the exuberance of vegetation, the profusion of trees and fruits and flowers*, the glare of burning skies, the freshness of the rainy season, the fury of storms, the serenity of Indian moonlight †, and the gigantic mould in which natural objects are generally cast—these and many other features are difficult to be realized by a European. We must also make allowance for the difference in eastern manners; though, after conceding a wide margin in this direction, it must be confessed that the disregard of all delicacy in laying bare the most revolting particulars of certain ancient legends which we now and then encounter in the Indian epics (especially in the Mahá-bhárata) is a serious blot, and one which never disfigures the pages of Homer, notwithstanding his occasional freedom of expression. Yet there are not wanting indications in the Indian epics of a higher degree of civilization than that represented in the Homeric poems. The battle-fields of the Rámáyaṇa and Mahá-bhárata, though abounding in childish exaggerations, are not made barbarous by wanton cruelties ‡; and the descriptions of Ayodhyá and Lanká imply far greater luxury and refinement than those of Sparta and Troy.

The constant interruption of the principal story (as before described) by tedious episodes, in both Rámáyaṇa and Mahá-bhárata, added to the rambling prolixity of the story itself, will always be regarded as the chief drawback in Hindú epic poetry, and constitutes one of the

* The immense profusion of flowers of all kinds is indicated by the number of botanical terms in a Sanskṛit dictionary. Some of the most common flowers and trees alluded to in epic poetry are, the chúta or mango; the aśoka (described by Sir William Jones); the kinśuka (butea frondosa, with beautiful red blossoms); the tamarind (amliká); the jasmine (of which there are many varieties, such as málati, játí, yúthiká, &c.); the kuruvaka (amaranth); the sandal (chandana); the jujube (karkandhu); the pomegranate (dáḍima); the kadamba (níṗa); the tamarisk (pichula); the vakula, karṇikára, śṛingáṭa, &c.

† There is a beautiful description of night in Rámáyaṇa (Gorr.) I. xxxvi. 15, &c.

‡ There is something savage in Achilles' treatment of Hector; and the cruelties permitted by Ulysses, in the 22d book of the Odyssey, are almost revolting. Compare with these Ráma's treatment of his fallen foe Rávaṇa, in the Yuddha-káṇḍa.

most marked features of distinction between it and the Greek. Even in this respect, however, the Iliad has not escaped the censure of critics. Many believe that this poem is the result of the fusion of different songs on one subject, long current in various localities, intermixed with later interpolations, something after the manner of the Mahá-bhárata. But the artistic instincts of the Greeks required that all the parts and appendages and more recent additions should be blended into one compact, homogeneous, and symmetrical whole. Although we have certainly in Homer occasional digressions or parentheses, such as the description of the 'shield of Achilles,' the 'story of Venus and Mars,' these are not like the Indian episodes. If not absolutely essential to the completeness of the epic conception, they appear to arise naturally out of the business of the plot, and cause no violent disruption of its unity. With eastern writers and compilers of legendary narratives, continuity was often designedly interrupted. They preferred to string together a number of distinct stories, like detached figures on a running frieze, rather than combine them into one harmonious outline, like the finished group on a medallion. They even purposely broke the sequence of each story; so that before one was ended another was commenced, and ere this was completed, others were interwoven; the result being a curious intertwining of stories within stories, the slender thread of an original narrative running through them all. A familiar instance of this is afforded by the 'Arabian Nights,' and by the well-known collection of tales called 'Hitopadeśa' (known in Europe as Pilpay's Fables); and the same tendency is observable in the composition of their epic poems—far more, however, in the Mahá-bhárata than in the Rámáyaṇa.

Passing on to a comparison of the plot and the personages of the Rámáyaṇa with those of the Iliad,—without supposing, as some have done, that either poem has been imitated from the other, it is certainly true, and so far remarkable, that the subject of both is a war undertaken to recover the wife of one of the warriors, carried off by a hero on the other side; and that Ráma, in this respect, corresponds to Menelaus, Sítá to Helen, Sparta to Ayodhyá, Lanká to Troy. It may even be true that some sort of analogy may be traced between the parts played by Agamemnon and Sugríva, Patroclus and Lakshmaṇa, Nestor and Jámbavat *. Again, Ulysses †, in one respect, may be compared to Hanumat; and Hector, as the bravest warrior on the Trojan side, may in some points be likened to Indrajit, in others to the indignant Vibhíshaṇa ‡. Other resemblances will be pointed out in the analysis; but these comparisons cannot be carried out to any extent without encountering difficulties at every step. Ráma's character has really nothing in common with that of Menelaus, and very little with that of Achilles; although, as the bravest and most powerful of the warriors, he is rather to be compared with the latter than the former hero. If in his anger he is occasionally Achillean, his whole nature is cast in a higher and less human mould than that of the Grecian hero. Sítá also rises in character far above Helen, and even above Penelope ‖, both in her sublime devotion and loyalty to her husband, and her indomitable patience and endurance under suffering and temptation. As for Bharata and Lakshmaṇa, they are models of fraternal duty; Kauśalyá of maternal tenderness; Daśaratha of paternal love: and it may be affirmed generally that the whole moral tone of the Rámáyaṇa is certainly above that of the Iliad. Again, in the Iliad the subject is really the anger of Achilles; and when that is satisfied the drama closes. The fall of Troy is not considered necessary to the completion of the plot. Whereas

* Jámbavat was the chief of the bears, who was always giving sage advice.

† When any work had to be done which required peculiar skill or stratagem, it was entrusted to πολύμητις Ὀδυσσεύς.

‡ Hector, like Vibhíshaṇa, was indignant with the ravisher, but he does not refuse to fight on his brother's side. It is on the strength of these analogies that M. Hippolyte Fauche, in the preface to his very commendable French translation of the Rámáyaṇa, concludes that the Rámáyaṇa was composed before the Homeric poems, and that Homer took his ideas from it. It is almost needless to say that this opinion appears to me wholly untenable.

‖ One cannot help suspecting Penelope of giving way to a little womanly vanity in allowing herself to be surrounded by so many suitors, though she repudiated their advances.

in the Rámáyaṇa the whole action points to the capture of Lanká and destruction of the ravisher. No one too can read either the Rámáyaṇa or Mahá-bhárata without feeling that they rise above the Homeric poems in this—that a deep religious meaning appears to underlie all the narrative, and that the wildest allegory may be intended to conceal a sublime moral, symbolizing the conflict between good and evil, and teaching the hopelessness of victory in so terrible a contest without purity of soul, self-abnegation, and the subjugation of the passions.

As to any parallel between the mythology of the epics of India and Europe—it is well known that Indra and S'iva offer points of analogy to Jupiter *; Durgá or Párvatí to Juno; Kṛishṇa to Apollo; Rati to Venus †; S'rí to Ceres; Pṛithiví to Cybele; Varuṇa to Neptune, and, in his earlier character, to Uranus; Saraswatí to Minerva; Kártikeya or Skanda to Mars ‡; Yama to Pluto; Kuvera to Plutus; Viśwakarma to Vulcan; Káma to Cupid; Nárada to Mercury ‖; Ushas, and in the later mythology Aruṇa, to Aurora; Váyu to Æolus; Ganeśa to Janus; the Aświní-kumáras§ to the Dioscuri, Castor and Pollux; Vaitaraṇí to Styx; Kailása and Meru to Ida and Olympus.

* Indra is always the Dyu-pati or Dyaush-pitar (Diespiter), who sends rain and wields the thunderbolt, and in the earlier mythology is the chief of the gods, like Zeus. Subsequently his worship was superseded by that of Kṛishṇa and S'iva.

† In one or two points Lakshmí may be compared to Venus.

‡ It is curious that Kártikeya, the war-god, is represented in Hindú mythology as the god of thieves. (See Mṛichchhakaṭi, Act III.) Indian thieves displayed and still display such skill and ingenuity, that a god like Mercury would appear to be a more appropriate patron. Kártikeya was the son of S'iva, just as Mars was the offspring of Jupiter.

‖ As Mercury was the inventor of the lyre, so Nárada was of the víṇá or lute.

§ These ever-youthful twin sons of the Sun, by his wife Sanjná, who was transformed into a mare (aświní), are very similar to the classical Dioscuri, belonging to heroic mythology, both by their exploits and the aid they render to their worshippers against their enemies. They are constantly, however, introduced in the Ṛig-veda, where they are connected with the sun, and may typify the two luminous points which precede the dawn, or perhaps the morning and evening star.

Yet in reality it is the mythology of the Indian poems that constitutes one of the principal features of contrast in comparing them with the Homeric. We cannot of course do more than indicate here the bare outlines of so wide and so interesting a subject as that of a comparative estimate of the mythologies of India and Greece. It need scarcely be pointed out that such comparison should begin with the Veda, and not with the epic poems. A careful study of the Vedic records proves beyond a doubt that the source of Asiatic and European mythologies is the same, just as the origin of Indo-European races is the same. In that primeval country, where the ancestors of Greeks and Hindús had their common home, men satisfied their first religious instincts by idealizing, personifying, and worshipping the principal powers and energies of nature—the wind, the storm, the fire, the sun—the elements on which, as an agricultural and pastoral race, their welfare depended. This was the simple religion of nature which the Áryan family carried with them when they separated, and which they cherished in their wanderings; and in this we must trace the germ of their subsequent mythological systems*. Once settled down in their new resting-places, simple elemental worship no longer satisfied the religious cravings of these giant-races, awaking to a consciousness of nascent national life. A richly peopled mythology arose in India and Greece as naturally as epic poetry itself. The one was the offspring of the other, and was in fact the mere poetical expression of those high aspirations which marked the Áryan character. Religious ideas—a sense of dependence on a higher Power, and a desire to realize his presence—grew with their growth and strengthened with their strength. Soon the Hindú, like the Greek, unguided by direct revelation, personified, deified, and worshipped not only the powers exhibited in external nature, but all the internal feelings, passions, moral and intellectual qualities and faculties of the mind. Soon he began to regard every grand or useful object as

* In a paper just published by Mr. C. Bruce, an ancient Homeric hymn to the Earth is shown to resemble strikingly a hymn in the Atharva-veda.

a mere visible manifestation of the supreme Providence presiding over the universe, and every departed hero or deceased benefactor as a mere incarnation of the same all-wise and omnipresent Ruler. Then, to give expression to the varied attributes and functions of this great Being, thus visibly manifested to the world, both Hindú and Greek peopled their pantheons with numerous divine and semi-divine creations, clothing them with male and female forms, and inventing in connexion with them various fanciful myths, fables, and allegories, which the undiscriminating multitude accepted as realities, without at all understanding the ideas they symbolized.

But in Greece, mythology, which was in many respects fully systematized when the Homeric poems were composed *, never passed certain limits, or outgrew (so to speak) a certain symmetry of outline. In the Iliad and the Odyssey, a god is little more than idealized humanity. His form and his actions are seldom out of keeping with this character. Hindú mythology, on the other hand, springing from the same source as that of Europe, but, spreading and ramifying with the rank luxuriance of an Indian forest, speedily outgrew all harmony of proportions, and surrounded itself with an intricate and impenetrable undergrowth of monstrous and confused allegory. Doubtless the gods of the Indian and Grecian epics preserve some traces of their common origin, resembling each other in various ways; interfering in human concerns, exhibiting human infirmities, taking part in the battles of their favourite heroes, furnishing them with celestial arms, or interposing directly to protect them. But even in the Rámáyaṇa, where Hindú mythology may be regarded as not fully developed, the shape and operations of divine and semi-divine beings are generally suggestive of the monstrous, the

---

* Herodotus says (Euterpe, 53) that "Homer and Hesiod *framed* the Greek Theogony, gave distinctive names to the gods, distributed functions to them, and described their forms." I conclude that by the verb *ποιεῖν*, Herodotus did not mean to imply that Homer *invented* the myths. At any rate, the received opinion I apprehend to be that Homer merely gave system to a mythology already current.

frightful, the hideous, and the incredible*: the deeds of its heroes, who are themselves half-gods, transport the imagination into the region of the wildest chimæra; and a whole pantheon presents itself, teeming with grotesque and unwieldy symbols, with horrible creations, half-animals half-gods, with man-eating ogres†, many-headed giants and disgusting demons, to an extent which the refined and delicate sensibilities of the Greeks and Romans could not have tolerated‡.

Moreover, in the Indian epics the boundaries between the natural and supernatural, between earth and heaven, between the divine, human, and even animal creations, are singularly vague and undefined; troops

* The human form, however idealised, was seldom thought adequate to the expression of divine attributes. Brahmá is four-faced, Siva three-eyed and sometimes five-headed; Indra has a thousand eyes, Kártikeya six faces, Rávaṇa ten heads, &c.; and it is very unusual to find a Hindú god with a limited number of arms.

† It is true that Homer now and then indulges in monstrous creations; but even the description of Polyphemus does not outrage all probability, like the exaggerated horrors of the demon Kabandha, in the 3d book of the Rámáyaṇa.

‡ This difference in the mythology becomes still more deserving of note, when it is borne in mind that the wildest fictions of the Rámáyaṇa and Mahá-bhárata are to this very day intimately bound up with the creed of the Hindús. It is probable that the more educated Hindús, like the more refined Greeks and Romans, regarded and still regard the fictions of mythology as allegorical or symbolical; but in Europe and Asia the mass of the people, not understanding symbols, or troubling themselves about the mystical significance of allegories, took these fictions for real stories, and accepted every thing in its literal and immediate meaning. Among European nations, however, even the ductile faith of the masses was sufficiently controlled by reason and common sense to prevent the poetry of religious men from attempting any great extravagance of allegory; and much as the Homeric poems are still admired, no one in any part of the world now dreams of placing the slightest faith in their legends, so as to connect them with religious opinions and practices. But the wildest mythological inventions of the Indian epics are still closely interwoven with *present* faith. In fact, the capacity of an uneducated Hindú for believing the grossest absurdities, and accepting the most monstrous fictions as realities, is apparently unlimited. Even a decent approximation to the actualities of real life is too insipid for his glowing imagination. Hence the absence of all history in the literature of India. A plain relation of facts has no charm whatever.

of deities and semi-divine personages appear on the stage on every occasion; gods, men, and animals are ever changing places *. In fact, it is not merely in a confused, exaggerated, and overgrown mythology that the difference between the Indian and Grecian epics lies. It is in the injudicious and excessive use of it, and the forced obtrusion of the wild ideas and doctrines connected with a boundless religious faith. In the Rámáyaṇa and Mahá-bhárata, the spiritual and the supernatural are every where so dominant and overpowering, that any thing merely human seems altogether out of place. In the Iliad and the Odyssey, the religious and supernatural element are perhaps scarcely less prevalent. The gods are continually interposing and superintending; but they do so as if they were themselves little removed from men, or at least without destroying the dramatic probability of the poem, or neutralizing its general air of plain matter-of-fact humanity. Again, granted that in Homer there is frequent mention of the future existence of the soul, and its condition of happiness or misery hereafter, and that the Homeric descriptions of disembodied spirits correspond in many points with the Hindú notions on the same subject †—yet even these doctrines do not stand out with such exaggerated reality in Homer as to make human concerns appear unreal; nor is there in his poems the slightest allusion to the soul's pre-existence in a former body, and its liability to

* Animals figure to a certain extent in Grecian mythology, and arrogate human functions. Thus Homer makes Xanthus, the horse of Achilles, speak in a human voice and warn him of his fate (Il. XIX. 404). But the line between animals and man is not so undefined as it is made in Hindú mythology by the doctrine of the transmigration of souls.

† See the following passages, which bear on the existence of the ψυχή after death as an εἴδωλον in Hades: Il. XXIII. 72, 104; Od. XI. 213, 476; XX. 355; XXIV. 14. It is curious that the Hindú notion of the restless state of the soul until the śráddha is performed (see note, p. 38) agrees with the ancient classical superstition that the ghosts of the dead wandered about as long as their bodies remained unburied, and were not suffered to mingle with those of the other dead. See Odyss. XI. 54: Il. XXIII. 72; and cf. Æn. VI. 325: Lucan I. 11.: Eur. Hec. 30.

pass into other bodies hereafter, which in Hindú poetry invests present actions with a mysterious meaning, and gives a deep distinctive colouring to Indian theology *.

Above all, although priests are occasionally mentioned in the Iliad and the Odyssey, there is wholly wanting in the Homeric poems any recognition of a regular hierarchy, or the necessity for a mediatorial caste of sacrificers †. This, which may be called the sacerdotal element of the Indian epics, is more or less woven into their very tissue. Priestcraft has been at work in these productions almost as much as the

---

* The essentially Asiatic doctrine of metempsychosis, which was little known among the Greeks till Pythagoras, may account for the mixing up of earth and heaven which prevails far more in Hindú than in classical mythology. Not only is a constant communication kept up between the two worlds, but such is their mutual interdependance that gods, men, and animals seem constantly to need each others' help. If distressed mortals are assisted out of their difficulties by divine interposition, the tables are often turned, and the poor gods, being themselves reduced to pitiful straits, are forced to implore the aid of mortal warriors in their conflicts with the demons. I need scarcely refer to the well-known examples of this in the Śakuntalá and Vikramorvaśí, &c. Again, not only are men often aided by animals which usurp human functions, but even the gods are dependant upon them, and are poetically described as using them for vehicles—Brahmá is carried on a swan; Vishṇu on an eagle, which is also half a man; Śiva on a bull. The dependance of the Hindú gods on mortals for *actual food* is only an extension of the same idea. They are represented as *living on the sacrifices* offered to them by human beings, and at every sacrificial ceremony assemble in troops, eager for their shares. In fact, sacrifice with the Hindús is not merely expiatory or placatory; it is necessary for the *actual support* of the gods. If there were no sacrifices the gods would be liable to starvation. This alone will account for the very natural interest they take in the destruction of the demons, whose great aim and object was to obstruct these sources of their sustenance. Much in the same way the ghosts of dead men, according to the Hindús, are supposed to depend on the living, and to be actually fed with cakes and libations at the *śráddha* ceremonies.

† A king, or any other individual, is allowed in Homer to perform a sacrifice without the help of priests. See Il. II. 411; III. 392. Nevertheless we read occasionally of a θυοσκόος, or 'sacrifice-viewer,' who prophesied from the appearance of the flame and the smoke at the sacrifice. See Il. XXIV. 221: Odyss. XXI. 144; XXII. 319.

imagination of the poet; and Bráhmanism, claiming a monopoly of all knowledge, human and divine, has appropriated this, as it has every other department of literature, and warped it to its own purposes. Its policy being to check the development of intellect, and keep the inferior castes in perpetual childhood, it encouraged an appetite for exaggeration more monstrous and absurd than would be tolerated in the most extravagant European fairy-tale. The more improbable the statement, the more childish delight it was calculated to awaken. This is more true of the Rámáyaṇa than of the Mahá-bhárata; but even in the later epic, full as it is of geographical, chronological, and historical details, few assertions can be trusted. Time is measured by millions of years, space by millions of miles; and if a battle has to be described, nothing is thought of it unless millions of soldiers, elephants, and horses are brought into the field *.

Even in the delineation of heroic character, where Hindú poets exhibit much skill, they cannot avoid ministering to the craving for the marvellous which is inseparable from their nature.

Homer's characters are like Shakespeare's. They are *true* heroes, if you will, but they are always *men*; never perfect, never free from human weaknesses, inconsistencies, and caprices of temper †. If their deeds are sometimes præterhuman, they do not commit improbabilities which are absolutely absurd. Moreover, he does not seem to delineate his characters; he allows them to delineate themselves. They stand out like photographs, in all the reality of nature. We are not so much told what they do or say ‡. They appear rather to speak and act for them-

---

* See extract from Aristotle's Poetics, p. 27, note †.

† How far more natural is Achilles, with all his faults, than Ráma, with his almost painful correctness of conduct! Even the cruel vengeance that Achilles perpetrates on the dead Hector strikes us as more likely to be true than Ráma's magnanimous treatment of the fallen Rávaṇa.

‡ Aristotle says that "among the many just claims of Homer to our praise, this is one—that he is the only poet who seems to have understood what part in his poem it was proper for him to take himself. The poet, in his own person, should speak as

selves. In the Hindú epics the poet gives us too long and too tedious descriptions in his own person; and, as a rule, his characters are either too good or too bad. True, even the better heroes sometimes commit what a European would call crimes; but if they sin, they do not sin like men *. We see in them no portraits of ourselves. The pictures are too much one colour. There are few gradations of light and shadow, and little artistic blending of opposite hues. On the one side we have all gods or demigods; on the other, all demons or fiends. We miss real human beings with mixed characters. There is no mirror held up to inconsistent humanity. Duryodhana and his ninety-nine brothers would be real men if they were not so uniformly vicious. Lakshmaṇa has perhaps the most natural character among the heroes of the Rámáyaṇa, and Bhíma among those of the Mahá-bhárata. In many respects the character of the latter is not unlike that of Achilles; but in drawing his most human heroes the Indian poet still displays a perpetual tendency to run into extravagance.

It must be admitted, however, that in exhibiting pictures of domestic life and manners the Sanskṛit epics are even more valuable than the Greek and Roman. In the delineation of women the Hindú poet throws aside all exaggerated colouring, and draws from nature. Kaikeyí, Kauśalyá, Mandodarí (the favourite wife of Rávaṇa †), and even

---

little as possible..... Homer, after a few preparatory lines, immediately introduces a man, a woman, or some other character; for all have their character." (Poetics III. 3.)

* The Páṇḍavas were certainly guilty of one inhuman act of treachery. In their anxiety to provide for their own escape from a horrible death, they enticed an outcaste woman and her five sons into their inflammable lac-house, and then burnt her alive. But the guilt of this transaction is neutralized to a Hindú by the woman being an outcaste; and besides, it is Bhíma who sets fire to the house. See the analysis at the end of this book. Ráma and Lakshmaṇa again were betrayed into a piece of cruelty in mutilating Śúrpanakhá; but for this the fiery Lakshmaṇa was responsible.

† What can be more natural than Mandodarí's lamentations over the dead body of Rávaṇa, and her allusions to his fatal passion for Sítá, in the 95th chapter of the 6th book of the Rámáyaṇa? (Gorresio's edition.)

the hump-backed Manthará, are all drawn to the very life. Sítá, Draupadí, and Damayantí engage our affections and our interest far more than Helen, or even than Penelope. Indeed, Hindú wives are generally perfect patterns of conjugal fidelity; nor can it be doubted that in these delightful portraits of the Pativratá or devoted wife we have true representations of the purity and simplicity of Hindú domestic manners in early times *. We may also gather from the epic poems many interesting hints as to the social position occupied by Hindú women before the Muhammadan conquest. No one can read the Rámáyaṇa and Mahá-bhárata without coming to the conclusion that the habit of secluding women, and of treating them as inferiors, is, to a certain extent, natural to all eastern nations, and prevailed in the earliest times †. Yet no one, at the same time, can fail to observe, that

* No doubt the devotion of a Hindú wife implied greater inferiority than is compatible with modern European ideas of independence. The extent to which this devotion was carried even in little matters is curiously exemplified by the story of Gándhárí, who out of sympathy for her blind husband never appeared in public without a veil over her face. Hence, during the grand sham-fight between the Kuru and Páṇḍu princes, Vidura stood by Dhṛitaráshṭra, and Kuntí by Gándhárí, to describe the scene to them (Astrasíkshá, 34).

† It was equally natural to the Greeks and Romans. Chivalry and reverence for the fair sex belonged only to European nations of northern origin, who were the first to hold 'inesse fœminis sanctum aliquid.' (Tac. Germ. 8.) That Hindú women in ancient times secluded themselves, except on certain occasions, may be inferred from the word *asúryampaśyá*, given by Páṇini as an epithet of a king's wife ('one who never sees the sun'); a very strong expression, stronger even than the *pardanishín* of the Muhammadans. It is to be observed also that in the Rámáyaṇa (VI. xcix. 33) there is clear allusion to some sort of seclusion being practised; and the term *Avarodha*, 'secluded or guarded place,' is used long before the time of the Muhammadans for the women's apartments. In the Ratnávali, however, the minister of Vatsa, with his chamberlain and the envoy from Ceylon, are admitted to an audience there in the presence of the queen and her damsels; and Ráma, although in the 99th chapter of the 6th book of the Rámáyaṇa he thinks it necessary to excuse himself for permitting his wife to expose herself to the gaze of the crowd, yet expressly (verse 34) enumerates various occasions on which it was allowable for a woman to show herself

women in India were subjected to less social restraint in former days than they are at present. True, the ancient lawgiver, Manu, speaks of women as having no will of their own, and totally unfit for independence; but he probably described a state of society which it was the aim of an arrogant priesthood to establish, rather than that which really existed in his own time. At a later period the pride of Bráhmanism, and still more recently the influence of Muhammadanism, deprived women of even such freedom as they once enjoyed; so that at the present day no Hindú woman has, *in theory*, any independence. It is not merely that she is not her own mistress: she is not her own property, and never, under any circumstances, can be. She belongs to her father first, who gives her away to her husband, to whom she belongs *for ever* *. She is not considered capable of so high a form of religion as man †, and she does not mix freely in society. But in

unveiled. I here translate the passage, as it bears very remarkably on this interesting subject. Ráma says to Vibhíshaṇa—"Neither houses, nor vestments, nor enclosing walls, nor ceremony, nor regal insignia (rája-satkára), are the screen (ávaraṇa) of a woman. It is her own virtue alone (that protects her). In great calamities (vyasaneshu), at marriages, at the public choice of a husband by maidens (of the Kshatriya caste), at a sacrifice, at assemblies (sansatsu), it is allowable for all the world to look upon women (stríṇám darśanam'sárvalaukikam)."

* Hence when her husband dies she cannot be remarried, as there is no one to give her away. In fact, the remarriage of Hindú widows, which is now permitted by law, is utterly opposed to all modern Hindú ideas about women; and there can be no doubt that the passing of this law was one cause of the mutiny of 1857. It is clear from the story of Damayantí, who appoints a second Swayamvara, that in early times remarriage was not necessarily a violation of propriety; though, from Damayantí's wonder that the new suitor should have failed to see through her artifice, and from her vexation at being supposed capable of a second marriage, it may be inferred that a second marriage was even then not altogether reputable.

† No doubt the inferior capacity of a woman as regards religion was implied in the epic poems, as well as in later works. A husband was said to be the wife's divinity, as well as her lord and master, and her best religion was to please him. See Sítá's speech, p. 13 of this book. See also the quotation from Mádhava Áchárya (who flourished in the 14th century), at p. 17, note *. Such verses as the following are com-

ancient times, when the epic songs were current in India, women were not confined to intercourse with their own families; they did very much as they pleased, travelled about, and showed themselves unreservedly in public *, and, if of the Kshatriya caste, were occasionally allowed to choose their own husbands from a number of assembled suitors †. It is clear, moreover, that in many instances there was considerable dignity and elevation about the female character, and that much mutual affection prevailed in families. Nothing can be more beautiful and touching than the pictures of domestic and social happiness in the Rámáyaṇa and Mahá-bhárata. Children are dutiful to their parents ‡ and submissive to their superiors; younger brothers are respectful

---

mon in Hindú literature: Bhartá hi paramam náryá bhúshaṇam, bhúshanais viná, 'a husband is a wife's chief ornament even without (other) ornaments.' Manu says (V. 151), Yasmai dadyát pitá tv enám bhrátá vánumate pituh, Tam śuśrúsheta jívantam sansthitam cha na langhayet, 'Him to whom her father may give her, or her brother with her father's consent, let her obey while he lives, and when he dies let her never slight him.' In book IV. 198, Manu classes women with Śúdras.

* Especially married women. A wife was required to obey her husband implicitly, but in other respects she was to be independent (swátantryam arhati, Mahá-bhár. I. 4741). Sítá, as we have seen, was allowed to show herself to the army; and, in illustration of what was said in a former note, we may here add that Śakuntalá appeared in the public court of king Dushyanta; Damayanti travelled about by herself; and in the Uttara-Ráma-charita, the mother of Ráma comes to the hermitage of Válmíki. It is certain that women were present at dramatic representations, visited the temples of the gods, and performed their ablutions with little privacy; which last custom they still practise, though Muhammadan women are prohibited from doing so. (Wilson, Hindú Theatre, vol. I. xliii.)

† The Swayamvara, however, appears to have been something exceptional, and only to have been allowed in the case of the daughters of kings or Kshatriyas. See Draupadí-swayamvara, 127: see also Mahá-bhár. I. 7926.

‡ Contrast with the respectful tone of Hindú children towards their parents, the harsh manner in which Telemachus generally speaks to his mother. Filial respect and affection is quite as noteworthy a feature in the Hindú character now as in ancient times. I have been assured by Indian officers that it is common for unmarried soldiers to stint themselves almost to starvation-point, that they may send home money to their aged

to elder brothers; parents are fondly attached to their children, watchful over their interests and ready to sacrifice themselves for their welfare; wives are loyal, devoted, and obedient to their husbands, yet show much independence of character, and do not hesitate to express their own opinions; husbands are tenderly affectionate towards their wives, and treat them with respect and courtesy; daughters and women generally are virtuous and modest, yet spirited and, when occasion requires, courageous; love and harmony reign throughout the family circle. Indeed, it is in depicting scenes of domestic affection, and expressing those universal feelings and emotions which belong to human nature in all time and in all places, that Sanskṛit epic poetry is unrivalled. In this respect not even Greek epos can compete with it. It is not often that Homer takes us out of the battle-field; and if we except the lamentations over the bodies of Patroclus and Hector, the visit of Priam to the tent of Achilles, and the parting of Hector and Andromache, there are no such pathetic passages in the Iliad as the death of the 'hermit-boy,' the pleadings of Sítá for permission to accompany her husband into exile, and the whole ordeal-scene at the end of the Rámáyaṇa. In the Indian epics such passages abound, and, besides giving a very high idea of the purity and happiness of domestic life in ancient India, indicate a capacity in Hindú women for the discharge of the most sacred and important social duties.

We must guard against the supposition that the women of India at the present day have altogether fallen from their ancient character. Notwithstanding the corrupting example of Muhammadanism, and the degrading tendency of modern Hindúism, some remarkable instances

---

parents. In fact, in proportion to the weakness or rather total absence of the *national* is the strength of the *family* bond. In England, where national life is strongest, children are far more independent, and less respectful to their parents. In this the Hindús might teach us a good lesson.

may still be found of moral, social, and even intellectual excellence *. These, however, are exceptions, and we may rest assured, that until Asiatic women, whether Hindú or Muhammadan, are elevated and educated, our efforts to raise Asiatic nations to the level of European will be fruitless †. Let us hope that when the Rámáyaṇa and Mahá-bhárata shall no longer be held sacred as repositories of faith and storehouses of religious tradition, the enlightened Hindú may still learn from these poems to honour the weaker sex; and that Indian women, restored to their ancient liberty and raised to a still higher position by becoming joint-partakers of Christ's religion, may do for our Eastern empire what they have done for Europe—soften, invigorate, and ennoble the character of its people.

* In some parts of India, especially in the Maráthí districts, there is still considerable freedom of thought and action allowed to women.

† Manu gives expression to a great truth when he says (III. 145), Sahasram tu pitṛín mátá gauraveṇátirichyate.

ANALYSIS OF THE RÁMÁYAṆA.

(Observe—The poem consists of seven books, but the seventh, or Uttara-káṇḍa, is generally admitted to be a later addition.)

FIRST BOOK or BÁLA-KÁṆḌA, also called ÁDI-KÁṆḌA.—The real story of the poem does not begin till the 5th chapter of this book *. The first four chapters are introductory, and are probably much later in date than the body of the poem. In the first chapter the poet Válmíki †, the author of the work, is represented as inquiring of the sage Nárada, "who is the bravest and best man that ever lived on the earth?" Nárada then relates briefly the history of Ráma; which Válmíki had not before heard. Soon afterwards Válmíki, walking near a river, sees a hunter shoot a

* As the northern recension of the Rámáyaṇa commenced by Schlegel is the older and purer, my references are to that as far as the end of book II. I have then referred to Gorresio's edition. The new Calcutta edition of the northern recension had not arrived at the Bodleian when I made my analysis. I have however inserted occasional references to it since, and should be inclined to add others, did I not feel convinced that this edition will never commend itself to the use of European students. Out of deference to native prejudices, it is printed to resemble a MS., and not a single word is divided—practical inconveniences, which, in my opinion, almost neutralize the advantage it possesses of a full commentary. M. Hippolyte Fauche deserves credit for his laborious translation into French of the whole edition of Gorresio; but I had not an opportunity of consulting his version, nor M. St. Hilaire's articles upon it in the 'Journal des Savants,' till I had nearly finished my own work.

† The author of an article in the Calcutta Review (XLV), to whom I am indebted for some valuable remarks on the Rámáyaṇa, thinks there is no doubt that Válmíki resided on the banks of the Jumná, near its confluence with the Ganges at Allahabad; and tradition has marked a hill in the district of Banda in Bundelkund, as his abode. He is said to have begun life as a highway robber, but repenting of his misdeeds, betook himself to a hermitage, on this hill, where he eventually received Sítá, the wife of Ráma, when banished by her over-sensitive husband. There were born her two sons, Kuśa and Lava (sometimes combined into one compound, thus—Kuśí-lavau), who were taught to sing the poem descriptive of their unknown father's actions, and from whom are traced the proudest Rajput castes. The reviewer thinks it not unlikely that Válmíki may have been contemporaneous with the heroes whom he describes; but this opinion seems to me to be based on insufficient data.

heron, and grieving for the poor bird he curses the hunter in language expressive of his sorrow (*śoka*). His words took the form of a verse, ever afterwards called *śloka*; and in this metre *, at the command of the god Brahmá, he composed the Rámáyaṇa, a poem celebrating, in 24,000 verses, the life and adventures (*ayana*) of Ráma, a prince of the solar race of kings, which commenced in Ikshwáku. The third chapter contains the Anukramaṇiká, or table of contents; and the fourth describes the appointment of two rhapsodists (Kuśa and Lava, really the children of Sítá and Ráma), who were to commit the whole poem to memory, and sing it at assemblies.

It may be useful here to give an abridgment of the genealogy of the solar race of kings, commencing with Ikshwáku, the son of the Manu Vaivaswata (the seventh Manu, or Manu of the present period). The latter was the son of Vivaswat (i. e. the sun, commonly called Súrya). The sun again was the son of the Muni Kaśyapa, who was the son of the Ṛishi Maríchi, who was the son of Brahmá. From Ikshwáku † sprang the two branches of the solar dynasty; that of Ayodhyá or Oude, which may be said to have commenced in Kakutstha, the grandson of Ikshwáku (as the latter's son Vikukshi, father of Kakutstha, did not reign), and that of Mithilá, or Videha (Tirhut) which commenced in another of Ikshwáku's sons, *Nimi*. Thirty-fifth in descent from Kakutstha came Sagara; fourth from him Bhagíratha; third from him Ambarísha; and fifteenth from him Raghu. We here repeat a portion of the genealogy in order—Maríchi, Kaśyapa, Vivaswat or Súrya, Vaivaswata, Ikshwáku [Vikukshi], Kakutstha [..................................], Sagara [..], Dilípa, Bhagíratha [..], Ambarísha [...............], Raghu, Aja, Daśaratha, Ráma. Hence Ráma is variously called, Kákutstha, Rághava, Dáśaratha or Dáśarathi.

The poem opens in the 5th chapter with a description of Ayodhyá or Oude, a city on the banks of the Sarayú ‡, the capital of the kingdom of Kośala, which belonged to Daśaratha, Ráma's father.

* That the Rámáyaṇa is reckoned by the Hindús to be one of the earliest Indian poems is shown by the circumstance that the invention of the common śloka metre, used in all subsequent heroic poems, is attributed to its author.

† This list agrees with the usual one as exhibited in Prinsep's table; but there is considerable variation in the genealogy, as given in Rámáyaṇa II. cx. For instance, the son of Ikshwáku is said to be Kukshi, and his son Vikukshi.

‡ Although Ayodhyá is the base of operations in the Rámáyaṇa, yet the poet carries us through a vast extent of country, conducting us now beyond the Sutlej into the Panjáb, now across the Vindhya mountains into the Dekkan, and across the Narbaddá and Godávarí to the most southern parts of India, even to the island of Ceylon. It is probable, however, that the geography of the poem is not always to be trusted. The river Sarayú is now called the Gogra.

We have next, in the 6th and 7th chapters, an eulogium on Daśaratha and his chosen counsellors; of whom the most eminent were Vaśishṭha, Vámadeva, Sumantra, and seven others. These are all Bráhmans, and direct the affairs of the government. King Daśaratha is without a son (viii. 1); a serious calamity in India, where a son is needed for the due performance of the śráddha or funeral ceremony necessary for the repose of the parent's soul after death (see note, p. 38), and where the very word for son (*putra* or *puttra*) is declared to mean one who delivers his father from hell *. The usual remedy for this misfortune was a great sacrifice conducted by Bráhmans, who receive enormous presents in return for the favour of the gods, which they are supposed thereby to procure †. Ṛishyaśṛinga therefore, a celebrated sage, married to Daśaratha's daughter Śántá (whose story is related in an episode, ix ‡), is called in to assist at the celebration of a great aśwamedha or horse-sacrifice.

---

* That is, from a particular hell called Put. Punnámno narakád yasmát pitaram tráyate sutah, Tasmát puttra iti proktah. Rám. I. 76 (Carey), quoted from Manu, book IX. 138. This is of course a mere fanciful etymology. But there is no doubt that the Hindús believe that the happiness of the dead depends on the performance of the śráddha ceremonies by their descendants. A man is therefore said to be in debt to his forefathers until he has a son. Then, and not till then, he is absolved from his debt to them—Esha vá anṛiṇo yah putríti śruteh.

† These sacrifices were purposely cumbered with a most tedious and intricate ceremonial, which none could perform but Bráhmans educated to the task. The Rákshasas were represented as eagerly on the watch for any flaw, defect, or mistake. If any occurred, the whole ceremony was seriously obstructed, and its efficacy destroyed.

‡ The episode of Ṛishyaśṛinga is very curious. "It so happened, that in the neighbouring kingdom of the Angi, now known as the district of Bhagulpore, in Bengal, there had been a great dearth, and the king, Lomapáda, had been assured that the only chance of obtaining rain was to entice this same ascetic from his retirement, and get him to marry the king's daughter, or rather the adopted child of Lomapáda, and real daughter of Daśaratha. This ascetic was the son of Vibháṇḍaka, a sainted mortal of frightful power; and he had begotten this son apparently without a mother, and had brought him up alone in the wilderness, where he had never seen nor even heard of the existence or fascinations of that interesting portion of the human race, called woman. The plan was to send a party of young females, disguised as ascetics, and coax the great saint from his retreat by those wiles which are all-powerful. The episode describing all this is most fantastic. The surprise and unsettlement of the mind, the entire interruption of devotions, and the heart's unrest, that befell the unhappy saint when he received his new visitants, is most graphically described; and we might laugh at the conceit of such being possible, had not a modern traveller in the Levant, Mr. Curzon, assured us of the existence of a similar case in one of the convents of Mount Athos in the nineteenth century. He there found a monk in middle life who had never set eyes on women, nor had any notion of them beyond what could be formed from a black and hideous altar-picture of

This was successfully conducted. We are told that "no oblation was neglected, nor any mistake committed; all was performed in exact conformity to the Veda*" (xiii. 10). The gods, with Indra at their head, assembled to receive their shares of the oblations (see note, p. 52), and being satisfied, promised four sons to Daśaratha (xiv. 9). The scene now changes to the Hindú Olympus, where a deputation of the gods waits on Brahmá, and represents to him that the universe is in danger of being destroyed by the chief of the Rákshasas, Rávaṇa. His power is described as so great that "where he is, there the sun does not give out its heat; the winds through fear of him do not blow; the fire ceases to burn; and the ocean, crowned with rolling billows, becomes motionless" (xiv. 17). This great demon could only be destroyed by man, as by a long course of penance he had obtained a boon from Brahmá, in virtue of which he was invulnerable by gods and divine beings of all kinds (xiv. 22). While the discussion of this matter is going on in heaven, Vishṇu joins the conclave, and, on being requested, promises to take the form of man, that he may kill Rávaṇa (xiv. 45). The next scene takes us back to the sacrifice. A supernatural being, tall as a mountain, rises in the fire, and presents a cup of divine páyasa or nectar to the priest, which the queens of Daśaratha are directed to drink † (xv. 20). Half is given to Kau-

---

the Virgin Mary. The cruel traveller, by an accurate description of the many charms of the fair sisterhood, entirely destroyed the poor solitary monk's peace of mind for the future. In the Hindú story they went further, for they enticed the ascetic away from his woods, put him on board a vessel on the broad Ganges, married him to the king's daughter, and brought him to Ayodhyá, to conduct the sacrifice." See Calcutta Review, XLV.

* The horse chosen for this purpose was let loose and allowed to roam about for a year. If no one was able during this period to seize it, it was deemed fit for sacrifice; but the seizure was sometimes effected by the god Indra, whose tenure of heaven was imperilled by the great power accruing to those who completed many aśwamedhas. Another year was consumed in preparations for the sacrifice. The description of the ceremony, in the 13th chap. (Calc. ed. 14), is curious. Many parts of the sacrifice, such as the *Pravargya* and *Upasada*, cannot be explained, as the nature of these rites is unknown to the pandits of the present day. Twenty-one yúpas or sacrificial posts were erected, to which were tied various animals, and especially the horse. Near the latter the queens of Daśaratha watched for a whole night. The marrow (vapá) of the horse [patatrin here = horse. According to the commentator, Calcutta edition, purá aśwánám pakshah santíti prasiddhyá evamvádah] was then taken out and dressed, and the horse itself appears to have been cut up and offered in the fire, and the king, smelling the smoke of the burning flesh, became absolved from his sins. Various other sacrifices seem to have accompanied the aśwamedha, such as the Chatushṭoma, Jyotishṭoma, Atirátra, Abhijit, &c. The most important part of the whole proceeding was the feasting and the largesses. King Daśaratha is described as giving to the priests a million cows, a hundred million pieces of gold, and four times as many pieces of silver.

† Of Daśaratha's three wives, the chief, Kauśalyá, is said to have been of his own race and

śalyá, who brings forth *Ráma*, possessed of half the nature of Vishṇu (and so called from the root *ram*, meaning 'to delight:' see Gorresio's edition, xix. 28); half the remaining part, or one-fourth, to Sumitrá, who brings forth *Lakshmaṇa* and *Śatrughna*, having each an eighth part of Vishṇu's essence; and the remaining quarter to Kaikeyí, who brings forth *Bharata*, with a fourth part of Vishṇu's essence *. The brothers are all deeply attached to each other; but Lakshmaṇa (often called Saumitri) is especially the companion of Ráma †, and Śatrughna of Bharata. Previously to the description of the birth of the princes there is a curious account of the creation of the monkeys, bears, and other semi-divine animals ‡, who were afterwards to become the allies of Ráma in his war with Rávaṇa. "These beings were supposed to be incarnations of various gods, and were in fact the progeny of the gods, demigods, divine serpents, and other mythical personages. Thus Su-gríva (the chief of them) was the son of the Sun; Báli of Indra; Tára of Vṛihaspati; Gandha-mádana of Kuvera; Nala of Viśwakarma; Níla of Fire; and the celebrated Hanumat, of the Wind. They appear to have been genii rather than animals, and could assume any form they pleased (Káma-rúpiṇah, xvi. 18): they could wield rocks, remove mountains, break the strongest trees, tear up the earth, mount the air and seize the clouds" (xvi. 24).

While Ráma and his brothers are still mere striplings, the sage Viśwámitra, son of Gádhi, presents himself at their father's court, and requests that Ráma will come to his hermitage to protect him and other devotees in the celebration of a sacrifice, which was impeded by the attacks of the Rákshasas ‖ (xx). Daśaratha at first flatly refuses to

---

country (probably so called from Kośala, the country of Daśaratha); the second, Kaikeyí, was the daughter of Aswapati, king of Kekaya, supposed to be in the Punjáb (whence the king himself is sometimes called Kekaya); and the third, Sumitrá, was probably from Magadha or Behár. The father of the last is said to have been a Vaiśya. Although in xix. the birth of Bharata *is* narrated *after* that of Ráma, he is supposed to have been born after the twins; and in xv. the nectar is taken to Sumitrá next to Kauśalyá. Schlegel considers that Bharata was eleven months junior to Ráma, and the twins only three months. See his note to xix. Probably the mother of Bharata was higher in rank than Sumitrá, which would give him the precedence.

* Avaśishṭárdham, in the text, must be taken to mean 'a half of the half,' as Kaikeyí certainly received a fourth part of the celestial food (xv. 21).

† He was to Ráma like another self. Rámasya Lakshmaṇo vahihpráṇa iváparah, na cha tena viná nidrám labhate, na tam viná mishṭam annam upánítam aśnáti (xix. 22).

‡ Described (xvi. 19) as *go-puchha*, 'with tails like oxen.'

‖ According to the Uttara-káṇḍa (Calc. ed. IV. 9. V. 21), Brahmá, after creating the waters, formed a race of beings called Rákshasas to guard them (raksh), and Viśwakarma assigned Lanká as their abode. But it is a noteworthy circumstance, that in Hindú mythology the principal employment and aim of all the malignant operations of evil spirits and demons was

let his son go (fearing the risk for one so young); but the anger of Viśwámitra is so terrible, that at length the king consents (xxii. xxiii). Ráma and Lakshmaṇa therefore are allowed to accompany Viśwámitra, who takes them along the course of the Sarayú or Gogra to the junction of that river with the Ganges. They passed the night on the bank; and Viśwámitra, who proved a most loquacious companion, explained the cause of the noise of the meeting of the waters (xxvi. 6). They lodged in a grove, where formerly Śiva performed penance. There Kámadeva, trying to influence Śiva with love, shot an arrow at him, and was reduced to ashes by a flash from his eye (xxv). When they had crossed the river, Ráma displayed his prowess by the slaughter of a giantess or fiend named Táḍaká: but it was only after long argument that he could be induced to kill a female (xxviii). This was his first exploit; and Viśwámitra in return presented him with a number of mystical weapons (xxix; see note, p. 27). Proceeding onwards, they arrived at the place where the sacrifice was to be performed, called 'the grove of perfection'* (xxxi. 28). Here Vishṇu, in a previous incarnation as the Vámana, or dwarf, had resided, when he became incarnate to deliver the world from the tyranny of Bali. The grove was now occupied by numbers of devotees, who were waiting the arrival of Ráma, to complete their great sacrifice. The demons were soon routed by the hero, and their leader Márícha (who was to appear again as an enemy of Ráma) was hurled by a blow from one of his mystical arrows to the distance of a hundred yojanas, into the ocean (xxxii. 17). When the sacred rites were accomplished, news was brought that Janaka, king of Mithilá, was about to perform a sacrifice, and, at a great assembly, to give his daughter Sítá † in marriage to any one who could bend the bow of Śiva (xxxiii. 4; and see pp. 5, 6, of this volume).

Viśwámitra proposed to take the young princes to the assembly ‡. On their way they encamped on the bank of the river Śoṇa, now known as the Sone (xxxiii. 20).

---

not to guard any thing, but rather to disturb the sacrifices and holy rites of devout men, and prevent their completion. (See note §, p. 9.) Viśwámitra himself might have conquered these demons; 'a word, a look of his might have reduced them to ashes;' but the slightest expression of anger on his part would have neutralized the effect of the sacrifice. A hero of the warrior caste, therefore, had to be present, to enable the ceremony to proceed.

* According to the Calcutta Review, in the district of Shahabád.

† Called Sítá because not born from a woman, but from a furrow while Janaka was ploughing (lxvi. 14). Dr. Weber thinks that the whole story of Ráma and Sítá is simply an allegory, denoting the introduction of agriculture and civilization into the south of India by immigrants from the north. He is also singular in believing that the Rámáyaṇa is posterior to the Mahá-bhárata.

‡ According to the Calcutta Review it was on his road home, as he resided in the hilly country on the banks of the river Kosi.

Here Viśwámitra tells his young companions the origin of the name of the city Kánya-Kubja, now called Kanouj, on the Ganges, sixty miles north of Cawnpore (xxxiv. 37). Next day they crossed the Sone, and journeyed through the district of the Ganges, where the episode of the origin of this river is introduced *. On the following day crossing the Ganges (xlv. 9) they entered Tirhut †, arriving the first night at Viśálá (xlv. 10; xlvii. 13), where they were hospitably received by king Sumati (xlvii. 20); and the history of the district is detailed by Viśwámitra (xlv. 14). Proceeding towards Mithilá (the capital of Tirhut), they passed through the hermitage of the sage Gautama (xlviii. 10), whose story is then told. (His wife Ahalyá was seduced by Indra, and the latter cursed in consequence ‡.) Thence proceeding onwards, they arrived at a great enclosure prepared for the sacrifice (yajna-váṭa) by king Janaka, where thousands of Bráhmans were collected. King Janaka there met them (l), and Śatánanda, son of Gautama, the domestic chaplain of Janaka, narrated to Ráma the history of Viśwámitra ‖. Thence with Janaka they proceeded to Mithilá, the capital of his kingdom (now known as Janakpore, in the kingdom of Nepál, just beyond the Tirhut district), and were there hospitably entertained. The story of the bending the bow of Śiva by Ráma is here told § (lvii; see p. 5 of this volume). In consequence of this exploit Sítá became the prize of Ráma (lxvii. 23); and messengers being sent to king Daśaratha (lxviii) to bid him to the wedding, he came accompanied by his two other sons, Bharata and Śatrughna. A sister of Sítá (Úrmilá) was given to Lakshmaṇa (lxxiii.

---

* See p. 13 of this volume.

† Or Sanskṛitice Tírabhukti, the province bounded by the banks of three rivers, the Gaṇḍak (Gaṇḍakí), the Ganges, and the Kosi (Kauśikí). The most ancient name of the district is *Videha*, its capital being Mithilá.

‡ This is one of the grossly indelicate stories of Hindú mythology.

‖ The various episodes which occur in this part of the poem are most interesting, especially this history of Viśwámitra, the birth of Kártikeya, god of war, the success of Bhagíratha in bringing down the Ganges from heaven (p. 14), the churning of the ocean and production of the nectar. The history of Viśwámitra includes the stories of Triśanku and that of Ambarisha. The last is very curious. Ambarisha, king of Ayodhyá, performed a sacrifice (lxii), but the victim being stolen by Indra (see note, p. 63), he is told by the priest that either the victim itself must be recovered, or a human victim substituted in its place. Ambarisha wanders over the earth in search of the real victim, and meets at last with a Bráhman named Richíka, to whom he offers a hundred thousand cattle for one of his sons. Richíka refuses to let his eldest son go, and his wife will not part with the youngest. Upon this the middle son, S'unahśephah, offers himself and is accepted. When about to be offered up as a sacrifice he is saved by Viśwámitra, who teaches him a prayer to Agni, and two hymns to Indra and Vishṇu.

§ In Bhavabhúti's drama, the Mahá-víra-charitra (Act I), the bow is represented as arriving, *self-conveyed*.

28); and two nieces of Janaka, daughters of his brother Kuśadhwaja (viz. Máṇḍaví and Śruta-kírti), became the brides of Bharata and Śatrughna respectively. The wedding is minutely described, as well as the pedigree of both families (lxx. lxxi), with special mention of the costly presents given to the Bráhmans and family priests (lxxii). After the ceremony king Janaka bestowed munificent dowries on his daughters (lxxiv. 2—6); and Daśaratha and his sons then set out on their return to Ayodhyá. Viśwámitra too took his leave, and retired towards the northern mountains * (lxxiv. 1).

On their way home Daśaratha and his sons are met by Paraśu-Ráma (regarded in the later mythology as a previous incarnation of Vishṇu; see note, p. 11), who was angry at the breaking of Śiva's † bow by Ráma-chandra, and challenged the latter to a trial of strength with another bow (once the property of Vishṇu ‡, lxxv. 13), telling him that if he could shoot an arrow from this bow he would consent to a personal combat. Ráma-chandra easily accomplished this feat also; and by so doing excluded Paraśu-Ráma from a seat in the celestial world ‖, but spared his life in consideration of his being a Bráhman (lxxvi. 6). On the party reaching Ayodhyá, Bharata was taken by his mother's brother, Yudhájit, to finish his education at the court of his maternal grandfather, Aśwapati or Kekaya, who lived in the city of Girivraja, said to be in the Punjáb (I. lxxvii. 18; II. lxviii. 21), and Śatrughna accompanied him.

SECOND BOOK or AYODHYÁ-KÁṆḌA.—At the commencement of this book we have an account of the circumstances which led the king Daśaratha, at the instigation of Bharata's mother, Kaikeyí, to countermand the intended inauguration of Ráma, as heir-apparent, and to decide on banishing him (i—xviii; and see p. 6 of this volume). It is remarkable that the virtues of Ráma had disarmed his stepmothers; and even the mother of Bharata (who was the king's favourite wife, xi. 6) felt no jealousy, until a humpbacked female slave named Manthará, like a fiend incarnate, instigated her to plot the degradation of Ráma, by suggesting that his elevation to the throne would involve the banishment or even death of Bharata, and her own disgrace (viii. 27). When all Kaikeyí's evil passions were thus roused, she tore

* That is, to the Nepál hills, and we hear no more of him.

† Paraśu-Ráma is elsewhere described as a disciple of Śiva. See Muir's Texts, vol. I. p. 157.

‡ Both the bows, however, were made by Viśwakarman (Vulcan); see Rám. I. lxxv. 11.

‖ It appears that somehow or other by the discharge of the arrow he was excluded from a seat in the celestial world, which he had earned by his penance, and consequently had to retire to the Himálaya mountains (lxxvi. 22): but the narrative is obscure; see p. 11 of this volume. The commentator to the Calcutta edition says—śara-mokshe gamishyámi pápasya tapasaś dagdhatvát puṇyasya cha śara-mokshena phala-pratibandhe jívan-mukto bhútwá gamishyámi ity arthaḥ.

off her jewels, and threw herself on the bare ground in 'the chamber of anger' (krodhágára), an apartment which (according to Ward) is still maintained in Hindú houses for wives who are out of humour with their husbands. (See Calcutta Review, XLV. 183.) There she is found by Daśaratha (x. 22), who in astonishment asks her if any one has insulted her (x. 28). She replies by reminding him that formerly, in a battle between the gods and demons, in which he had aided the gods, he was dangerously wounded, and that she had then watched by his bedside, and that he then promised her two boons, the fulfilment of which she now required, viz. the installation of Bharata, and the banishment of Ráma for fourteen years to the forest of Daṇḍaka as a tápasa or devotee (xi. 23 and 24). A tremendous quarrel then ensues between the king and Kaikeyí* (xii); but the king is obliged to abide by his promise, and gives orders for the banishment of Ráma (xviii). The mother of Ráma (Kauśalyá) is heart-broken: his friends counsel him to rebel, and the fiery Lakshmaṇa urges resistance; but the good Ráma listens to no one, and thinks only of his duty to his father.

Ráma therefore is banished to the woods, and his wife Sítá and her brother Lakshmaṇa insist on accompanying him (xxxi. xxxii). They set off for their fourteen years of exile, escorted at first by the citizens, and encamp the first night on the river Tamasá (now the Tonse, on which Azimgurh is situated, xlv). Ráma, hopeless of persuading the citizens to return, crosses the river in the night while they are asleep (xlvi. 20—28), hastens to the Gomatí (Goomtee, xlix. 10), and thence to the Ganges (l. 11) at Sungroor (in the district of Allábahád), then called Śringavera. Here was the extremity of his father's kingdom; and here he made his charioteer Sumantra return (lii. 94), with a forgiving message to his father, urging him to send for the absent Bharata and inaugurate him as king (lii. 32), and to be kind to the stepmother who was the author of his own exile † (lii. 23). Here at Śringavera, on the Ganges (lxxxiii. 19), Guha, king of the Nishádas, received them hospitably (l. 22). They

* All the misfortunes of king Daśaratha are the result of polygamy; whereas Ráma was satisfied with one wife, the blameless Sítá, and remained ever faithful to her. In this Ráma is a contrast to the heroes of the Mahá-bhárata.

† Before commencing their forest-life, Ráma and Lakshmaṇa, in obedience to the desire of Kaikeyí (xl. 23), clothed themselves in bark-garments, and tied their hair so as to form a jaṭá or knot, projecting like a kind of horn over their foreheads, after the fashion of Hindú devotees (lii. 61). How many centuries have passed since the two brothers began their memorable journey, and yet every step of it is known, and traversed annually by thousands of pilgrims! strong indeed are the ties of religion, when entwined with the legends of a country! Those who have followed the path of Ráma from the Gogra to Ceylon, stand out as marked men among their countrymen. It is this that gives the Rámáyaṇa a strange interest; the story still lives: whereas no one now, in any part of the world, puts faith in the legends of Homer. (See Calcutta Review, XLV.)

slept under an Ingudi tree (l), and next day Guha ferried them across the Ganges (lii. 69), and thence they soon reached the sacred junction of the Ganges and the Jumná, called by Hindús Prayága (liv. 5), where now stands the celebrated city of Alláhabád *, and where then stood the hermitage of the sage Bharadwája. He also treated them hospitably (liv. 42); and, with his approval, they determined on fixing their first residence on the hill Chitra-kúṭa (Chuteerkote, liv. 28), about two days' march beyond the river Jumná (also called Kálindí). They therefore crossed that river (lv) on a great raft (sumaháplava, lv. 14) into the district of Bandah (in Bundelkund) †, and, advancing into the forest (lv. 32), arrived at Chitra-kúṭa, where they erected their hermitage and commenced a forest-life, surrounded by various anchorites, whom they protected in the performance of their sacrifices ‡ (lvi).

When Ráma's charioteer arrived at Ayodhyá with the empty chariot (lvii), king Daśaratha was so affected, that after relating (lxiii) how in his youth he had accidentally killed a hermit's son, and incurred in consequence the father's curse (see p. 6 of this volume), his spirit sank within him, and he died (lxiv). The lamentations of the women soon proclaimed the event (lxv). The absent Bharata was sent for from the house of his maternal grandfather in the city of Girivraja ‖ (lxviii. 21). He was seven days on his journey home (lxxi. 18); and when on reaching home he heard of his brother's banishment, he was horror-struck, and heaped imprecations on his astonished mother, who expected only praise from her son (lxxviii and lxxiv). Meanwhile Satrughna seized Manthará, the humpbacked slave, dragged her along the ground, and would have killed her (lxxviii. 16), but was prevented by Bharata (lxxviii.

---

* This spot is also called Triveṇí, because the sacred river Saraswatí is said to join the other two rivers underground.

† The spot where they crossed is still shown in the Pergunnah of Mow. (Calcutta Review, XLV.) In fact, temples and shrines every where mark their steps.

‡ The isolated hill Chitra-kúṭa is the holiest spot of the worshippers of Ráma: it is crowded with temples and shrines of Ráma and Lakshmaṇa. Every cavern is connected with their names; the heights swarm with monkeys, and some of the wild-fruits are still called Sítá-phal. It is situated on a river called the Pisuní, described as the Mandákiní (xcv), fifty miles south-east of the town of Bandah in Bundelkund, lat. 25.12, long. 80.47. The river is lined with ghats and flights of stairs suitable for religious ablutions.

‖ This, as before mentioned, was the capital of the country of his mother Kaikeyí, and is also called Raja-gṛiha. It was somewhere beyond the Vipáśá or Beeás, but not beyond the Chandrabhágá or Chenáb. (See Calc. Review, XLV.) The locality is much disputed. Lassen connects the Kekeyí with the Kathai, who are mentioned by Arrian, and are identified with the Khatree caste, in the Punjáb. It was evidently beyond the Sutlej and the Beeás, as Bharata in returning is described as crossing the former river (see lxxi. 2); and the messengers who went to fetch him are described as passing the Vipáśá (lxviii. 19).

21). The two brothers then went to Kauśalyá, pronounced before her the most terrible execrations against those who had procured Ráma's banishment, and assured her of their determination to bring him back (lxxv).

Before the last occurrences Bharata, on the twelfth day, had performed the śráddha or funeral ceremonies (lxxvii. 1), which a son alone could lawfully discharge, and which were necessary to secure the rest and happiness of a deceased parent's soul. Soon afterwards (on the fourteenth day) the ministers assembled, and decided that Bharata was to assume the government (lxxix), but he declined to deprive his elder brother Ráma of his rightful inheritance, and declared his intention of setting out for the forest with a complete army (chatur-anga) to bring Ráma back, and his determination to undergo himself the fourteen years exile in the forest (lxxix. 8, 9).

When the army was prepared they started (lxxxii. lxxxiii), and on reaching Śringavera on the Ganges they roused the anger of Guha, king of the Nishádas, who fancied they were marching against Ráma (lxxxiv and lxxxv. 7). When he learned the real object of the expedition, he praised Bharata, and pointed out to him the spot, on the bare ground under the Ingudí tree, where his brother and Sitá had rested. Bharata was much affected at the sight, and expressed his sentiments in touching language (lxxxviii; see also l). Next day they crossed the Ganges, and following Ráma's steps came to the hermitage of Bharadwája at Prayága (lxxxix. xc), who, by the power of his devotion, created a magnificent palace, and compelled the gods to supply a splendid feast for the whole army (xci). They were feasted with flesh meat and spirituous liquors, and food of all kinds, such as in later times no twice-born man was allowed to touch; and all the dancing-girls, damsels, and garlands of Indra's paradise were in requisition on the occasion (xci. 45. 50). Next they crossed the Jumná, and approached Chitra-kúṭa (see note ‡, p. 69), where the noise of the coming army at first alarmed the exiles (xcvii. 8). The impetuous Lakshmaṇa broke out into anger (xcvii. 17), but Ráma calmed him (xcviii); and presently Bharata and Śatrughna stood before them (c). Ráma's first inquiry was about his father (ci). Bharata then broke the sad news of his father's death, and begged him to return to Ayodhyá and assume the kingdom (cii).

Then ensued a generous contest between the brothers; Bharata imploring Ráma to accept the throne, and Ráma insisting on the duty of making good his father's vow (cvi. cvii). Here the Bráhman Jáváli, in a short discourse, tried to instil infidel, atheistic, and irreligious sentiments into Ráma, hoping to shake his resolution; but Ráma indignantly rebuked him (cviii). In the end Bharata yielded, but only consented to take charge of the kingdom as a deposit. He bore away on his head Ráma's shoes *

* In the northern recension Bharata is made to bring with him a pair of shoes adorned with gold (hema-bhúshita, cxli. 21). These he presents to Ráma, begging him to put them

in token of this (cxiii. 1), and took up his abode outside Ayodhyá, at Nandi-gráma, putting on a bark dress, and wearing the matted hair of a devotee, until the return of the rightful king (cxv). Before dismissing him, the forgiving Ráma entreated him not to indulge angry feelings towards his mother for having caused the family calamities—'Cherish thy mother Kaikeyí, show no resentment towards her; thou art adjured to this by me and Sítá' (cxii. 27). This ends the second book or *Ayodhyá-káṇḍa;* which is certainly the best and most free from exaggerations in the whole poem.

THIRD BOOK or ARAṆYA-KÁṆḌA.—After their departure the hermits who lived near Ráma came to him and notified their intention of leaving their present abode, which had become too much infested by Rákshasas (i). Ráma, finding his retreat lonely without them, and wishing to remove further from his family, determined on journeying southwards to the great forest of Daṇḍaka, which in early times extended throughout the whole centre of India, from the Ganges to the Godávarí. The first day they reached the hermitage of Anasúyá, the wife of the Ṛishi Atri, a female devotee, who gave Sítá some beautifying ointment * (ii. iii). Proceeding south through the jungle they entered the forest of Daṇḍaka (v), and there came into collision with a giant, Virádha, representing one of the powerful aborigines (see note, p. 10), who was killed by Lakshmaṇa, and buried, at his own request, in a pit (*avaṭa*), to ensure his happiness in a future life (viii. 20). Next they came to the hermitage of an aged ascetic, S'arabhanga, who was mounting the pile to anticipate death and beatitude; but fate had decreed that he should see Ráma ere his felicity could be achieved. He hailed the hero as one long expected, directed him to seek the hermitage of Sutíkshṇa, then mounted the pile †, and when his body was consumed reappeared in a glittering shape (ix). After this, Ráma promised security to numerous

on; which Ráma accordingly does, and then returns them to Bharata, who upon that bows to the shoes and says, "For fourteen years I will wear the matted hair and dress of an ascetic, feeding on roots and fruits, and dwelling outside the city, and committing the kingdom to thy shoes. After the fourteenth year, if I do not see you again, I will enter the fire" (cxii. 26). The book ends by recording that Bharata never transacted any state-business or received any presents without first laying every thing before the shoes (cxv. 25). In the Bengal version the sage S'arabhanga brings the shoes, which are made of Kuśa grass, and gives them to Ráma, who puts them on and then presents to his brother (cxxiii. 20—21).

* According to the Calcutta Reviewer, her cell is still shown on the Pisuni river, in Bundelkund, on the edge of the Bandah district.

† The spot where this took place is still known as the hermitage of Sarbhang, on the edge of the Bandah district. (Calcutta Review.)

ascetics who were molested by the Rákshasas (x). He then crossed the Tamasá river (Tonse), and proceeded to the hermitage of Sutíkshṇa, where was the celebrated Rámagiri, or hill of Ráma * (now known as Ramtek, near Nagpore). In this neighbourhood, moving from one hermitage to another, passed ten years of Ráma's banishment (xv. 28). In the description of the quiet life of the exiles, we find that their morning and evening devotions were never omitted, and that Sítá dutifully waited on her husband and brother-in-law, never eating till they had finished †. (See Gorresio's edition, II. lvi. 31.) When they travelled, Ráma walked first, Sítá in the middle, and Lakshmaṇa behind (xv. 1). On one occasion Ráma passed near a lake called Panchápsaras, under which an ascetic named Mandakarṇi had built a secret chamber for five celestial damsels, who had seduced him from his devotions (xv. 17). At length, by the advice of Sutíkshṇa, they moved westward to visit the hermitage of the sage Agastya, near the Vindhya mountains. He presented Ráma with a bow and weapons, and advised him to live for the remainder of his exile in the neighbourhood of Janasthána at Panchavatí on the Godáveri ‡ (xix). Whilst Ráma was on his way to Panchavatí he met the celebrated vulture Jaṭáyus (son of Garuḍa), who, out of a former regard for his father Daśaratha, now declared his friendship for Ráma, and his intention to aid him and protect Sítá. This district was in fact infested by Rákshasas, and, amongst others, by Rávaṇa's sister, Śúrpa-ṇakhá, who became smitten with love for Ráma. He of course repelled her, telling her that he was already married (xxiv. 1); but this only roused the jealousy of Śúrpa-ṇakhá, who made an attack on Sítá, and so excited the brothers, that the fiery Lakshmaṇa thoughtlessly cut off her ears and nose ‖ (xxiv. 22). Śúrpa-ṇakhá, smarting with pain, demanded vengeance from her brothers Khara and Dúshaṇa, who had been appointed by her elder brother Rávaṇa to guard the district. Thereupon they attacked Ráma and Lakshmaṇa, but were both destroyed with their entire army of 14,000 Rákshasas (xxx. 21). Still bent on revenge, Śúrpa-ṇakhá repaired to her brother Rávaṇa, the demon-monarch of Ceylon (for whose destruction Vishṇu had taken the form of Ráma).

The description of Rávaṇa, in the 36th chapter of the Araṇya-káṇḍa, is as follows §: This mighty demon "had ten faces, twenty arms, copper-coloured eyes, a

* Celebrated, at least in Sanskṛit literature, as the place of exile of the Yaksha in the Meghadúta.

† This custom remains unaltered to the present day. Compare Manu IV. 43: 'Let him not eat with his wife, nor look at her eating.'

‡ A spot now known as Násik, in the Bombay presidency, between Bombay and Agra. (Calcutta Review.)

‖ It was from this circumstance that Panchavatí is now called Násik (násiká).

§ As we have before remarked, Rávaṇa may be regarded as the Satan of the Rámáyaṇa,

huge chest, and white teeth, like the young moon. His form was as a thick cloud, or a mountain, or the god of Death with open mouth. He had all the marks of royalty; but his body bore the impress of wounds inflicted by all the divine arms in his warfare with the gods. It was scarred by the thunderbolt of Indra, by the tusks of (Indra's) elephant Airávata, and by the discus of Vishṇu. His strength was so great that he could agitate the seas and split the tops of mountains. He was a breaker of all laws, and a ravisher of other men's wives. He once penetrated into Bhogavatí (the serpent-capital of Pátála), conquered the great serpent Vásuki, and carried off the beloved wife of Takshaka. He defeated Vaiśravaṇa (i. e. his own brother Kuvera, the god of Wealth), and carried off his self-moving chariot called Pushpaka. He devastated the divine groves of Chitra-ratha, and the gardens of the gods. Tall as a mountain-peak he stopped with his arms the sun and moon in their course, and prevented their rising. The sun, when it passed over his residence, drew in its beams in terror. He underwent severe austerities in the forest of Gokarṇa for ten thousand years, standing in the midst of five fires with his feet in the air; whence he was released by Brahmá, and obtained from him the power of taking what shape he pleased *." (Compare Calcutta edition, xxxii.)

The better to secure the mighty Rávaṇa's cooperation, Śúrpa-ṇakhá succeeded in inspiring him with a passion for Sítá (xxxviii. 17), whom he determined to carry off. Having with difficulty secured the aid of another demon, Márícha, who was the son of the Tádaká (I. xxvii. 8) formerly killed by Ráma, and had himself been hurled into the sea by Ráma in his first battle with the Rákshasas (I. xxxii. 17), Rávaṇa transported himself and his accomplice in the aërial car, Pushpaka, to the forest near Ráma's dwelling (xlviii. 6). Márícha then assumed the form of a beautiful golden deer, which so captivated Sítá (xlviii. 11) that Ráma was induced to leave her with Lakshmaṇa,

---

as Duryodhana of the Mahá-bhárata; and one cannot help comparing part of this description with Milton's portrait of Satan. The majestic imagery of the English poet stands out in striking contrast to the wild hyperbole of Válmíki.

* It appears from chap. liii. of the Araṇya-káṇḍa, that Rávaṇa was the son of Viśravas, who was the son of the sage Pulastya, who was the son of Brahmá. Hence Rávaṇa was the brother of the god Kuvera (though by a different mother); and in verse 30 he calls himself his brother and enemy. Both he and Kuvera are sometimes called Paulastya. Vibhíshaṇa and Kumbha-karṇa were also brothers of Rávaṇa. According to the Puráṇas (Vishṇu-p., p. 83, note) Ilavilá was the mother of Kuvera, and Keśiní of the other three brothers. The story goes, that Rávaṇa so tyrannized over all the gods that he made each of them perform some menial work in his household; thus Agni was his cook, Varuṇa supplied water, Kuvera furnished cash, Vayu swept the house, &c. (See Moore's Pantheon, p. 333. See also the Mahá-bhárata account at p. 411, vol. IV. of Muir's Texts.)

that he might catch the deer for her, or kill it. Mortally wounded by his arrow, the deer uttered cries for help, feigning Ráma's voice (l. 22), which so alarmed Sítá that she persuaded Lakshmaṇa against his will to leave her alone and go to the assistance of his brother. Meanwhile Rávaṇa approached in the guise of a religious mendicant. All nature seemed petrified with terror as he advanced (lii. 10, 11); and when Sítá's eyes fell on the stranger, she started (lii. 48), but was lulled to confidence by his mendicant's dress, and offered him food and water (lii. 51). Suddenly Rávaṇa declared himself (liii). Then throwing off his disguise (lv. 3), he avowed his intention to make her his queen. Sítá's indignation burst forth, but her wrath was powerless against the fierce Rávaṇa, who took her up in his arms, placed her in his self-moving car, and bore her through the sky to his capital. As Sítá was carried along, she invoked heaven and earth, mountains and streams, in the most beautiful language (lv. 43). The gods and saints came to look on, and were struck with horror at the violence done to her (lviii. 14, 15), but they stood in awe of the ravisher, and knew that this was part of the plan for his destruction. All nature shuddered, various prodigies occurred, the sun's disk paled, darkness overspread the heavens (lviii. 16—43). It was the short-lived triumph of evil over good. Even the great Creator Brahmá roused himself, and exclaimed, 'Sin is consummated'* (lviii. 17). Rávaṇa, however, did not escape with his prize without a battle; for the semi-divine bird Jaṭáyus, who had before promised to protect Sítá (xx), and was awaked from his slumber by the rushing of Rávaṇa's car, placed himself in the way and attempted to rescue her, but was defeated and mortally wounded (lvi). Before they reached Lanká Sítá contrived to drop among some monkey-chiefs, collected together on a mountain, her ornaments and upper garment (lx. 6). Arrived in the demon-city, Rávaṇa forced Sítá to inspect all the wonders and beauties of his capital (lxi), and then promised to make them hers, if she would consent to be his queen. Again indignantly rejected, he becomes enraged, and delivers her over to the guardianship of a troop of frightful Rákshasís or female furies, who are described as horrible in appearance and cannibal in their propensities (lxii. 29—38). Tormented by them, she must have died of despair, had not Brahmá in compassion sent Indra to her with the god of Sleep†, and a vessel containing celestial food (lxiii. 7, 8) to support her strength.

Terrible was the wrath of the usually gentle Ráma when on his return he found that Sítá had been carried off (lxix). At first he blamed Lakshmaṇa for leaving her alone (lxvi), but was satisfied with his explanation; and the brothers then set off in pur-

* As if he had said, 'It was necessary that the offence should come, that the salvation of man should be wrought.' (See Calcutta Review, XLV.)

† Similarly in the Odyssey (IV. 795) Minerva sends a dream to console and animate Penelope.

suit. They learned from the dying Jaṭáyus, whom they soon encountered (and whom Ráma at first suspected of having killed Sítá, lxxii. 11), the name of the ravisher of Sítá (lxxii. 18), but not his abode. They then commenced a long search, and proceeding southwards fell in with a headless fiend (Kabandha) named Danu, the son of the goddess Śrí (lxxv. 24); described as "covered with hair, vast as a mountain, without head or neck, having a mouth armed with immense teeth in the middle of his belly, arms a league long, and one enormous glaring eye in his breast" (lxxiv. 16). This terrific creature placed himself across the path of the two brothers, and seizing them in his arms would have devoured them, had they not succeeded in cutting off his arms, and thereby wounding him mortally. Before his death he told the brothers that they were his appointed deliverers, and narrated his history. He had propitiated Brahmá by penance, and had received from him the gift of 'long life.' Then, filled with pride, he challenged Indra, whose thunderbolt striking his head and thighs caused them to enter his body (lxxv. 27). Having the gift of long life, he could not die in any ordinary way; but Indra promised that he should be released in a battle with Ráma and Lakshmaṇa. After his death his body was burnt by the brothers, and reappearing in a heavenly shape, he recommended Ráma to proceed southwards by the river Pampá, to the dwelling of Sugríva, king of the apes * (see p. 64), on the hill Ṛishyamúka, and to assist him in his war against his brother Báli, who had usurped his kingdom, carried off his wife Rumá (IV. viii. 31), and driven him to take refuge in the mountains (lxxvi). Ráma accordingly journeyed on towards Ṛishyamúka, passing on the banks of the Pampá a deserted hermitage, in which still lingered an old female ascetic, named Sarvarí, who only waited for his arrival to secure heaven by immolating herself † (lxxvii. 32).

* Like Hanumat, his celebrated follower, he is described as Káma-rúpí, i. e. endowed with the faculty of putting off his monkey-form and assuming any shape he pleased (lxxv. 66).

† We may note here, that there are several instances of self-immolation by fire in the Rámáyaṇa, although we do not read of the 'post-cremation' of widows. Here is another example that Ráma was 'the expected one,' on whose coming the happiness of the human race depended. Old ascetics lived just long enough to see his day, and then, rejoicing, committed themselves to the flames. The Kabandha only waited to be delivered by Ráma; and here, on the margin of a lake, was a hermitage, long since deserted by its occupants, but every thing in it preserved unfaded, and one old woman detained in life to greet him. She ministered to him, and then entering the fire ascended to heaven. Ráma's fate was to be always suffering and giving up self and earthly possessions, and yet looked for, welcomed, and honoured. (See Calcutta Review, XLV.) Some of the legends concerning Kṛishṇa are said to have been composed by distorting certain particulars in the life of Christ detailed in the Gospels; but with greater plausibility might the history of Ráma be thought to have been embellished from this source.

FOURTH BOOK or KISHKINDHYÁ-KÁṆḌA.—When the monkey-king Sugríva saw the two brothers approaching Ṛishyamúka, he took them for spies sent by his brother Báli, and in great alarm leaped from the summit of the hill and fled to the mountain Malaya, where he was joined by his whole army of monkeys (i. 16). Hanumat, son of the Wind, one of his followers, undertook to go back, and, assuming the form of a religious mendicant, gain the confidence of the two strangers. This he did, and proposed to take them before Sugríva. The brothers mounted on his back, and he carried them like the wind to Malaya (iii. 29), where they were introduced to Sugríva, who informed them that he had witnessed the flight of a Rákshasa carrying off Sítá through the air, and picked up her upper vestment and jewels when they were dropped by her (v. 10). He could not, however, tell the name of the Rákshasa, nor the place of his abode (vi. 2). At the sight of the memorials of his wife, Ráma was agitated with deep emotion, and promised, in return for this service, to conquer Báli and re-establish Sugríva on the throne. When Sugríva doubted of Ráma's ability to cope with the terrible Báli, who had killed the great giant Dundubhi (himself more than a match for the Ocean and the mighty Himálaya, ix. 40. 52), Ráma gave two proofs of his strength. First he kicked the huge skeleton of Dundubhi (which Sugríva had preserved), with one stroke of his foot, to the distance of a hundred yojanas (ix. 92), and then shot an arrow with such force that it pierced seven palm-trees, divided a mountain, and penetrated to the infernal regions, thence returning of its own accord, in the form of a shining swan, to his quiver (xi. 5, 6).

Sugríva, convinced of Ráma's power, provoked Báli to join battle. The latter was killed by one of Ráma's arrows, and in dying acknowledged his fault and asked his brother's forgiveness, and commending his son Angada and his wife Tárá to his care (xxi). The lamentations of Tárá over her husband's body are beautifully described (xxii). Sugríva is now reinstated in the throne at Kishkindhyá, his capital city (supposed to have been situated north of Mysore *), and invites Ráma and Lakshmaṇa to live with him there (xxv. 7). Ráma, however, replies that he has promised not to enter any town for fourteen years (xxv. 9), and retires with his brother to the mountain Prasravaṇa (xxvi. 1), where he continues during the rainy season, having received a promise from Sugríva that in the autumn he will assist him with his armies in conquering the Rákshasas and recovering Sítá.

The rainy season ended, Sugríva summons his armies; and, in ordering them to search every corner of the earth, describes minutely the geography of India †. He

* Somewhere in that strip of British territory which separates the kingdom of Mysore from the Nizám's territory. (Calcutta Review.)

† This is an interesting part of the poem. Much of the geography may be verified, but a great deal is probably fanciful. Countries and people are mentioned about whom nothing is accurately known.

marshals his troops in four great divisions. The first he sends north, under Vinata (xl. 14). The second, south, under various generals, especially Hanumat, Jámbavat (son of Brahmá, chief of the bears), Níla, Nala, Tára, and Angada, son of Báli, heir to the monkey-throne (xli. 2—5; liii. 6). The third, west, under Susheṇa (xliii. 2). The fourth, north, under Śatabali (xlv. 5). But his most particular directions are given to Hanumat and the party proceeding southwards (xli. 6); and such confidence has Ráma in the courage and skill of Hanumat, that he gives him his ring to show to Sítá, in case of his being successful in discovering her (xlii. 15).

After a time three divisions of the army return *re infectá* (xlvii). That under Hanumat and Angada alone accomplish any thing, and meet with various adventures. Exploring the Vindhya mountains, they light on a huge magic cave, inhabited by an anchorite named Swayam-prabhá (li. 17), in which every single thing, including flowers, fruits, and trees, was made of gold. In order to escape from this enchanted grotto alive, they had to follow the directions of the anchorite, and cover up their faces (hasta-ruddha-mukháh, liii. 1). On emerging from the cavern and beholding the ocean before them they fall into despondency, fearing the anger of Sugríva, should they return without finding Sítá. Angada, who as heir to the throne is the nominal leader of the party, breaks out into abuse of Sugríva (lv. 10), and counsels re-entering the cavern and starving themselves to death. Hanumat opposes all his eloquence to the evil counsels of Angada (liv), but without effect (lv). Happily, however, in the midst of their difficulties they encounter the king of the vultures, Sampáti, the elder brother of Jaṭáyus (lvi), with his son Supárśwa (lxii). He tells them his own wonderful history (lviii—lxii), and informs them that Sítá is at Lanká, in the palace of Rávaṇa, and that his own sight is so piercing that he is able to see her there at the distance of a hundred yojanas off (lviii. 33). Overjoyed at this intelligence, Angada leads his army southwards to the margin of the sea, which separates India from Ceylon (lxiii. 27).

FIFTH BOOK or SUNDARA-KAṆḌA*.—On arriving at the sea-shore opposite to Ceylon, the army of monkeys holds a consultation. How were they to cross the straits, represented as a hundred yojanas in width? (i). Various monkeys offer to leap across, but only Hanumat is found capable of clearing the entire distance.

* This is one of the longest and most tediously 'spun out' in the whole poem. Its prolixity, however, is to the Hindú mind a great recommendation. Otherwise there is nothing to distinguish this book as '*par excellence*,' 'the beautiful' book of the poem. The veneration in which it is held by so many millions of our Indian fellow-subjects to this very day must be my apology for following out the chain of absurdities to the end.

He undertakes the feat without hesitation, and promises to search for Sítá in Rávaṇa's capital (iii). In flying through the air he meets with two or three adventures, the description of which, for wild exaggeration and absurd fiction, can hardly be matched in any child's fairy-tale extant. His progress is first opposed by the mother of the Nágas, a Rákshasí called Surasá, who attempts to swallow him bodily, and, in order to take in the enormously increasing bulk of the monkey-general, distends her mouth to a hundred leagues *. Upon this Hanumat suddenly contracts himself to the size of a thumb, and without more ado darts through her huge carcase (vi. 25), and comes out at her right ear (lvi. 27). The mountain Maináka (called also Hiraṇya-nábha) next raises itself in the middle of the sea, to form a resting-place for his feet (vii). Lastly, another monstrous Rákshasí, named Sinhiká, hoping to appease her appetite by a suitable meal (viii. 2), proceeds deliberately to swallow Hanumat, who plunges into her body, tears out her entrails, and slips out again with the rapidity of thought (viii. 10, 11).

At length Hanumat reaches the opposite coast (ix), and at night reduces his before colossal form to the size of a cat (Vṛishadanśa-pramáṇa, ix. 47), that he may creep into the marvellous city of Lanká, built by Viśwakarman †, and containing within itself all the treasures and rarities of the world. He contemplates the magnificence of the capital of the Rákshasas, and visits various palaces (xii. 6—16), examining their inmates. Some of the Rákshasas fill him with disgust, but others were beautiful to look upon; some were noble in their aspect and behaviour, others the reverse (xi. 15). "Some had long arms and frightful shapes; some were prodigiously fat, others excessively thin; some dwarfish, others enormously tall and humpbacked; some had only one eye, others only one ear; some enormous paunches, and flaccid, pendent breasts; others long projecting teeth, and crooked thighs; some could assume many forms at will; others were beautiful and of great splendour" (x. 18, 19. See also xvii. 24, &c.; where they are further described as biped, triped, quadruped, with heads of serpents, donkeys, horses, elephants, and every other imaginable deformity). After inspecting the palaces of Kumbha-karṇa and Vibhíshaṇa (xii. 8), Hanumat arrives at that of Rávaṇa. The residence of the demon-king was itself a city, and in the midst of it the self-moving car Pushpaka (half a yojana in length, and the same in width), which contained within itself the actual palace of Rávaṇa, and all the

* A kind of 'swelling-match' takes place between Hanumat and Surasá. The latter commences by opening her mouth to the moderate dimensions of ten leagues (yojanas). Upon which Hanumat distends himself to the extent of twenty. Surasá then enlarges the aperture of her jaws to thirty leagues, but still finds it impossible to swallow the monkey-chief, who increases his bulk to forty leagues, and so on.

† The Hindú Vulcan.

women's apartments (xiii. 2. 6, &c.; xv), described with the most extravagant hyperbole. There he beholds Rávaṇa himself asleep on a crystal throne (xiv); but nowhere can he detect the hiding-place of Sítá. At last he discovers her in a grove of Aśokas, guarded by female Rákshasas of hideous and disgusting shapes (xvii). There she sat like a penitent on the ground in profound reverie, dressed in the garb of widowhood, without ornaments, her hair collected in a single braid* (xviii. 10, 11). Hidden in the trees, he becomes a spectator of an interview between the demon-king and Sítá. Rávaṇa presses her to yield to his wishes † (xxii). She sternly rebukes him, and exhorts him to save himself from Ráma's vengeance (xxiii). He is lashed to fury by her contempt, gives her two months to consider, and swears that if she then refuses him, "he will have her cut into pieces for his breakfast" ‡ (xxiv. 8). Meanwhile he delivers her over to the female furies, her guardians, who first attempt to coax, and then menace her. "Her only reply is, 'I cannot renounce my husband, who to me is a divinity'" (xxv. 12; see last note, p. 56). The rage of the female demons is then frightful; some threaten to devour her, some to strangle her: but she only bursts forth into long and rapturous praises of her husband, and expressions of devotion to him (xxvi. xxviii). One good Rákshasí ‖, however (named Trijaṭá), advises them to desist, relates a dream, and prophesies the destruction of Rávaṇa (xxvii).

After this the Rákshasís go to sleep; and Hanumat, seated in the branches of a neighbouring tree, discovers himself (xxx. 13). At first Sítá suspects some new snare; but Hanumat shows her Ráma's ring, gains her confidence, consoles and animates her, satisfies all her inquiries, and obtains a token from her to take back to her husband, viz. a single jewel which she had preserved in her braided hair (xxxvi. 72, 73). He offers to carry her on his back, and transport her at once into the presence of Ráma (xxxv. 23); but she modestly replies that she cannot voluntarily submit to touch the person of any one but her husband (xxxv. 45). Hanumat then takes his leave; but, before rejoining his companions, gives the Rákshasas a proof of what they were to expect from the prowess of a hero who had such a messenger at his command. He devastates the Aśoka grove, tears up the trees, destroys the houses, grinds the hills to powder (xxxvii. 41), and then challenges the Rákshasas to fight. Rávaṇa dispatches an army of 80,000 Rákshasas against him, which Hanumat de-

* "She appeared like Rohiṇí oppressed by the planet Mars, or like memory clouded, or prosperity ruined, or hope departed, or knowledge obstructed" (xviii. 6, &c.).

† When one remembers that Rávaṇa had ten heads, one is tempted to ask with which of his mouths he made love?

‡ Dwábhyám úrdhwam tu másábhyám bhartáram mám anichchhatím, Mama twám prátarásáya súdáś chhetsyanti khaṇḍaśaḥ.

‖ In the Mahá-bhárata (Vana-parva, 16146) she is called Dharma-jná.

feats (xxxviii). He then sends against him the mighty Rákshasa Jambu-málí, and after him the sons of his own ministers, and five other generals in succession; all of whom are killed by Hanumat (xxxix. xl. xli). Next Aksha, the heir-apparent, marches against the heroic monkey, wounds him, but meets in the end with the same fate as the others (xlii). Lastly, Rávaṇa despatches the bravest of his sons, Indrajit, to the battle; and Hanumat at length falls into the hands of the Rákshasas, struck to the ground by the enchanted arrow of Brahmá (xliv; see note *, p. 27). He is then taken before Rávaṇa (xlv), and announcing himself as the ambassador of Sugríva, warns the ravisher of Sítá that nothing can save him from the vengeance of Ráma (xlvii). Rávaṇa, infuriated, orders him to be put to death; but Vibhíshaṇa reminds his brother that the life of ambassadors is sacred (xlviii). Upon this, it is decided to punish Hanumat by setting fire to his tail, as monkeys hold that appendage in great esteem (xlix. 3). This is done (xlix. 5); but Sítá adjures the fire to be good to her protector (xlix. 21—24). Hanumat is then marched in procession through the city; suddenly he contracts himself, slips out of the hands of his guards, mounts on the roofs of the palaces, and with his burning tail sets the whole city on fire (l). He then satisfies himself that Sítá has not perished in the conflagration, reassures her, bids her adieu, and, springing from the mountain Arishṭa (which, staggering under the shock, and crushed by his weight, sinks into the earth), darts through the sky, rejoins his companions on the opposite coast, and recounts to them the narrative of his adventures (liv. lv. lvi). The monkeys, rejoined by Hanumat, set out for Kishkindhyá, and on their way receive permission from Angada to signalize the success of their expedition by running riot in 'the grove of honey' (Madhu-vana), guarded by the monkey Dadhi-mukha; where, feasting to their hearts' content, they speedily intoxicate themselves (lx). After this escapade they return to Sugríva, and then for the first time Ráma learns the hiding-place of Sítá (lxvi). Hanumat describes his interview with her, and, to attest the truth of his story, gives Sítá's token to Ráma, who praises him (lxx), inquires about the fortifications of Lanká (lxxii), and soon marches southward, attended by Sugríva and his army of monkeys, to deliver Sítá; Níla being sent on with a detachment in advance (lxxiii).

Crossing the Vindhya and Malaya mountains, they soon arrive at Mahendra, on the borders of the sea, where their progress is for the present stayed (lxxiv. lxxv). Meanwhile Rávaṇa consults with his ministers; and Nikashá, his mother, advises Vibhíshaṇa to recommend the restoration of Sítá (lxxvi). But Prahasta, Indrajit, Virúpáksha, and others, counsel war, and promise to kill Ráma and Lakshmaṇa, and exterminate the apes (lxxix. lxxx). After a long altercation, Rávaṇa is so enraged with his brother Vibhíshaṇa, who again and again urges conciliation, that he rises in a fury and kicks him from his seat (lxxxvii. 2). Smarting under this outrage, Vibhíshaṇa left Lanká, and flew through the air to Kailása *, to the court of his relative Kuvera (god of Riches), where the god S'iva also at that time happened to be present. The latter directs him to join Ráma and desert Rávaṇa; which Vibhíshaṇa accordingly does (lxxxix. 40—58). He is at first taken for a spy, and Sugríva recommends Ráma to put him to death (lxxxix. 70); but Ráma accepts him as an ally, and embraces him † (xcii. 1).

They then consult together how to transport the army across the sea. For three days and nights Ráma underwent rigorous penance on the shore, hoping to propitiate the god of the Ocean, and induce him to appear (xciii. 1); but the Ocean remained unimpressible, until Ráma, enraged, shot one of his fiery arrows into the water, filling the sea-monsters with terror, wounding the Dánavas in the depths of Pátála, and causing such a commotion in the deep, that the god was forced to present himself, attended by his marine ministers (xciv. 1), and promised to support a pier or bridge ‡, by means of which the army might be transported across.

Nala, son of Viśwakarman, was charged with the construction of the pier (xciv. 15). Thousands of monkey bridge-builders, flying through the sky in every direction, tore up rocks and trees and threw them into the water. In bringing huge crags from the Himálayas, some were accidentally dropped, and remain to this day monuments of the exploit ‖. At length a pier was formed twenty yojanas long and ten wide (xcv. 11—15), by which the whole army crossed, Vibhíshaṇa taking the lead. The gods, Ṛishis, Pitṛis, &c., looked on, and uttered the celebrated prophecy—'As long as the sea shall remain, so long shall this pier (*setu*) endure, and the fame of Ráma be proclaimed' § (xcv. 35).

* In Hindú mythology Kailása is represented as the abode of both Kuvera and S'iva.

† It appears that when along with Rávaṇa he propitiated Brahmá by his penances, the god granted them both boons; and the boon chosen by Vibhíshaṇa was, that he should never, even in the greatest calamity, set his mind on wickedness. (See Mahá-bhár. III. 15918)

‡ The Ocean at first objected to a regular *setu* or embankment (xciv. 8), though a pier (described as a *setu*) was afterwards constructed: the line of rocks in the channel is certainly known in India as Ráma-setu. In maps it is called 'Adam's bridge.'

‖ Every where in India are scattered isolated blocks, attributed by the natives to Ráma's bridge-builders. More than this, the hill Govardhana, near Muttra, and the whole Kymar range in central India are firmly believed to have arisen from the same cause.

§ Ráma also made the same prophecy, calling it the bridge of Nala. (Yuddha-k. cviii. 16.) "In the midst of the arm of the sea is the island Ramesurum, or the pillar of Ráma, of as great repute and renown as the pillars of the western Hercules. There to this day stands a temple of massive Cyclopean workmanship, said to have been built by the hero, the idol of which is washed daily with water from the Ganges. From the highest point is a commanding view of the ocean, and the interminable black line of rocks stretching across the gulf of

SIXTH BOOK or YUDDHA-KÁṆḌA.—As soon as Ráma's army has crossed into the island of Lanká, Rávaṇa dispatches two spies (Súka and Sáraṇa) disguised as monkeys into the enemy's camp (i. 6). Vibhíshaṇa discovers them, and wishes to have them killed, but Ráma spares their lives, and sends them back after showing them all his army (i. 31). They return to Lanká, and enumerate to Rávaṇa, from the top of his palace, all the heroes whom he sees preparing to fight against him in the plains below * (ii. iii. iv). He is angry with them for praising the courage of the enemy, and, dismissing them with reproaches (v. 13), sends Sárdúla and other spies disguised as before. They are discovered, beaten, and forced to return like those who preceded them (v. 25). Rávaṇa now determines to make a last effort to induce Sítá to yield to his proposals, and causes to be made by magic a false head of Ráma and a false bow, which he casts at her feet, pretending that he has killed her husband and destroyed his army (vii). Sítá is at first overwhelmed with grief; but Rávaṇa being suddenly called away by one of his ministers, the head vanishes, and a Rákshasí named Saramá consoles Sítá (ix). A terrible sound of drums and conch-shells is now heard in Ráma's camp, the army preparing for the attack (x. 35). The noise alarms Rávaṇa, who summons his counsellors; and an old minister, his maternal grandfather, named Mályavat, advises him to make peace (xi. 34). Rávaṇa is indignant with Mályavat, and proceeds to organize the defence of the city (xii). Ráma also makes ready for the attack. He learns from spies the position of the enemy and the plan of their defence (xiii), and ascends with his chiefs the hill Suvelá, which commands Lanká. After ascertaining the position of the Rákshasas (xiv. xv), he distributes his army accordingly, reserving to himself the task of attacking Rávaṇa in person by the northern gate of the city (xiii. 29). But first he sends Angada to summon Rávaṇa to restore Sítá (xvi. 83); which he refuses to do, and in his fury gives orders to seize and punish the envoy. Angada breaks away from the Rákshasas who hold him, kicks down the top of the palace, and flies back (xvi. 90). Ráma's army now approaches the city, which was situated on the hill Trikúṭa (xv. 22), and several skirmishes and engagements take place (xvii. xviii).

Manaar. Thither, from all parts of India, wander the pilgrims, who are smitten with the wondrous love of travel to sacred shrines. From Chuteerkote, near the Jumná, it is roughly calculated to be no less than one hundred stages. We have conversed with some who have accomplished the great feat: but many never return; they either die by the way, or their courage and strength evaporates in some roadside hermitage. Whatever may be its origin, there is the reefy barrier, compelling every vessel, from or to the mouths of the Ganges, to circumnavigate the island of Ceylon." (See Calcutta Review, XLV.)

* This will remind the classical scholar of a similar enumeration of the Grecian warriors by Helen in Homer III. 165, &c.

In one of these, Indrajit, Rávaṇa's most powerful son, makes himself invisible by means of his skill in magic, and pierces with his enchanted weapons, in the form of serpents *, a great number of warriors, and among them Ráma and Lakshmaṇa, who fall, covered with wounds, and appear to be dead (xix. xx). The whole army is in despair at the sight of the fallen brothers; and Sítá is forced by her cruel guardians into the car Pushpaka, that she may be transported to the field of battle, and made to witness the heart-rending spectacle of her husband and brother-in-law apparently lifeless (xxii; Calc. ed. xlvii). But they are not dead. They are only spell-bound, as well as wounded by the magic arrows. Ráma is roused from his stupor by the Wind, who whispers in his ear that he is Vishṇu incarnate † (xxvi. 9). Ráma then invokes Garuḍa, who delivers the two brothers from the serpent-like arrows, and heals their wounds (xxvi. 17).

The battle recommences, and Rávaṇa, who has made several abortive attacks by means of his generals Dhúmráksha, Akampana, and Prahasta (all of whom are killed, xxviii—xxxii), resolves to take the field in person, notwithstanding the entreaties of his favourite wife Mandodarí, who advises him to restore Sítá (xxxiii). He sallies forth accordingly, and attacks and wounds successively Sugríva (xxxvi. 15), Hanumat (45), Níla (56), and Lakshmaṇa (86); but being in his turn wounded by Ráma, who rescues his brother (xxxvi. 115), Rávaṇa is forced to re-enter Lanká, humiliated and dispirited.

Rávaṇa then decides on availing himself of the services of his gigantic brother Kumbha-karṇa; but how to awake him is the difficulty, as he is buried in deep sleep for six months together (xxxvii. 19), and then only awakes for a short time, that he may gorge himself with enormous quantities of food ‡. The messengers try to enter

* According to the Hanuman-nāṭaka (p. 91 Calc. ed.) these weapons were a kind of rope, which when thrown at an enemy became transformed into a serpent and retained him in its folds. This play agrees with the 108th chapter of the Yuddha-káṇḍa in calling Indrajit, the wielder of these weapons, by his first name of Megha-náda. Indrajit's victory over Indra is described Uttara-káṇḍa xxxiv. (Calc. ed.). His original name of Megha-náda was then changed by Brahmá to Indrajit.

† This is probably an interpolation; it is wanting in the Calcutta edition, where Ráma recovers consciousness while the monkeys are watching him. Muir's Texts, IV. pp. 385. 387.

‡ Rámáyaṇa xxxvii. 14 (Calc. ed. lxi. 28) makes his long slumber the consequence of a curse laid upon him by Brahmá; but according to the Mahá-bhárata he had performed penance, like his brothers Rávaṇa and Vibhíshaṇa; and being allowed, like them, to choose a boon, he asked for long slumber (mahatí nidrá). (See Mahá-bhár. III. 15916. See also Uttara-káṇḍa, ch. x. Calc. ed.) His figure is a favourite one in village representations of the siege of Lanká, and he is generally exhibited asleep. (Calc. Rev. XLV.) The description of him in the Rámáyaṇa is ridiculously extravagant and exaggerated.

his room, but are blown away from the door by the wind caused by the deep breathing of the sleeping monster (xxxvii. 24). At last, after violent efforts, they force an entrance; and ten thousand Rákshasas make every sort of din in his ears, by beating drums, &c. Then they hammer his limbs with mallets, dance upon him, cause a thousand elephants to walk over his body, pile heaps of food under his very nose; but all without effect. Nothing avails but the touch of some beautiful women, who eventually succeed in rousing him * (xxxvii. 63). Kumbha-karṇa tries to dissuade his brother to desist from any further contest with Ráma, giving him to understand that he is Vishṇu incarnate (xl. 50); but the infatuated Rávaṇa declares that if Ráma be very Vishṇu he will kill him (xli. 22). Kumbha-karṇa then consents to go out to battle. He displays extraordinary valour, routs, wounds, and even devours † thousands of the monkey-army, but is ultimately conquered and killed by Ráma (xlvi).

Rávaṇa is overcome with grief at his brother's death (xlvii. 2), and next sends four of his own sons to the battle, viz. Triśiras, Devántaka, Narántaka, and Atikáya, who were all slain (xlviii—li). Indrajit, the bravest of his sons, then took the field again, and again by means of his magical weapons, inflicted terrible wounds on all the leaders of Ráma's army; viz. Sugríva, Angada, Níla, Jámbavat, Nala, Tára, Sarabha, Susheṇa, Panasa, Gandhamádana, Dwivida, Keśarí, Sampáti, Vinata, Ṛishabha; as well as on Ráma and Lakshmaṇa (lii. liii. 10—13), leaving them for dead. At this achievement Rávaṇa and the Rákshasas were overjoyed, and the monkey-army in despair; but Vibhíshaṇa and Hanumat still survive, and, visiting the battle-field at night (liii. 7), find the chief of the bears (Jámbavat) covered with wounds, but still conscious. He entreats Hanumat to fly towards the Himálaya mountains. There, on a golden hill called Ṛishabha, which was the very crest of Kailása (liii. 34, &c.), he would find four medicinal herbs, by virtue of which all the dead and wounded might be restored (liii. 39). Accordingly Hanumat flies there; but the divine plants, suspecting his object, render themselves invisible (liii. 59). Upon this the irritated monkey tears up the mountain-peak, and bears it, with all its contents, into the camp of Ráma and Lakshmaṇa; who, with all the dead and wounded chiefs, are instantly restored by the exhalations issuing from the healing plants (liii. 67). After this the chiefs of Ráma's army make a grand night-attack on Lanká, and fire the town (liv). A terrific mêlée ensues, in which the sons of Kumbha-karṇa, Kumbha and Nikumbha,

* In the Calcutta version of the Hanuman-náṭaka, they awake him by pouring hot oil into his ear-holes (p. 87).

† Like all the Rákshasas, he is cannibal in his propensities. In his youthful days he was wont to go about eating Ṛishis (Uttara-k. viii. 38, Calc. ed.); and here he is described as seizing the monkeys in his arms, and swallowing them whole, though they manage to escape through his ears and nose (xlvi. 33, 34).

and another demon, Makarákshа, are slain (lv. 87; lvi. lvii. lviii. 49). Lanká would now have fallen, had not Indrajit made a sally and routed the monkey-army. He then again turns his skill in magic to account by creating a false image of Sítá, which he carries in his car, and kills before Hanumat (lx. 27). The monkey-army is terrified, and Ráma, when he hears the news, becomes unconscious (lxii. 10). Lakshmaṇa revives him; and Vibhíshaṇa, who knows his nephew's arts, explains the deceit and reassures them (lxii. lxiii). At last Indrajit, notwithstanding his magic and his valour, is killed in a great combat with Lakshmaṇa (lxvii—lxx). Rávaṇa is beside himself with grief and fury at the death of his brave son, and is about to kill Sítá in revenge, but his ministers prevent him (lxxii).

As a last resource, Rávaṇa determines to go out again in person to the battle (lxxv). He skirmishes a little with Ráma, both heroes attacking each other with magic arrows (lxxix). Rávaṇa then engages with Lakshmaṇa, whom he transfixes through the breast with a fiery enchanted dart (lxxx. 34). Ráma, infuriated at the fall of his brother, after trying in vain to extract the dart, attacks Rávaṇa, and a drawn battle ensues (lxxxi). The physician (vaidya) Susheṇa is then sent for, who examines the wound, pronounces that Lakshmaṇa is not dead, and that a celebrated medicinal plant (mahaushadhi), growing on the northern mountain Gandha-mádana, will cure him (lxxxii. 37). Hanumat undertakes to fetch it, and accordingly flies there.

Passing over Ayodhyá and Nandigráma, he is observed by Bharata, who seeing a strange object in the sky prepares to shoot it (lxxxii. 94); but Hanumat descends, and, arresting the arrow, gives Bharata tidings of his brothers. On reaching Gandhamádana, he is attacked by a terrible Rákshasa named Kála-nemi, sent by Rávaṇa to kill Hanumat. This demon first takes the form of an anchorite, and persuades Hanumat to drink some water out of a lake, where there is a monstrous crocodile. Hanumat, however, kills both the crocodile and Kála-nemi (lxxxii. 158. 183), and afterwards destroys 30,000 Gandharvas, who attack him (lxxxiii. 19). He then looks about for the plant, and finding it nowhere (21), takes up the whole mountain bodily in his arms (lxxxiii. 25), and deposits it, with its rocks, metals, forests, lions, elephants, and tigers, at the feet of Susheṇa (40), who knows well where to look for the plant, gathers it, and makes Lakshmaṇa breathe its healing exhalations (56, 57). The monkeys then obtain leave to ascend the mountain, and regale themselves with its fruits and examine its hermitages (lxxxiv. 4). After which Hanumat flies back with the mountain, and restores it to its place, killing with his feet and tail some more Rákshasas, who attack him on his way while he carries the mountain, and is unable to use his hands (lxxxiv. 23, 24).

At length the great battle between Ráma and Rávaṇa takes place. The gods assemble to take the side of the former, and all the demons and evil spirits back their own champion (lxxxvii. 8). Rávaṇa is mounted on a magic car, drawn by horses having human *faces* (manushya-vadanair hayaih, lxxxvi. 3); and, in order that the two champions may fight on an equality, Indra sends his own car, driven by his charioteer Mátali, for the use of Ráma (lxxxvi. 8). Both armies cease fighting, that they may look on (xci. 2); but the gods and demons in the sky, taking the part of either warrior, renew their ancient strife * (lxxxvii. 6, 7). The heroes now overwhelm each other with arrows. Ráma cuts off a hundred heads from Rávaṇa successively; but no sooner is one cut off than another appears in its place † (xcii. 24), and the battle, which had already lasted seven days and seven nights without interruption, might have been endlessly protracted, had not Mátali informed Ráma that Rávaṇa was not vulnerable in the head (xcii. 41). Thereupon Ráma shot off the terrible arrow of Brahmá ‡, given to him by the sage Agastya, and the demon-king fell dead (xcii. 58). As usual, the old hackneyed prodigies precede his fall (see note, p. 28); and when the victory is consummated a perfect deluge of flowers covers the conqueror. The lamentations of the women over Rávaṇa, and especially of his favourite wife Mandodarí, are well described (xciv. xcv). The generous Ráma causes magnificent obsequies to be performed over the body of his enemy, which is duly consumed by fire ‖ (xcvi), and then places Vibhíshaṇa on the throne of Lanká (xcvii. 15). Ráma then sends Hanumat with a message to Sítá, and afterwards Vibhíshaṇa brings her into his presence in a litter (śiviká); but Ráma allows her to come before him on foot, that she may be seen by all the army. The monkeys and bears crowd round her, admiring her incomparable beauty, the cause of so much toil, danger, and suffering to themselves § (xcix. 15, 16). On seeing her, Ráma is deeply moved; three feelings distract him, joy, grief, and anger (xcix. 19), and he does not ad-

* This is just what takes place in the Iliad before the great battle between Achilles and Hector, the gods taking their respective places on either side (Il. XX).

† This reminds one of Hercules and the Hydra.

‡ Here called *paitámaham astram*, and described as having the wind for its feathers, the fire and the sun for its point, the air for its body, and the mountains Meru and Mandara for its weight (xcii. 45). It had the very convenient property of returning to its owner's quiver after doing its work. (See xcii. 59, and note *, p. 17.) There appear to have been various forms of this unerring weapon, as it was also used by Indrajit against Hanumat in Sundara-káṇḍa xliv. We may suppose it to have been another arrow consecrated by the same formula, addressed to Brahmá.

‖ Contrast this with Achilles' treatment of the fallen Hector.

§ The whole scene is very similar to that in Iliad III. 121, &c., where Helen shows herself on the rampart, and calls forth much the same kind of admiration.

dress his wife. Sítá, conscious of her purity, is hurt by his cold reception of her and bursts into tears, uttering only the words, 'há áryaputra' (xcix. 52). Ráma then haughtily informs her, that having satisfied his honour by the destruction of the ravisher, he can do no more. In short, he declines to take back his wife, whom he suspects of contamination, after so long a residence in Rávaṇa's capital (c). Sítá asserts her innocence in the most dignified and touching language, and begs Lakshmaṇa to prepare a pyre (ci. 20), that she may prove her purity. She enters the flames, invoking Agni (ci. 30); upon which all the gods with the old king Daśaratha appear (cii. 2), and reveal to Ráma his divine nature *, telling him that he is Náráyaṇa (cii. 12), and that Sítá is Lakshmí (30). Agni, the god of Fire, then presents himself, holding Sítá, whom he places in Ráma's arms unhurt † (ciii. 1—5). Ráma is now overjoyed, and declares that he only consented to the ordeal that he might establish his wife's innocence in the eyes of the world (ciii. 17). The old king Daśaratha then blesses his son, gives him good advice, and returns to heaven (civ); while Indra, at the request of Ráma, restores to life all the monkeys and bears killed during the war (cv). Ráma and Lakshmaṇa, along with Vibhíshaṇa, Sugríva, and all the allies, now mount the self-moving car Pushpaka, which contained a whole palace or rather city within itself, and set out on their return to Ayodhyá; Ráma, to beguile the way as they travelled through the sky, describing to Sítá all the scenes of their late adventures lying beneath their feet ‡ (cviii). On their reaching the hermitage of Bharadwája at Prayága, Ráma stops the car; and the fourteen years of his banishment having now expired (cix), sends forward Hanumat to announce his return to Bharata, who was still living at Nandigráma, undergoing austere penance. Bharata hastens to meet his brother, and, in token of delivering over the power which he still holds on trust for him, places on Ráma's feet the two shoes (cxi. 46; and compare note, p. 70).

* He never appears to be conscious of it, until the gods enlighten him. (See cii. 10.) This is not the case with Kṛishṇa in the Mahá-bhárata.

† The whole description of Sítá's repudiation by Ráma is certainly one of the finest scenes in the Rámáyaṇa. These touches of nature surprise us constantly in the midst of a wilderness of exaggeration.

‡ Kálidása, who must have lived at least five hundred years after Válmíki, devotes nearly the whole of the 13th chapter of the Raghu-vanśa to this subject, which he makes a convenient pretext for displaying his geographical and topographical knowledge, as in the Megha-dúta. Bhava-bhúti does the same in the 7th act of his drama, Mahá-víra-charitra; and Murári the same in his play on the same subject. It may be suspected that a good deal of matter at the end of the Yuddha-káṇḍa is modern, as the descriptions do not always agree with what precedes. Ráma here calls Indrajit by his original name of Megha-náda (cviii. 9; and compare note *, p. 83).

Ráma and the three brothers are now once more reunited * (cxi); and Ráma, accompanied by them and by Sítá and the monkeys, who assume human forms (cxii. 28), makes a magnificent entry into Ayodhyá. He is then solemnly crowned, associates Lakshmaṇa in the empire, and, before dismissing his allies, bestows splendid presents on them (cxii). Hanumat, at his own request, receives as a reward the gift of perpetual life and youth (cxii. 101). Every one returns happy and loaded with gifts to his own home, and Ráma commences a glorious reign at Ayodhyá (cxiii).

SEVENTH BOOK or UTTARA-KÁṆḌA.—Although this book (as we have already stated) is probably a comparatively modern addition, a short account of its contents is here given †. It commences with a history of Rávaṇa and the Rákshasas; for an epitome of which, see Dr. Muir's Sanskṛit Texts, vol. IV. p. 413. Ráma being duly crowned at Ayodhyá, seemed likely to enter upon a life of quiet enjoyment with his wife. But this would not have satisfied the Hindú conception of the impossibility of finding rest in this world (see p. 28 of this volume), nor harmonised with the idea of the man born to suffering and self-denial. Inquiring one day what his subjects thought of his deeds, he was told that they approved every thing but his taking back his wife after her long residence with Rávaṇa. The scrupulously correct and over-sensitive Ráma, though convinced of his wife's fidelity, and though she was soon to become a mother, felt quite unable to allow cause of offence in such a matter. Torn by contending feelings, he at last determined on sending her for the rest of her life to the hermitage of Válmíki (Calc. ed. chap. lv); whither indeed she had herself before expressed a wish to go for rest and refreshment. Lakshmaṇa conducted her there, and then broke to her the sad news of her husband's determination to live apart from her. In the hermitage of the poet were born her twin sons, Kuśa and Lava; who, though deserted by their father, bore upon their persons the marks of their high birth, and being taught to recite the Rámáyaṇa, unconsciously celebrated his actions. (See p. 60.) At length one day the twins wandered accidentally to Ayodhyá, where reciting their poem before their father, they were recognised by him. Once more he sent for Sítá to his presence, that in a public assembly she might assert her innocence before the people. She was brought by Válmíki himself, and having adjured the goddess Earth to attest her purity, the ground opened and received her (Calc. ed. chap. cx). Ráma had but this one devoted wife; and now

* This reunion forms the most striking scene in the dramatic representation at the annual festival of the Dasserah in the north-west provinces, and is called 'Bharat-miláp.'

† It forms the subject of Bhava-bhúti's celebrated drama, the Uttara-Ráma-charitra. A great deal of the former narrative appears to be repeated in parts of this book.

that she was gone he could not remain behind. But he did not die a natural death. The story of his translation to heaven is thus told*: "One day Time, in the form of an ascetic, comes to his palace-gate (cxvi. 1), and asks, as the messenger of the great Ṛishi (Brahmá), to see Ráma (3). He is admitted and received with honour (9), but says, when asked what he has to communicate, that his message must be delivered in private, and that any one who witnesses the interview is to lose his life (13). Ráma informs Lakshmaṇa of all this, and desires him to stand outside. Time then tells Ráma (cxvii. 1) that he has been sent by Brahmá to say that when he (Ráma, i. e. Vishṇu), after destroying the worlds, was sleeping on the ocean, he had formed him (Brahmá) from the lotus springing from his navel, and committed to him the work of creation (4—7); that he (Brahmá) had then entreated Ráma to assume the function of Preserver, and that the latter had in consequence become Vishṇu, being born as the son of Aditi (10), and had determined to deliver mankind by destroying Rávaṇa, and to live on earth ten thousand and ten hundred years; that period, adds Time, was now on the eve of expiration (13), and Ráma could either, at his pleasure, prolong his stay on earth, or ascend to heaven and rule over the gods (15). Ráma replies (18), that he had been born for the good of the three worlds, and would now return to the place whence he had come, as it was his function to fulfil the purposes of the gods. While they are speaking, the irritable Ṛishi Durvásas comes, and insists on seeing Ráma immediately, under a threat, if refused, of cursing Ráma and all his family (cxviii. 1). Lakshmaṇa, preferring to save his kinsman, though knowing that his own death must be the consequence of interrupting the interview of Ráma with Time, enters the palace, and reports the Ṛishi's message to Ráma (8). Ráma comes out; and when Durvásas has got the food he wished, and departed, Ráma reflects with great distress on the words of Time, which require that Lakshmaṇa should die (16). Lakshmaṇa, however (cxix. 2), exhorts Ráma not to grieve, but to abandon him, and not break his own promise. The counsellors concurring in this advice (9), Ráma abandons Lakshmaṇa, who goes to the river Sarayú, suppresses all his senses, and is conveyed bodily by Indra to heaven. The gods are delighted by the arrival of the fourth part of Vishṇu (19). Ráma then resolves to instal Bharata as his successor, and retire to the forest and follow Lakshmaṇa (cxx. 1). Bharata, however, refuses the succession, and determines to accompany his brother (8). Ráma's subjects are filled with grief, and say they also will follow him wherever he goes (12). Messengers are sent to Śatrughna, the other brother, and he also resolves to accompany Ráma (cxxi. 1—14); who at length sets out in procession from his capital with all the ceremonial appropriate to the 'great departure' (*mahá-prasthána*, cxxii. 1),

* I have extracted this from Dr. Muir's Sanskrit Texts, vol. IV. p. 407.

silent, indifferent to external objects, joyless, with Srí on his right, the goddess Earth on his left, Energy in front, attended by all his weapons in human shapes, by the Vedas in the forms of Bráhmans, by the Gáyatrí, the Omkára, the Vashaṭkára, by Ṛishis, by his women, female slaves, eunuchs, and servants. Bharata with his family, and Satrughna, follow, together with Bráhmans bearing the sacred fire, and the whole of the people of the country, and even with animals, &c. &c. Ráma, with all these attendants, comes to the banks of the Sarayú (cxxiii). Brahmá, with all the gods, in innumerable celestial cars, now appears, and all the sky is refulgent with the divine splendour. Pure and fragrant breezes blow, a shower of flowers falls. Ráma enters the waters of the Sarayú; and Brahmá utters a voice from the sky, saying, 'Approach, Vishṇu; Rághava, thou hast happily arrived, with thy god-like brothers. Enter thine own body as Vishṇu, or the eternal æther. For thou art the abode of the worlds (*loka-gatih*): no one comprehends thee, the inconceivable and imperishable, except the large-eyed Máyá, thy primeval spouse.' Hearing these words, Ráma enters the glory of Vishṇu (*Vaishṇavam tejas*) with his body and his followers. He then asks Brahmá to find an abode for the people who had accompanied him from devotion to his person; and Brahmá appoints them a celestial residence accordingly."

SUMMARY OF THE LEADING STORY

OF

THE MAHÁ-BHÁRATA.

THIS poem (which was recited by Vaiśampáyana, the pupil of Vyása, to Janamejaya, the great-grandson of Arjuna) is divided into eighteen books. To which has been added a supplement called Harivanśa (see p. 40). It is in celebration of the lunar race of kings, as the Rámáyaṇa is of the solar; and some knowledge of their genealogy is essential to the comprehension of the story. Soma, the moon, the progenitor of the lunar race, who reigned at Hastinápur, was the child of the Ṛishi, *Atri*, and father of Budha, who married Ilá or Iḍá, daughter of the solar prince Ikshwáku, and had by her a son, Aila or Purúravas. The latter had a son by Urvaśí named *Áyus*, from whom came Nahusha, the father of Yayáti. The latter had two sons, Puru and Yadu, from whom proceeded the two branches of the lunar line. In the line of *Yadu* we need only mention the last three princes, Sura, Vasudeva *, and Kṛishṇa with his brother Balaráma. Fifteenth in the other line—that of *Puru*—came Dushyanta, father of the great Bharata, from whom India to this day is called Bhárata-varsha. Ninth from Bharata came Kuru, and fourteenth from him Śántanu. This Śántanu had by his wife Satyavatí, a son named Vichitra-vírya. Bhíshma (also called Śántanava, Deva-vrata, &c.), who renounced the right of succession and took

---

* Pṛithá or Kuntí, wife of Páṇḍu, and mother of three of the Páṇḍu princes, was a sister of Vasudeva, and therefore aunt of Kṛishṇa.

the vow of a Brahmachárí *, was the son of S'ántanu by a former wife, the goddess Gangá, whence one of his names is Gángeya. Satyavatí also had, before her marriage with S'ántanu, borne Vyása to the sage Parás'ara; so that Vichitra-vírya, Bhíshma, and Vyása were half-brothers †; and Vyása, although he retired into the wilderness, to live a life of contemplation, promised his mother that he would place himself at her disposal whenever she required his services. Satyavatí had recourse to him when her son Vichitra-vírya died childless, and requested him to pay his addresses to Vichitra-vírya's two widows, named Ambiká and Ambáliká. He consented, and had by them respectively two children, Dhṛitaráshṭra, who was born blind, and Páṇḍu, who was born with a pale complexion ‡. When Satyavatí begged Vyása to become the father of a third son (who should be without any defect), the elder wife, terrified by Vyása's austere appearance, sent him one of her slave-girls, dressed in her own clothes; and this girl was the mother of Vidura (whence he is sometimes called Kshattṛi ‖). Dhṛitaráshṭra, Páṇḍu, and Vidura were thus brothers, sons of Vyása, the supposed author or compiler of the Mahá-bhárata. Vyása after this retired again to the woods; but, gifted with divine prescience, appeared both to his sons and grandsons whenever they were in difficulties, and needed his advice and assistance. To make the genealogy more clear, it may be well to repeat it in a tabular form :—

* I. e. perpetual celibacy. Adya-prabhṛiti me brahmacharyam bhavishyati; Aputrasyápi me loká bhavishyanty akshayá divi. (Mahá-bhár. I. 4060.)

† Parás'ara met with Satyavatí when quite a girl, as he was crossing the river Jumná in a boat. The result of their intercourse was a child, Vyása, who was called Kṛishṇa, from his swarthy complexion, and Dwaipáyana, because he was brought forth by Satyavatí on an island (dwípa) in the Jumná. (See Mahá-bhár. I. 2416, 2417, and 4235.)

‡ The mother of Páṇḍu was also called Kaus'alyá; and this name (which was that of the mother of Ráma-chandra) seems also to be applied to the mother of Dhṛitaráshṭra. Paleness of complexion, in the eyes of a Hindú, would be regarded as a kind of leprosy, and was therefore almost as great a defect as blindness. The reason given for these defects is very curious. Ambiká was so terrified by the swarthy complexion and shaggy aspect of the sage Vyása (not to speak of the *gandha* emitted by his body), that when he visited her she closed her eyes, and did not venture to open them while he was with her. In consequence of this assumed blindness her child was born blind. Ambáliká, on the other hand, though she kept her eyes open, became so colourless with fright, that her son was born with a pale complexion. (See Mahá-bhár. I. 4275—4290.) Páṇḍu seems to have been in other respects good looking—Sá deví kumáram ajíjanat páṇḍu-lakshaṇa-sampannam dípyamánam vara-s'riyá.

‖ Vyása was so much pleased with this slave-girl that he pronounced her free, and declared that her child, Vidura, should be sarva-buddhimatám varah. Kshattṛi, although in Manu the child of a S'údra father and Bráhman mother, signifies here the child of a Bráhman father and S'údra mother.

Atri (the muni, generally reckoned among the seven Rishis or sages).

Soma (or chandra), the moon.

Budha (or Mercury), married Ilá or Idá, daughter of Ikshwáku.

Purúravas or Aila (married the nymph U'rvasí).

Áyus.

Nahusha.

Yayáti (husband of S'armishthá and Devayání).

Line of Puru.	Line of Yadu.
Puru (king in Pratishthána)	Yadu
Dushyanta (h. of S'akuntalá)	Vrishni
Bharata	Devaráta
Hastin (built Hastinápur)	Andhaka
Kuru	S'úra
S'ántanu	

Vasudeva, brother of Kuntí or Prithá, also called Anaka-dundubhi.

Krishna and Balaráma, with whom, by the quarrels of the Yádavas, the line becomes extinct. They were cotemporary with the sons of Pándu and Dhritaráshtra.

Line of Puru and Kuru continued.

S'ántanu—Satyavatí

| Chitrángada* | Vichitra-virya, son of both, died childless. | Vyása, son of Satyavatí, married the two widows of Vichitra-virya. | Bhíshma, called S'ántanava and Gángeya, as son of S'ántanu by Gangá. | Kripa † |

Dhritaráshtra—Gándhárí	Kuntí or Prithá—Pándu—Mádrí	Vidura, called Kshattrí.
	Karna Yudhish-thira Bhíma Arjuna Nakula Sahadeva	

Duryodhana and 99 other sons.

* Chitrángada reigned a very short time after the death of S'ántanu. He was so arrogant and proud of his strength that he defied gods and men; upon which the king of the Gandharbas, his namesake, came down to fight with him and killed him.

† Kripa and his sister Kripá, wife of Drona, were adopted children of S'ántanu (see Mahábhár. I. 5087; and see note ‡, p. 97).

FIRST BOOK or ÁDI-PARVA.—Dhṛitaráshṭra and Páṇḍu were brought up by their uncle Bhíshma*, who in the meanwhile conducted the government of Hastinápur† (4349). Dhṛitaráshṭra was the first-born, but at first renounced the throne, in consequence of his blindness (4361). Vidura being the son of a Śúdra woman, could not succeed, and Páṇḍu therefore became king (4361). In the meantime Dhṛitaráshṭra married Gándhárí (also called Saubaleyí or Saubalí, daughter of Subala, king of Gándhára); who when she heard that her future husband was blind, to show her respect for him, bound her own eyes with a handkerchief, and always remained blindfolded in his presence‡. Soon afterwards, at a swayamvara held by king Kuntibhoja, his adopted daughter, Pṛithá or Kuntí, chose Páṇḍu for her husband (4418). She was the child of a Yádava prince, Śúra, who gave her to his childless cousin Kuntibhoja; under whose care she was brought up. One day, before her marriage, she paid such respect and attention to a powerful sage named Durvásas, a guest in her father's house, that he gave her a charm and taught her an incantation, by virtue of which she was to have a child by any god she liked to invoke. Out of curiosity, she invoked the Sun, by whom she had a child, who was born clothed in armour‖. Pṛithá (or Kuntí), afraid of the censure of her relatives, deserted the child, and exposed it in the river. It was found by Adhiratha, a charioteer (*súta*), and nurtured by his wife Rádhá; whence the child was afterwards called Rádheya, though named by his foster-parents Vasusheṇa. When he was grown up, Indra tricked him out of his armour (which he wanted for his son Arjuna) by appealing to his generosity in the guise of a Bráhman. Indra in return conferred upon him enormous strength (*śakti*), and changed his name to Karṇa§ (4383—4411).

After Páṇḍu's marriage to Pṛithá, his uncle Bhíshma, wishing him to take a second wife, made an expedition to Śalya, king of Madra, and prevailed upon him to bestow his sister Mádrí upon Páṇḍu, in exchange for vast sums of money and jewels

* Dhṛitaráshṭraścha Páṇḍuścha Viduraścha mahámatiḥ Janma-prabhṛiti Bhíshmeṇa putravat paripálitáḥ (4353). They were all three thoroughly educated by Bhíshma. Dhṛitaráshṭra is described as excelling all others in strength (4356), Páṇḍu as excelling in the use of the bow, and Vidura as pre-eminent for virtue (4358).

† Hastinápur is also called Gajasáhwaya and Nágasáhwaya.

‡ Sá paṭam ádáya kṛitwá bahuguṇam tadá Babandha netre swe rájan pativrata-paráyaṇá (4376). She is described as so devoted to her husband that Vácha 'pi purushán anyán suvratá nánwakírtayat.

‖ The Sun afterwards restored to her her maidenhood (kanyátwa). See 4400.

§ He is also called Vaikartana, as son of Vikartana or the Sun, and sometimes Vṛisha. Karṇa is described (4405) as worshipping the Sun till he scorched his own back (áprishṭhatápát). Compare Hitop. book II. v. 32.

(4438). Soon after this second marriage Páṇḍu undertook a great campaign, in which he conquered the Daśárnas, Magadha, Káśi, Mithilá or Videha, and subjugated so many countries, that the kingdom of Hastinápur became under him as glorious and extensive as formerly under Bharata (4461). Having acquired enormous wealth, which he distributed to Bhíshma, Vidura, and Dhritaráshṭra, Páṇḍu retired to the woods, to indulge his passion for hunting, and lived with his two wives as a forester on the southern slope of the Himálayas. The blind Dhritaráshṭra, who had a very useful charioteer named Sanjaya, was then obliged, with the assistance of Bhíshma as his regent, to take the reins of government. After this, Bhíshma promoted the marriage of Vidura with a beautiful slave-girl belonging to king Devaka*.

We have next an account of the birth of Dhritaráshṭra's sons. One day the sage Vyása was hospitably entertained by the queen Gándhárí, and in return granted her a boon. She chose to be the mother of a hundred sons, and soon afterwards became pregnant (4490). After two years' gestation she produced a mass of flesh, which was divided by Vyása into a hundred and one pieces (as big as the joint of a thumb), and placed in jars (kuṇḍeshu). In due time the eldest son, Duryodhana (sometimes called Suyodhana; see p. 20 of this volume), was born, but not till after the birth of Prithá's son Yudhishṭhira. At Duryodhana's birth various evil omens of the usual hackneyed description occurred; jackals yelled, donkeys brayed, whirlwinds blew, and the sky seemed on fire (4509). Dhritaráshṭra, alarmed, called his ministers together, who recommended him to abandon the child, but could not persuade him to do so. In another month the remaining ninety-nine sons were born † from the remaining jars, and one daughter, called Duhśalá (afterwards married to Jayadratha). Dhritaráshṭra had also one other son, named Yuyutsu, born in the usual way from a woman of the Vaiśyá caste (4522), making altogether a hundred and two children.

We have next the account of the birth of the five reputed sons of Páṇḍu. One day, on a hunting expedition, Páṇḍu transfixed with five arrows a male and female deer, engaged in amorous sport together. These turned out to be a certain sage and his wife, who had taken the form of these animals. The sage cursed Páṇḍu, and predicted that he would die in the conjugal embraces of one of his wives (4588). In consequence of this curse, Páṇḍu took the vow of a Brahmachárí ‡, abandoned sensual pleasures, gave all his property to the Bráhmans, and became a hermit. He

* Vidura is one of the best characters in the Mahá-bhárata, always ready with good advice (hitopadeśa), both for the Páṇḍavas and for his brother Dhritaráshṭra. His disposition leads him always to take the part of the Páṇḍu princes, and warn them of the evil designs of their cousins.

† Their names are all detailed at 4540.

‡ The brahmacharya-vrata, or vow of continence.

kept apart from Pṛithá (also called Kuntí), and from his other wife, Mádrí; but, with his approval, the former made use of the charm and incantation formerly given to her by Durvásas (see p. 94, l. 13), and had three sons, Yudhishṭhira, Bhíma, and Arjuna, by the three deities, Dharma, Váyu, and Indra respectively (see p. 99, last note). Yudhishṭhira was born first, and before Dhṛitaráshṭra's eldest son Duryodhana. At his birth a heavenly voice was heard, which said, 'This is the best of virtuous men.' Bhíma, the son of Pṛithá and Váyu, was born on the same day as Duryodhana (4776). Soon after his birth, his mother accidentally let him fall, when a great prodigy occurred—indicative of the vast strength which was to distinguish him—for the body of the child falling on a rock shivered it to atoms. On the birth of Arjuna auspicious omens were manifested; showers of flowers fell *, celestial minstrels filled the air with harmony, and a heavenly voice sounded his praises and future glory (4792).

Mádrí, the other wife of Páṇḍu, was now anxious to have children, and was told by Pṛithá (Kuntí) to think on any god she pleased (4849). She chose the two Aświns †, who appeared to her, and were the fathers of her twin sons Nakula and Sahadeva ‡. While these five princes were still children, Páṇḍu, forgetting the curse of the sage whom he had killed in the form of a deer, ventured one day to embrace Mádrí, and died in her arms (4877). She and Kuntí then had a dispute for the honour of becoming a satí (suttee), which ended in Mádrí burning herself with her husband's corpse (4896); and Pṛithá (also called Kuntí), with the five Páṇḍu princes, were taken by the Ṛishis, or holy men—companions of Páṇḍu—to Hastinápur, where they were presented to Dhṛitaráshṭra, and all the circumstances of their birth and of the death of Páṇḍu narrated (4918). The news of the death of his brother was received by Dhṛitaráshṭra with much apparent sorrow; he gave orders for the due performance of the funeral rites, and allowed the five young princes and their mother

* Showers of flowers are as common in Indian poetry as showers of blood; the one indicating good, the other portending evil.

† The Aświnau are the twin sons of Súrya, the sun, by his wife Sanjná, transformed to a mare. They are endowed with perpetual youth and beauty, and are the physicians of the gods. See the last note, p. 47; and compare the explanations in *Nirukta*, XII. 1. p. 170, Roth's edit.

‡ The five Páṇḍu princes are known by various other names in the Mahá-bhárata, some of which it may be useful here to note. Yudhishṭhira is also called, Dharmarája, Dharmaputra, and sometimes simply Rájan. His charioteer was called Indrasena. Bhíma's other names are, Bhímasena, Vṛikodara, Báhuśálin. Arjuna is also called, Kiríṭin, Phálguna, Jishṇu, Dhananjaya, Bíbhatsu, Savyasáchin, Pákaśásani, Guḍákeśa, Śweta-váhana, Nara, and sometimes *par excellence* Pártha, though Bhíma and Yudhishṭhira, as sons of Pṛithá, had also this title. Nakula and Sahadeva are called Mádreyau (as sons of Mádrí), and sometimes Yamau (the twins). The name *Kaurava* is sometimes applied to the Páṇḍu princes as well as to the sons of Dhṛitaráshṭra.

to live with his own family. The cousins were in the habit of playing together; but in their boyish sports the Páṇḍu princes excelled the sons of Dhṛitaráshṭra (4978), which excited much ill feeling; and the spiteful Duryodhana, even when a boy, tried to destroy Bhíma by mixing poison in his food (5008), and then throwing him into the water when stupified by its effects. Bhíma, however, was not drowned, but descended to the abode of the nágas (or serpents), who freed him from the influence of the poison (5052), and gave him a liquid to drink which endued him with the strength of ten thousand nágas *. After this, Duryodhana, Karṇa, and S'akuni † devised various schemes for destroying the Páṇḍu princes, but without success (5068).

We have next the account of the coming of Droṇa to Hastinápur. He was a Bráhman, the son of Bharadwája ‡, and being well skilled in the use of the bow and other warlike weapons, was chosen by Bhíshma (who acted as Dhṛitaráshṭra's regent) to train all the young princes, both Kauravas and Páṇḍavas, in warlike exercises. An account of the tournament at which, their education being completed, they exhibited their skill, is given at p. 21. The fee which Droṇa required for their instruction was, that they should capture Drupada king of Panchála, who had insulted him (5446). They therefore invaded Drupada's territory and took him prisoner (5502); but Droṇa spared his life, and gave him back half his kingdom. (This Drupada was afterwards to become the father-in-law of the five Páṇḍavas ‖.) After this, Yudhishṭhira was installed by Dhṛitaráshṭra as Yuvarája or heir-apparent (5518), and by his exploits soon eclipsed the glory of his father Páṇḍu's reign (5519). Meanwhile Bhíma learnt the use of the club and the sword from his cousin Balaráma (5520);

---

* Tasmán nágáyutabalo raṇe 'dhṛishyo bhavishyasi (5054).

† S'akuni was the brother of Gándhárí, and therefore maternal uncle (mátula) of the Kaurava princes. He was the counsellor of Duryodhana. He is often called Saubala, as Gándhárí is called Saubalí.

‡ Droṇa married Kṛipá, sister of Kṛipa, and had by her a son, Aswatthámán. Kṛipa and Kṛipá were the children of a great sage, S'aradvat (called Gautama as son of Gotama). He performed very severe penance, and thereby frightened Indra, who sent a nymph to tempt him (5076), but without success. However, twins were born to the sage in a clump of grass (śarastamba), who were found by king S'ántanu, and out of pity (kṛipá) taken home and reared as his own. He called them Kṛipa and Kṛipá. The former became one of the privy council at Hastinápur, and is sometimes called Gautama, sometimes S'áradvata.

‖ Burning with resentment, Drupada endeavoured to procure the birth of a son, to avenge his defeat and bring about the destruction of Droṇa. Two Bráhmans undertook a sacrifice for him, and two children were born from the midst of the altar, out of the sacrificial fire, a son, Dhṛishṭa-dyumna, and a daughter, Kṛishṇá or Draupadí, afterwards the wife of the Páṇḍavas.

but Arjuna, by the help of Droṇa, who gave him magical weapons (5525), excelled all in skill and the use of arms. The great renown gained by the Páṇḍu princes excited the jealousy and ill-will of Dhṛitaráshṭra (5542), but won the affections of the citizens (5657). The latter met together, and after consultation declared that as Dhṛitaráshṭra was blind he ought not to conduct the government, and that as Bhishma had formerly declined the throne he ought not to be allowed to act as regent (5660). They therefore proposed to crown Yudhishṭhira at once *. When Duryodhana heard of this, he consulted with Karṇa, Śakuni, and Duḥśásana, how he might remove Yudhishṭhira out of the way, and secure the throne for himself. At his urgent solicitation, Dhṛitaráshṭra was induced to send the Páṇḍava princes on an excursion to the city of Váraṇávata, pretending that he wished them to see the beauties of that town, and to be present at a festival there (5705). Meanwhile Duryodhana instigated his friend Purochana to precede them, and to prepare a house for their reception, which he was to fill secretly with hemp, resin, and other combustible substances, plastering the walls with mortar composed of oil, fat, and lac (*lákshá* or *jatu*). When the princes were asleep in this house, and unsuspicious of danger, he was to set it on fire (5730). The five Páṇḍavas and their mother left Hastinápur amid the tears and regrets of the citizens, and in eight days arrived at Váraṇávata, where, after great demonstrations of respect from the inhabitants, they were conducted by Purochana to the house of lac. Having been warned by Vidura, they soon discovered the dangerous character of the structure (5781), and with the assistance of a miner (*khanaka*) sent by Vidura, dug an underground passage, by which to escape from the interior (5813). Then having invited a degraded outcaste woman (*nishádí*) with her five sons to a feast, and having stupified them with wine, they first set fire to the house of Purochana †, and then to their own. Purochana was burnt, and the woman with her five sons, but they themselves escaped by the secret passage (*surungá*). The charred bodies of the woman and her sons being afterwards found, it was supposed that the Páṇḍava princes had perished in the conflagration (5864), and their funeral ceremonies were performed by Dhṛitaráshṭra. Meanwhile they hurried off to the woods; Bhíma, the strong one, carrying his mother and the twins, and leading his other brothers by the hands (5839) when through fatigue they could not move on. Whilst his mother and brothers were asleep under a fig-tree, Bhíma had an encounter with a hideous giant named Hiḍimba, whom he slew (6038). Afterwards he married Hiḍimbá, the sister of this monster, and had a son by her named Ghaṭotkacha (6072).

* Te vayam Páṇḍava-jyeshṭham abhishinchámá.

† It is worthy of remark, that Bhíma is the one to set fire to the houses.

By the advice of their grandfather Vyása, the Páṇḍava princes next took up their abode in the house of a Bráhman at a city called Ekachakrá. There they lived for a long time in the guise of mendicant Bráhmans, safe from the persecution of Duryodhana. Every day they went out to beg for food given as alms (*bhaiksha*), which their mother Kuntí divided at night, giving half of the whole to Bhíma as his share * (6108). While resident in the house of the Bráhman, Bhíma delivered his family and the city of Ekachakrá from the Rákshasa named Baka (or Vaka), who every day devoured one of the citizens, and terrified the whole neighbourhood (see p. 33 of this volume).

After this Vyása appeared to his grandsons, and informed them that Draupadí, the daughter of Drupada, king of Panchála, was destined to be their common wife †. In a long discourse he explained that in real fact she had been in a former life the daughter of a sage, and had performed a most severe penance, in order that a husband might fall to her lot. S'iva, pleased with her penance, had appeared to her, and had promised her, instead of one, five husbands. When the maiden replied that she wanted only one husband, the god answered, "Five times you said to me, Grant me a husband; therefore in another body you will obtain five husbands" (6433 and 7322). This Ṛishi's daughter was thereupon born in the family of Drupada as a maiden of the most distinguished beauty, and was destined to be the wife of the Páṇḍavas ‡.

---

* From his enormous appetite Bhíma was called 'wolf-stomached' (Vṛikodara). His portion was always one half of the whole dish intended for the family meal, because he was *Nágarskaba-tulya-rúpa*, 'equal in size to the chief of the Nágas' (see 7161).

† Polyandria is still practised among some hill-tribes in the Himálaya range near Simla, and in other barren mountainous regions, such as Bhotan, where a large population could not be supported. It prevails also among the Nair (Náyar) tribe in Malabar. Our forefathers, or at least the ancient Britons, according to Cæsar, were given to the same practice: 'Uxores habent deni duodenique inter se communes,' &c. De Bello Gallico, V. 14.

‡ Vyása, who is the type and representative of strict Bráhmanism, was obliged to explain at length the necessity for the marriage of Draupadí to five husbands (which is called a sûkshma-dharma, 7246). He also gifted Drupada with divine intuition (*chakshur divyam*) to perceive the divinity of the Páṇḍavas and penetrate the mystic meaning of what otherwise he would have regarded as a serious violation of the laws and institutions of the Bráhmans (7313). Hence Drupada became aware of his daughter's former birth, as described above, and that Arjuna was really a part or avatár of Indra (S'akrasyáṃśa), and that all his brothers were also portions of the same god. Draupadí herself, although nominally the daughter of Drupada, was really born, like her brother Dhṛishṭa-dyumna, out of the midst of the sacrificial fire (vedi-madhyát, 6931), and was a form of Lakshmí. In no other way could her supernatural birth, and the divine perfume which exhaled from her person, and was perceived a league off (krośa-mátrát pravátí, 6934. 7311), be accounted for. Vyása at the same time explained the mysterious birth of Kṛishṇa and Baladeva;—how the god Vishṇu pulled out two

In obedience to the directions of their grandfather, the five Páṇḍavas quitted Eka-chakrá, and betook themselves to the court of king Drupada, where Draupadí was about to hold her swayamvara. (See the description of this at p. 22.) Arjuna being chosen by Draupadí, they returned with her to their mother, who being inside the house, and fancying that they had brought alms, called out to them, 'Share it between you' (*Bhunkteti sametya sarve*, 7132). The words of a parent, thus spoken, could not be set aside without evil consequences; and Drupada, at the persuasion of Vyása, who acquainted him with the divine destination of his daughter *, consented to her becoming the common wife of the five Páṇḍu princes. She was first married by the family-priest Dhaumya to Yudhishṭhira (7340), and then, according to priority of birth, to the other four †.

The Páṇḍavas, being now strengthened by their alliance with the powerful king of Panchála, threw off their disguises; and king Dhṛitaráshṭra thought it more politic to settle all differences by dividing his kingdom between them and his own sons. He gave up Hastinápur to the latter, presided over by Duryodhana, and permitted

---

of his own hairs, one white and the other black, which entered into two women of the family of the Yádavas (Devakí and Rohiṇí), and became, the white one Baladeva and the black one Kṛishṇa. (See 7307; and compare Vishṇu-puráṇa, book V. ch. 1.) In the Márkaṇḍeya-puráṇa (ch. 5) it is shown how the five Páṇḍavas could be all portions of Indra, and yet four of them sons of other gods. When Indra killed the son of Twashṭṛi (or Viśwakarman as Prajápati, the Creator), his punishment for this *brahmahatyá* was that all his *tejas*, 'manly vigour,' deserted him, and entered Dharma, the god of Justice. The son of Twashṭṛi was reproduced as the demon Vṛitra, and again slain by Indra; as a punishment for which his *bala*, 'strength,' left him, and entered *Máruta*, 'the Wind.' Lastly, when Indra violated Ahalyá, the wife of the sage Gautama, his *rúpa*, 'beauty,' abandoned him, and entered the Násatyas or Aświns. When Dharma gave back the *tejas* of Indra, Yudhishṭhira was born; when the Wind gave up Indra's *bala*, Bhíma was born; and when the Aświns restored the *rúpa* of Indra, Nakula and Sahadeva were born. Arjuna was born as half the essence of Indra. Hence, as they were all portions of one deity, there could be no harm in Draupadí becoming the wife of all five.

* See the last note. Drupada at first objected. Yudhishṭhira's excuse for himself and his brothers is remarkable; *púrveshám anupúrvyeṇa yátam vartmánuyámahe* (7146).

† She had a son by each of the five brothers—Prativindhya by Yudhishṭhira; Sutasoma by Bhíma; S'rutakarman by Arjuna; S'atáníka by Nakula; S'rutasena by Sahadeva (8039). Arjuna had also another wife, Subhadrá, the sister of Kṛishṇa, with whom he eloped when on a visit to Kṛishṇa at Dwáraká. By her he had a son, Abhimanyu. He had also a son named Irávat by the serpent-nymph Ulúpí. Bhíma had also a son, Ghaṭotkacha, by the Rákshasí Hiḍimbá (see bottom of p. 98); and the others had children by different wives (see Vishṇu-puráṇa, p. 459). Arjuna's son Abhimanyu had a son Paríkshit, who was the father of Janamejaya. Paríkshit died of the bite of a snake; and the Bhágavata-puráṇa was narrated to him between the bite and his death.

the five Páṇḍavas to occupy a district near the Jumná, called Kháṇḍavaprastha, where they built Indraprastha (the modern Delhi), and, under Yudhishṭhira as their leader, subjugated much of the adjacent territory by predatory incursions (6573).

While they were living happily together, after these successes, the divine seer Nárada * came to them, and admonished them to take care that Draupadí was never the cause of their disunion, lest the same fate should befal them which happened to two brothers of the Daitya race, Sunda and Upasunda. Their story is then narrated †.

The remainder of the first book is filled with the adventures of Arjuna, who, to fulfil a vow, went to reside for twelve years in the forest (7775). One day, when he was bathing in the Ganges, he was carried off by the serpent-nymph Ulúpí, daughter of the king of the Nágas, whom he married (7809). Afterwards he married Chitrángadá, daughter of the king of Maṇipura (7826), and had a child by her named Babhruváhana (7883).

In the course of his wanderings Arjuna came to Prabhása, a place of pilgrimage in the west of India, where he met Kṛishṇa ‡, who here first formed a friendship with him (7888), and took him to his city Dwáraká (7899), where he received him as a visitor into his own house (7905). Soon afterwards, some of the relatives of Kṛishṇa celebrated a festival in the mountain Raivataka, to which both Arjuna and Kṛishṇa went. There they saw Balaráma in a state of intoxication (*kshíva*) ‖ with his wife Revatí (8912); and there they saw Subhadrá, Kṛishṇa's sister. Her beauty excited the love of Arjuna, who, after obtaining Kṛishṇa's leave, carried her off and married her (7937). In the twelfth year of his absence he returned with her to Indraprastha. Kṛishṇa and Balaráma followed him there, to celebrate Arjuna's marriage with Subhadrá, who in due time bore a son, named Abhimanyu (8025).

The Páṇḍavas and all the people of Indraprastha then lived happily for some time under the rule of Yudhishṭhira (8050). One day Arjuna and Kṛishṇa went to bathe in the Jumná, and were resting themselves after sporting in the stream, when they were accosted by the god Agni in the form of a Bráhman, who begged them to help him in his attempts to burn the Kháṇḍava forest, sacred to Indra. It appeared that Agni's vigour had been exhausted by devouring too many oblations at a great sacri-

* Nárada was one of the ten divine Ṛishis, sons of Brahmá. He was a friend of Kṛishṇa, and was inventor of the víṇá or lute. He often acts as a messenger of the gods.

† It is briefly told in the 4th book of the Hitopadeśa.

‡ It may be useful to enumerate some of the other names by which Kṛishṇa is known in the Mahá-bhárata, as follows: Vásudeva, Keśava, Govinda, Janárdana, Dámodara, Dáśárha, Náráyaṇa, Hṛishíkeśa, Purushottama, Mádhava, Madhusúdana, Achyuta. (See Udyoga-p. 2560.) In the Draupadí-haraṇa (75) Kṛishṇa and Arjuna are called *Kṛishṇau*.

‖ Compare Meghadúta, v. 51, where Balaráma's fondness for wine is alluded to.

fice, and Brahmá had revealed to him that there was only one way of recovering his strength, namely, by consuming the whole Kháṇḍava forest with all its inhabitants (8149). This he had attempted to do, but was always frustrated by Indra, who by deluging the forest extinguished the fire. Agni therefore craved the assistance of Arjuna and Kṛishṇa. Arjuna agreed to help him, provided Agni furnished him with a chariot, a bow, and divine arms. Upon this Agni applied to the god Varuṇa, who gave him the bow called Gáṇḍíva, two quivers called Akshayyau*, and a chariot having an ape for its standard (*kapi-lakshaṇa*). These had been given to Varuṇa by Soma, and now being handed over by Varuṇa to Agni, were by him given to Arjuna (8183). Agni at the same time gave to Kṛishṇa as a weapon the celebrated discus (*chakra*) called Vajranábha, Sudarśana, &c. (8196), and a club called Kaumodakí (8200). With the assistance of these weapons, Arjuna and Kṛishṇa fought with Indra (8207), who, unable to overcome them, could no longer prevent Agni from completing the burning of the forest, and thereby recovering his energy.

SECOND BOOK or SABHÁ-PARVA.—This commences by describing how Arjuna and his brothers conquered various kings and subdued various countries (983) in the neighbourhood of Indraprastha. Yudhishṭhira, elated with these successes, undertook, with the assistance of Kṛishṇa (1223), to celebrate the Rájasúya, a great sacrifice, at which his own inauguration as paramount sovereign was to be performed. He could not, however, perform the Rájasúya till after the destruction of a tyrannical and powerful king named Jarásandha (626), who was the determined foe of Kṛishṇa, but was challenged and slain by Bhíma. See Muir's Texts, vol. IV. p. 245.

Afterwards a great assembly (*sabhá*) was held; various princes attended, and brought either rich presents or tribute (1264). Among those who came were Bhíshma, Dhṛitaráshṭra and his hundred sons, Subala (king of Gandhára), Śakuni, Drupada, Śalya, Droṇa, Kṛipa, Jayadratha, Kuntibhoja, Śiśupála, and others from the extreme south and north (Dráviḍa, Ceylon, and Kásmír, 1271)†. On the day of the inauguration (*abhisheka*) Bhíshma, at the suggestion of the sage Nárada, proposed that a respectful oblation (*argha*) should be prepared and offered in token of worship to the best and strongest person present; whom he declared to be Kṛishṇa. To this the Páṇḍavas readily agreed; and Sahadeva was commissioned to present the offering. Śiśupála, however, (also called Sunítha,) opposed the worship of Kṛishṇa (1336. 1414); and, after denouncing him as a contemptible and ill-instructed person (1340),

* Sometimes called *akshayye*, as *ishudhi* is either masc. or fem.

† The details in this part of the poem are interesting and curious as throwing light on the geographical divisions and political condition of India at an early epoch.

challenged him to fight; but Kṛishṇa instantly struck off his head with his discus *. The events of the Rájasúya having cemented the alliance between Kṛishṇa and the Páṇḍavas (1625), the former, at the completion of the ceremony, returned to Dwáraká.

After this, in a conversation between Duryodhana and S'akuni, in which the former expressed his determination to get rid of the Páṇḍavas, S'akuni, who was skilful at dice (*akshakuśala*), persuaded Duryodhana to contrive that Yudhishṭhira, who was very fond of gambling (*dyútapriya*), should play with him (S'akuni) (1721). Dhṛitaráshṭra was then persuaded to hold another assembly (*sabhá*) at Hastinápur; and Vidura was sent to the Páṇḍavas, to invite them to be present (1993). They consented to attend; and Yudhishṭhira was easily prevailed on by Duryodhana to play with S'akuni. By degrees Yudhishṭhira staked every thing, his territory, his possessions, and last of all Draupadí. All were successively lost; and Draupadí, who was then regarded as a slave, was treated with great indignity by Duḥśásana. He dragged her by the hair of the head into the assembly (2229. 2235); upon which Bhíma, who witnessed this insult, swore that he would one day dash Duḥśásana to pieces and drink his blood † (2302). In the end a compromise was agreed upon. The kingdom was given up to Duryodhana for twelve years; and the five Páṇḍavas, with Draupadí, were required to live for that period in the woods, and to pass the thirteenth concealed under assumed names in various disguises. This concludes the Sabhá-parva.

THIRD BOOK OR VANA-PARVA.—This, which is one of the longest of the eighteen, describes the life of the Páṇḍavas in the woods. They retired to the Kámyaka forest, and took up their abode on the banks of the Saraswatí (242), resolved to conquer back their kingdom at the end of the thirteenth year, if Duryodhana was not willing to give it up.

While they were resident there, Arjuna, at the advice of his grandfather Vyása, and at the desire of Yudhishṭhira (1459), went to the Himálaya mountains (1495), that he might perform there severe penance, and thereby obtain celestial arms from Indra, to secure his victory over the Kuru princes. On arriving at Indrakíla (the

* Duryodhana also, in a subsequent part of the Mahá-bhárata, shows his scepticism in regard to the divine nature of Kṛishṇa (Udyoga-p. 4368). The story of S'iśupála and his destruction by Kṛishṇa forms the subject of the celebrated poem of Mágha. All the particulars of the narrative as told in this book of the Mahá-bhárata are given by Dr. Muir in his Sanskṛit Texts, vol. IV. p. 171—180. The Vishṇu-puráṇa identifies S'iśupála with the demons Hiraṇya-kaśipu and Rávaṇa (Wilson's transl. p. 437).

† This threat he fulfilled. The incident is noticeable as it is the subject of the drama called Veṇí-sanhára.

mountain Mandara), a voice in the sky called out to him to stop (1498), and Indra appeared to him, promising to give him the desired arms if by his austerities he was able to obtain a sight of the god Śiva (1513). Upon this Arjuna commenced a course of severe penance (1538); and after some time Śiva, to reward him and prove his bravery, approached him as a Kiráta or wild mountaineer living by the chase, at the moment that a demon named Múka, in the form of a boar, was making an attack upon him. Śiva and Arjuna both shot together at the boar, which fell dead, and both claimed to have hit him first. This served as a pretext for Śiva, as the Kiráta, to quarrel with Arjuna, and have a battle with him. Arjuna fought long with the Kiráta *, but could not conquer him. At last he recognised the god, and threw himself at his feet. Śiva, pleased with his bravery, granted him a boon; and Arjuna asked for the celebrated weapon Páśupata, to enable him to conquer Karṇa and the Kuru princes in war. Śiva granted his request, and disappeared † (1650-1664). Then the guardians of the four regions (*lokapáláh*), Indra, Yama, Varuṇa, and Kuvera, presented themselves (1670), and each enriched Arjuna with his peculiar weapons. Indra afterwards sent his chariot, with his charioteer Mátali, to convey Arjuna from the mountain Mandara to his heavenly palace (1715). Arjuna mounted the car (as his ancestor Dushyanta had done before him), and, amid instructive conversations with Mátali, arrived at the abode of his divine father, who embraced him, placed him near himself on his throne, and permitted him to be present at a heavenly festival.

Many other beautiful episodes are introduced into the Vana-parva; and long stories are narrated, such as that of Nala, to amuse and console the Páṇḍu princes in their banishment. An attempt to carry off Draupadí by Jayadratha, while the five brothers are absent on a shooting excursion, resembles in some respects the story of Sítá's forcible abduction by Rávaṇa in the Rámáyaṇa (15572). The whole story of the Rámáyaṇa is also told in this book (15945).

FOURTH BOOK or VIRÁṬA-PARVA.—This describes the thirteenth year of exile, and recounts the adventures of the Páṇḍavas, who are obliged to live for this year incognito. They journeyed to the court of king Viráṭa, and entered his service in different disguises—Yudhishṭhira as master of the ceremonies and superintendent of the games (Sabhástára); Bhíma as cook (Paurogava); Nakula as groom or farrier (Aśwabandha); Sahadeva as herdsman (Go-sankhyátṛi); Arjuna as eunuch or companion and teacher of the women (Shaṇḍaka); and Draupadí as servant-maid and

* This scene forms the subject of a celebrated poem by Bháravi called the Kirátárjuníya.

† Since writing the above I have received from Dr. Muir the greater portion of the 4th volume of his Sanskrit Texts, now passing through the press. Part of the episode has been translated by him at p. 194.

needle-woman (Sairindhrí, 77). Before offering themselves to Viráṭa, they deposited their bows and weapons in a Samí-tree growing in a cemetery, and hung a dead body in the branches to prevent any one from approaching it (170. 2147). Yudhishṭhira called himself a Bráhman and took the name of Kanka (23); Arjuna named himself Vṛihannalá (54), and as a eunuch (*tṛitíyám prakṛitim gataḥ*) adopted a sort of woman's dress, putting bracelets on his arms and ear-rings in his ears (53), in order, as he said, to hide the scars caused by his bow-string (52). He undertook in this capacity to teach dancing, music, and singing to the daughter of Viráṭa and the other women of the palace (305), and soon gained their good graces (310).

Viráṭa's capital was called Matsya (or sometimes Upaplavya). There, four months after the arrival of the Páṇḍavas, a great festival was held, at which a number of wrestlers (*malla*) exhibited their prowess. Bhíma then astonished Viráṭa by dashing to the ground and killing the strongest of the wrestlers named Jímúta (362). Ten months of the year thus passed away (373), when one day Draupadí, who acted as servant-maid to the queen Sudeshṇá, was seen by Viráṭa's general named Kíchaka. He fell in love with her (376), and tried every artifice to seduce her without effect, till at last, pretending to favour his advances, she agreed to meet him at a certain dancing-room (*nartanágára*, 735), having first consulted with Bhíma, who dressed himself in her clothes, kept the assignation for her, and had a tremendous fight (*báhu-yuddha*) with Kíchaka, pounding him with his fists into an undistinguishable mass of flesh. Bhíma then returned privately to his kitchen (786), and Draupadí to explain the death of Kíchaka, declared that he had been killed by her husbands, the Gandharvas (787). Upon this the relatives of Kíchaka made a great uproar, and attempted to burn Draupadí with the body; but Bhíma came to her rescue, tore up a tree* for a weapon, and slew more than a hundred men.

The scene now shifts and takes us back to Duryodhana and the Kurus. The spies who had been sent to ascertain, if possible, the retreat of the Páṇḍavas, and so prevent the fulfilment of the compact which required them to preserve their incognito, returned without discovering them. Having heard, however, the story of the death of Kíchaka, the spies repeated it at an assembly. Upon this, Suśarman king of Trigarta, whose country had been often ravaged by Kíchaka, proposed to make a raid into Viráṭa's territory for the sake of plunder, and to carry off his cattle (980). This he did (999), and Viráṭa, accompanied by all the Páṇḍavas except Arjuna (their thirteenth year of exile being just about to expire, 1001), invaded Trigarta to recover his property (1036). A great battle was fought, and Viráṭa was taken prisoner by Suśarman (1076). Bhíma as usual tore up a tree and prepared to rescue him; but Yudhishṭhira advised him not

* This was Bhíma's favourite way of exhibiting his enormous strength.

to display his strength too conspicuously, lest he should be recognized (1084). He then took a bow, pursued Suśarman, defeated him, released Viráṭa, and recovered the cattle (1117). Viráṭa then expressed his gratitude to the Páṇḍavas (whose real names he was still ignorant of) and promised them rewards (1132).

In the mean time, while Viráṭa and the four Páṇḍavas were still absent at Trigarta, Duryodhana and his brothers made an expedition against Viráṭa's capital, Matsya, and carried off more cattle. Uttara (called also Bhúminjaya) the son of Viráṭa, (in the absence of his father,) determined to follow and attack the Kuru army, if any one could be found to act as his charioteer. Vṛihannalá (Arjuna) undertook this office (1227), and promised to bring back fine clothes and ornaments for Uttará and the other women of the palace (1226). When they arrived in sight of the Kuru army, the courage of Uttara (who was a mere youth) failed him; he refused to fight (1241), and jumping from the chariot, ran away (1258). Vṛihannalá pursued him, forced him to return, and made him act as charioteer (1279), while he himself (Arjuna) undertook to fight the Kauravas. Then the usual prodigies took place, terror seized Bhíshma, Duryodhana, and their followers, who suspected that Vṛihannalá was Arjuna in disguise (1286), and even the horses shed tears* (1290). Duryodhana, however, declared that if he turned out to be Arjuna, he would have to wander in exile for a second period of twelve years (1300). Meanwhile Arjuna made Uttara drive to the Śamí-tree, in which his bow Gáṇḍíva and other arms were concealed (1306). There, having recovered his weapons, he revealed himself to Uttara (1371), and explained also the disguises of his brothers and Draupadí. Uttara, then, to test his veracity, inquired whether he could repeat Arjuna's ten names, and what each meant (1373). Arjuna enumerated them (Arjuna, Phálguna, Jishṇu, Kiríṭin, Swetaváhana, Bibhatsu, Vijaya, Kṛishṇa, Savya-sáchin, Dhananjaya), and explained their derivation † (1380—1390). Uttara then declared that he was satisfied, and no longer afraid of the Kuru army (1393).

Arjuna next put off his bracelets and woman's attire, strung his bow Gáṇḍíva, and assumed all his other weapons, which are described as addressing him suppliantly, and saying, "we are your servants, ready to carry out your commands ‡" (1421). He also

---

* Compare Homer, Iliad XVII, 426.

† See Arjuna's other names in the last note, p. 96. With reference to note *, p. 19, I should state that the explanation here given of the name Arjuna is Prithivyám chaturantáyám varṇo me durlabhah samah, karomi karma śuklam cha tena mám Arjunam viduh. In the note at p. 96 I have omitted the name Vijaya, but I have alluded to Arjuna's name Kṛishṇa in the note at p. 101. This name is thus explained: Krishṇa ityeva daśamam náma chakre pitá mama, Kṛishṇávadátasya satah priyatwád bálakasya vai.

‡ Compare Rámáyaṇa I. xxix, where these magical weapons also address Ráma. See note, p. 27.

removed Uttara's standard and placed his own ape-emblazoned banner in front of the chariot (1438). Then a great battle between Arjuna and the Kauravas took place, in which the brother of Karṇa was killed by Arjuna (1678). Single combats also took place between Arjuna and the following heroes: Kṛipa (1790), Droṇa (1846), Aśwatthâman (1902), Karṇa (1939), Duhśásana (1989), Vikarṇa (1992), Bhíshma (2040), and Duryodhana (2090). In all these contests Arjuna was victorious. At length the whole Kuru army fled before him (2138), and all the property and cattle of Viráṭa was recovered. Arjuna then told Uttara to conceal the real circumstances of the battle, and to make himself out to Viráṭa as the victor (2145); and having returned to the Samí-tree, he re-deposited his arms and re-assumed the disguise of Vṛihannalá (2150). Next he desired Uttara to send messengers to his father's capital announcing his victory (2157). Meanwhile Viráṭa himself with the four Páṇḍavas returned home from Trigarta; and hearing that Uttara had gone to fight the Kuru army with only a eunuch for his charioteer, was much alarmed for his safety (2174), and dispatched a whole army to aid him. But Yudhishṭhira astonished him by saying that with Vṛihannalá he was more than a match for all the Kauravas, gods, and Asuras together (2176).

Soon afterwards, Uttara's messengers arrived and announced his victory (2177), which so delighted Viráṭa that he ordered the whole city to be decorated, and sent his daughter Uttará with a procession of women and minstrels to meet his son (2189). Meanwhile he called to Kanka (i.e. Yudhishṭhira as the Sabhástára) to bring dice, that he might mark his joy by a game. Kanka advised him not to play, and as a warning related the story of Yudhishṭhira (2195); but in the end they played together, and during the game (2198) Viráṭa began to praise his son's courage. Upon this, Yudhishṭhira hinted that he could have done nothing without Vṛihannalá, which so enraged Viráṭa, that he aimed a severe blow at Yudhishṭhira's nose with one of the dice (2208). The nose bled profusely, but Yudhishṭhira caught the blood in his hands, and Draupadí, who happened to be near, received it in a golden vessel (2211). Soon afterwards Uttara arrived, and seeing Kanka covered with blood, asked the reason (2222). Viráṭa explained, and Uttara then made his father beg Kanka's pardon (2225). The latter was appeased, but declared that if the blood had touched the ground, Viráṭa and all his kingdom must have perished (2227). Viráṭa then broke out into a long eulogy of his son's courage; but Uttara stopped him, and declared that he deserved no credit for the victory, as the son of some deity had forced him to return when he was running away in terror, and had conquered the Kuru army for him (2242). Viráṭa asked where this divine being was (2252). Uttara replied that he had vanished, but had promised to re-appear in a day or two (2254). Vṛihannalá (Arjuna) then gave to Uttara all the garments and costly articles which they had taken in battle (2257). On the third day after this, Viráṭa held a great assembly, at which the five Páṇḍavas attended, and took their seats with the other princes (2262). Viráṭa (who did not yet know their real rank) was at first angry at this presumption (2266): Arjuna then revealed who they were. Viráṭa was delighted, embraced the Páṇḍavas, offered them all his possessions, and to Arjuna his daughter Uttará in marriage. Arjuna declined *, but accepted her for his son Abhimanyu, whose wife she became (2355). The book closes with a description of the marriage festivities, to which Kṛishṇa and Balaráma were invited (2356).

FIFTH BOOK or UDYOGA-PARVA.—This book opens with a description of an assembly of princes called by Viráṭa, at which the Páṇḍavas, Kṛishṇa and Balaráma, were present. A consultation is held as to what course the Páṇḍavas were to take; and Kṛishṇa, in a speech, advised that they should not go to war with their kinsmen until they had sent an ambassador to Duryodhana, summoning him to restore half the kingdom (24). Balaráma supported Kṛishṇa's opinion (28), recommended conciliation (*sáman*), and suggested that Yudhishṭhira should try another game at dice with Śakuni (36). This speech excited the indignation of Sátyaki, who in an angry tone counselled war (40). Drupada supported him (66), and recommended that they should anticipate Duryodhana by sending messengers to various kings and princes, urging them to collect armies and come to their aid (70). Kṛishṇa approved the counsel of Drupada, but inclined to negotiation rather than to a fratricidal war; he declared that he had only joined the assembled princes to be present at the marriage; and that as he was related to both the Páṇḍavas and Kauravas, he should now return home and await the course of events, without joining either side (93). He accordingly returned to Dwáraká with Balaráma and his followers (100). Viráṭa and Drupada then sent messengers to all their allies, and collected their forces from all parts (102). The sons of Dhṛitaráshṭra did the same. After this, the family-priest of Drupada was dispatched by the Páṇḍavas as an ambassador to king Dhṛitaráshṭra at Hastinápur, to try the effect of negotiation (127).

Meanwhile Kṛishṇa and Balaráma returned to Dwáraká (131). Duryodhana determined to follow Kṛishṇa there, hoping to prevail on him to fight on the side of the Kuru army. On the very day that Duryodhana arrived in Dwáraká, Arjuna came there also, and it happened that they both reached the door of Kṛishṇa's apartment, where he was asleep, at the same moment (135). Duryodhana succeeded in entering first, and took up his station at Kṛishṇa's head. Arjuna followed behind, and stood reverently at Kṛishṇa's feet (137). On awaking, Kṛishṇa's eyes first fell on Arjuna (138).

* Giving as his reason that she had trusted to him like a father when he had lived with her in the women's apartments, as eunuch (2328).

He then asked them both the object of their visit. Duryodhana thereupon requested his aid in battle, declaring that although Kṛishṇa was equally related to Arjuna, yet that, as he (Duryodhana) had entered the room first, he was entitled to the priority. Kṛishṇa answered that, as he had seen Arjuna first, he should give Arjuna the first choice of two things. On the one side, he placed himself, stipulating that he was to lay down his weapons and abstain from fighting. On the other, he placed his army of a hundred million (*arbuda*) warriors, named Náráyaṇas. Arjuna, without hesitation, chose Kṛishṇa; and Duryodhana, with glee, accepted the army, thinking that as Kṛishṇa was pledged not to fight, he would be unable to help the Páṇḍavas in battle (154).

Duryodhana next went to Balaráma and asked his aid; but Balaráma declared that both he and Kṛishṇa had determined to take no part in the strife* (159). When Duryodhana was gone, Kṛishṇa expressed his surprise that Arjuna should have chosen him (Kṛishṇa), although pledged not to fight (*ayudhyamánam*). Arjuna replied, that he did so in the hope that Kṛishṇa would act as his charioteer, from which he expected to gain as much in prestige as if he had received material assistance. Kṛishṇa then consented to do so (170), and with Arjuna joined Yudhishṭhira, who with his brothers was still living in the country of Viráṭa.

Śalya, king of Madra, and brother of Mádrí, now arrived with a large army to aid his relatives, the Páṇḍavas, but Duryodhana by an artifice contrived to make him pledge himself to take the side of the Kauravas. He, however, promised Yudhishṭhira to assist Arjuna when engaged in single combat with Karṇa, by acting as charioteer to the latter, and discouraging him (215). Śalya then, to console Yudhishṭhira for the sufferings he and his brothers had endured, related, in a long episode, the troubles of the god Indra, his conflict with a three-headed son of Twashṭṛi, named Triśiras, and with the demon Vṛitra, &c. (229—553).

We have next an account of the arrival at Hastinápur of the Bráhman ambassador sent by Drupada and the Páṇḍavas. He made a speech before the assembled Kuru princes (604), calling on Bhíshma and Dhṛitaráshṭra to give back to the Páṇḍavas their paternal inheritance (*paitṛikam dhanam*). He declared that the Páṇḍavas were desirous to forgive and forget (*pṛishṭhataḥ kṛi*) all past wrongs, and to return to their possessions without destroying their kindred in battle. Still, if war was forced on them, they had eleven armies ready to fight (620). Karṇa, in reply to this, made an angry speech, saying, that the Páṇḍavas had brought upon themselves the hardships they had undergone, and that the time was not yet expired during which

* Compare Megha-dúta, v. 51, where Balaráma is described as Bandhu-prityá samara-vimukha.

they were bound by agreement to wander in the forest (636). "Duryodhana," he added, "would give up the whole earth even to an enemy, if justice required it, but would not yield a fraction through fear" (635). Bhíshma rebuked Karṇa for his fiery speech, and counselled caution, lest, killed by Arjuna in battle, 'they should be made to eat the dust' (640). Dhṛitaráshṭra agreed with Bhíshma, and determined on sending Sanjaya (his charioteer, also called Gávalgaṇi) as an ambassador with kind messages to the Páṇḍavas, to Viráṭa, and to Kṛishṇa (684). Sanjaya accordingly arrived at Upaplavya, where the Páṇḍavas were dwelling with Viráṭa, and delivered the compliments with which he was charged. Yudhishṭhira * made a civil speech in return (690), and asked what message he had brought from Dhṛitaráshṭra. Sanjaya replied, that Dhṛitaráshṭra wished for peace, to which Yudhishṭhira rejoined, that neither did he desire war (738). A long conversation ensued, in which Sanjaya exhorted the Páṇḍavas to pacification (*śáman*). Yudhishṭhira said that he could not abandon his duty (*dharma*), and that he would be guided by the advice of Kṛishṇa. The latter then made a speech (809), in which he expressed himself equally desirous of pacification, but thought it impossible to avoid war, in consequence of the grasping avaricious nature of Dhṛitaráshṭra and his sons (811), and of the wrongs suffered at their hands by Draupadí and the Páṇḍavas (844). He also observed that the duty (*dharma*) of a Kshatriya was to fight. The colloquy ended by Yudhishṭhira sending back the following message to the Kauravas. "Peace and friendship shall be between us, provided that we receive back our share of the kingdom, together with five towns †, one for each of the brothers (935). We are prepared either for peace or for war, for mildness or severity" (938).

Sanjaya then returned to Dhṛitaráshṭra, but being fatigued with his journey (969), declined to deliver his message till the next day in full assembly. This caused Dhṛitaráshṭra to pass a sleepless anxious night; and to while away the time he sent for Vidura, who entertained him with a tedious didactic discourse (contained in the section called *Prajágara-parva*, 972—1564 ‡), at the end of which, Dhṛitaráshṭra asked to be instructed on certain mysterious points relative to the immortality of the soul and its union with the body. Vidura declared that, being the son of a Śúdrá woman, he was prohibited from discoursing on such matters (1569); but a Ṛishi named Sanatsujáta appeared at his summons, and helped to pass the remainder of the night by a long metaphysical disquisition (1578—1790).

---

* I have omitted in note ‡, p. 96, a name of Yudhishṭhira here used, viz. Ajáta-śatru.

† The five townships (*grámáḥ*) claimed by the Páṇḍavas were Kuśasthala (elsewhere Avisthala), Vṛikasthala, Mákandí, Váraṇávata, and Avasána.

‡ Many verses in the Hitopadeśa are taken from this and other moral discourses of Vidura.

Next day an assembly was held at which all the Kauravas were present, and Sanjaya detailed in the most minute manner all that had passed in his interview with the Páṇḍavas*. Considerable confusion then arose among the Kuru party, some counselling war, others peace. This is described at great length. Bhíshma declared that Arjuna as an incarnation of Nara, and Kṛishṇa as a form of Náráyaṇa, were invincible (1936; see Muir's Texts, vol. IV. p. 196). Dhṛitaráshṭra was for conciliation, and blamed Duryodhana and his other sons for their infatuation (2257). Sanjaya described the forces he saw collected on the side of the Páṇḍavas (2233), and enumerated the principal chiefs, viz. Kṛishṇa, Chekitána, Sátyaki (called Yuyudhána†), Satyajit, Drupada, with his son Dhṛishṭadyumna, S'ikhaṇḍin, Viráṭa, with his sons S'ankha and Uttara, Súryadatta, Madiráśwa, Abhimanyu or Saubhadra (son of Arjuna), Járásandhi, Dhṛishṭa-ketu king of Chedi, the five Kaikeyas (brothers), Uttamaujas, Yudhámanyu, &c., of whom Dhṛishṭadyumna (remembering the insult received by his sister) was the most eager for the war, and was continually urging the Páṇḍavas to commence hostilities (2278). The Páṇḍu forces were to be distributed so that each division should be ranged in opposition to certain sections of the Kuru army (2243). Yudhishṭhira was to oppose S'alya king of Madra; Bhíma was to do battle with Duryodhana and his brothers; Arjuna was to be ranged against Karṇa, Aśwatthámán (son of Droṇa), Vikarṇa, and Jayadratha. Other great chiefs on the Kuru side were Bhíshma, Droṇa, Somadatta, Kṛipa, &c.

Before any actual declaration of war, the Páṇḍavas held a final consultation, at which Arjuna begged Kṛishṇa to undertake the office of a mediator, hoping to settle the matter by negotiation (2802). Sahadeva, supported by Sátyaki, advocated immediate war (2862); and Draupadí too, who could not forget the insult she had received (see p. 103, l. 14), deprecated all attempts at conciliation. Arjuna however still persisted in requesting Kṛishṇa to make the attempt, as he (Kṛishṇa) was regarded as equally friendly to both sides (2920). "If Duryodhana," he said, "refuses to listen to your conciliatory language, and to consult his own interest, then let nothing save him from his fate." Kṛishṇa then consented to set out for Hastinápur as mediator.

Then follows a description of his departure in a splendid chariot, accompanied by Sátyaki†, who was told by Kṛishṇa to stow away in the car the śankha, chakra, gadá, and all Kṛishṇa's other weapons, for fear of treachery on the part of Duryodhana (2931). The chariot was followed for a short distance by the Páṇḍavas, and met

* Much matter is here interpolated; for instance, a long speech made by Arjuna, in which he prophecied various incidents of the coming war, and the remorse of Duryodhana.

† Sátyaki, also called *Yuyudhána* and *S'aineya*, was son of Satyaka, and grandson of S'ini (2930). He belonged to the same family as Kṛishṇa.

midway by Paraśu-ráma and various Ṛishis (2984), who informed Kṛishṇa of their resolution to be present at the coming congress of Kuru princes. Kṛishṇa halted for the night at Vṛikasthala (3012), where he received honour from the inhabitants. When Dhṛitaráshṭra heard of his approach, he declared his intention of presenting him with magnificent presents (3040). Duryodhana, however, deprecated all such expressions of devotion, and hinted that he should detain Kṛishṇa as a prisoner (3090). Both Dhṛitaráshṭra and Bhíshma were horrified at this speech, and declared that, both as ambassador and relative, he was worthy of all respect. Next day, all except Duryodhana went out to meet Kṛishṇa; and the latter, thus escorted, entered the house of Dhṛitaráshṭra. He and Vidura honoured him, and made friendly inquiries after the Páṇḍavas (3123). In the afternoon Kṛishṇa paid a visit to his father's sister Kuntí (or Pṛithá, the mother of Yudhishṭhira, Arjuna, and Bhíma), and consoled her in a long conversation (3128—3234). Kṛishṇa then visited the house of Duryodhana, but refused to accept his hospitality or to eat with him (3247). He declared that he would eat with no one except Vidura, to whose house he next went, and was there entertained (3274). Kṛishṇa then told Vidura the object of his journey, and his desire to effect a reconciliation between the rival cousins (3324).

After that, we have an account of Kṛishṇa's retiring to rest in the house of Vidura, and of his performing all the appointed religious ceremonies on awaking in the morning (3334). He then dressed himself, put on the jewel Kaustabha (3343), and set out for the assembly. Next follows a description of the great congress. The Ṛishis, headed by Nárada, appeared in the sky, and were accommodated with seats in the assembly (3370—3375). Duryodhana and Karṇa sat together on one seat, a little apart from Kṛishṇa. The latter opened the proceedings by a speech, which commenced thus: "Let there be peace (*śama*) between the Kurus and Páṇḍavas" (3386): then, looking towards Dhṛitaráshṭra, he said, "It rests with you and me to effect a reconciliation" (3396). When he had concluded a long harangue, all remained riveted and thrilled by his eloquence (3448). None ventured to reply.

Paraśu-ráma then broke silence, and related the story of king Dambhodbhava (3450; see Muir's Texts, vol. IV. p. 198). He ended by declaring that Arjuna and Kṛishṇa were Nara and Náráyaṇa, and therefore invincible (3496).

The sage Kaṇwa then addressed Duryodhana, praised Kṛishṇa and Arjuna, recommended peace, and related the story of Mátali (3511—3710). Duryodhana knitted his brow at this speech, then, to show his scorn, struck his thigh, and looking at Karṇa, burst out into a loud laugh (3711). Upon that, Nárada rebuked his obstinacy, related the history of Gálava, a disciple of Viśwámitra, and that of Yayáti, both of whom suffered by their pride and obstinacy (3720—4116), and recommended him to make peace with the Páṇḍavas (4118). Dhṛitaráshṭra then declared that he concurred in the opinion of the Ṛishis, but that he had no power over his wicked son Duryodhana. He therefore begged Kṛishṇa to try his influence once more. Thereupon Kṛishṇa made another effort to persuade Duryodhana (4128), and was seconded by Bhíshma (4187), Vidura, Droṇa, and Dhṛitaráshṭra, who all joined their entreaties (4194—4231). But all to no effect; Duryodhana only made an angry reply, and refused to give up any territory: "It was not our fault," he said, "if the Páṇḍavas were conquered at dice" (4241). Kṛishṇa's wrath then rose in earnest (4259). Duhśásana, alarmed, said to Duryodhana, "If you will not consent to peace, the Kauravas will deliver you, and Karṇa, and me, bound, into the hands of the Páṇḍavas" (4281). Upon that, Duryodhana rose up and left the assembly, followed by his brothers (4287).

The queen Gándhárí was then sent for, that she might make an effort to appease her son (4315). Acceding to her request, Duryodhana returned to the assembly, his eyes red with anger (4326). Gándhárí then addressed him, entreating him to give up half the kingdom to the Páṇḍavas (4353). Spurning her advice, he went away again in a fury (4364), and consulted with Karṇa, Śakuni, and Duhśásana, how he might seize Kṛishṇa by force and imprison him (4368). Dhṛitaráshṭra suspecting his intention, ordered him to be summoned again to the assembly, and rebuked him sternly (4396). Kṛishṇa then addressing him, said, "You think that I am alone, but know that the Páṇḍavas, Andhakas, Vṛishṇis, Ádityas, Rudras, Vasus, and Ṛishis are all present here in me." Thereupon he laughed aloud, and flames of fire, of the size of a thumb, settled on him. Brahmá appeared on his forehead, Rudra on his breast, the guardians of the world on his arms, Agni was generated from his mouth; the Ádityas, Sádhyas, Vasus, Aświns, Maruts with Indra, Viśwadevas, Yakshas, Gandharvas, and Rákshasas were also manifested around him; Arjuna was produced from his right arm; Balaráma from his left arm; Bhíma, Yudhishṭhira, and the sons of Mádrí from his back; flames of fire issued from his eyes, nose, and ears; and the sun's rays from the pores of his skin* (4419—4430). At this awful sight, the assembled princes were obliged to close their eyes; but the blind Dhṛitaráshṭra was gifted by Kṛishṇa with divine vision, that he might behold the glorious spectacle of his identification with every form (4437). Then a great earthquake and other portents occurred (4439), and the congress broke up. Kṛishṇa, having suppressed his divinity, re-assumed his human form and departed. Before rejoining the Páṇḍavas, he paid a farewell visit to his father's sister Pṛithá, and told her all that had happened (4459). She narrated to him the stories of Muchukunda and Vidulá (4467—4668), after which Kṛishṇa set out on his return. He took Karṇa with him for some distance in his chariot, hoping to

* This remarkable passage, identifying Vishṇu with every thing in the universe, may be a later interpolation.

persuade him to take part with the Páṇḍavas as a sixth brother (4737). But, notwithstanding all Kṛishṇa's arguments, Karṇa would not be persuaded; and, leaving the chariot, returned to the sons of Dhṛitaráshṭra (4883).

We have next an account of an interview between Karṇa and Pṛithá. She revealed to him the story of his birth (see p. 94 of this volume), and begged him not to fight against his half-brothers. A heavenly voice, issuing from the sun, confirmed her story, bidding Karṇa obey his mother (4960). Karṇa at first wavered; but the thought that men would call him a coward for deserting the Kuru party made him resolve not to take part with the Páṇḍavas. He however promised not to join in mortal combat with any but Arjuna (4949).

Kṛishṇa's return to the Páṇḍavas at Upaplavya is next described (8957). He recounted all that had taken place at Hastinápur, and informed Yudhishṭhira that the army of Duryodhana was assembling at Kurukshetra (5095).

Yudhishṭhira, hearing this, proceeded to marshal his forces, which consisted of seven full armies (*akshauhiṇís*), over which the following were appointed generals: Drupada, Dhṛishṭadyumna, Viráṭa, Śikhaṇḍin, Sátyaki, Chekitána, and Bhíma (5101). By the advice of Kṛishṇa, Dhṛishṭadyumna was appointed general-in-chief, to lead them to Kurukshetra, where they formed a camp (5145—5175).

Soon afterwards, Balaráma declared his resolution to retire from the contest. Both Bhíma and Duryodhana, he said, were his pupils in the use of the mace; he had an equal regard for both, and he could not look on while the Kauravas were being destroyed; he should therefore make a pilgrimage to the banks of the Saraswatí, and there wait the end of the war (5348).

We have next a description of the coming of Rukmin, son of the king of Bhoja, to the camp of the Páṇḍavas. He had a wonderful bow, called Vijaya (5359), and offered himself to Yudhishṭhira as an ally.

Then follows an account of how Ulúka was sent by Duryodhana to the Páṇḍavas, with a hostile message, challenging them to battle (5407—5713).

Meanwhile Bhíshma consented to accept the generalship of the Kuru army (5719). Though averse to fighting against his kinsmen, he could not as a Kshatriya abstain from joining in the war, when once commenced. As the oldest warrior on the field *, he was well acquainted with the chiefs on each side, and, at the request of Duryo-

* Bhíshma, though really the grand-uncle of the Kuru and Páṇḍu princes, is often styled their grandfather (*pitámaha*); and though really the uncle of Dhṛitaráshṭra and Páṇḍu, is sometimes styled their father. He is a kind of Priam in caution and sagacity, but like a hardy old veteran, never consents to leave the fighting to others.

dhana, enumerated all the chariots and combatants of both Kauravas and Páṇḍavas (5714—5940).

Bhíshma then told Duryodhana that although he was willing to fight, he could never bring himself either to kill the sons of Kuntí, or to fight with the son of Drupada, Śikhaṇḍin, who was first born as a female, and afterwards changed to a male (5940). To explain his reasons for not fighting with Śikhaṇḍin, he related the story of Ambá, daughter of the king of Káśi, who with her two sisters, Ambiká and Ambáliká, (afterwards wives of Vichitra-vírya, and mothers of Dhṛitaráshṭra and Páṇḍu, see p. 92 of this volume,) had been carried off by Bhíshma at a swayamvara, that he might marry them to his brother Vichitra-vírya (5950).

The eldest, Ambá, on reaching Hastinápur, told Bhíshma that she had affianced herself to the king of Śálwa, and begged so piteously to be released and sent to him, that Bhíshma consented. When, however, she presented herself to her affianced lord, he refused to receive her, hearing that she had been carried off by Bhíshma. Ambá then wandered about disconsolate, not knowing where to take refuge. At last she was told by an ascetic to apply to Paraśu-Ráma (6047). He told her that she should be born in the family of Drupada as a girl, and should afterwards become a man, and kill Bhíshma, in revenge for the disgrace he had brought upon her (7383).

In the course of this long episode we have a description of a single combat between Bhíshma and Paraśu-Ráma (7142), as well as the story of Śikhaṇḍin's birth and transformation (7391).

SIXTH BOOK or BHI'SHMA-PARVA.—Before the armies joined battle, Vyása appeared to his son Dhṛitaráshṭra, who was greatly dejected at the prospect of the war, consoled him, and offered to confer sight upon him, that he might view the combat. Dhṛitaráshṭra declined witnessing the slaughter of his kindred, and Vyása then said that he would endow Sanjaya (Dhṛitaráshṭra's charioteer) with the faculty of knowing every thing that took place, making him invulnerable, and enabling him to transport himself by a thought at any time to any part of the field of battle (43—47).

We have then an account of all the prodigies which occurred before the fight. These exceeded in horror all the usual hackneyed portents. Not only did showers of blood fall (21), not only was thunder heard in a cloudless sky (67), but the moon looked like fire, asses were born from cows, cows from mares, jackals from dogs, &c. &c. (50—113).

Sanjaya then entertained Dhṛitaráshṭra with a long description of the earth in general, and Bhárata-varsha (India) in particular, its geography, botany, zoology, &c. &c. (163—893). Part of this is translated in Wilson's Vishṇu-Puráṇa, p. 179.

The armies now met on Kurukshetra, a vast plain north-west of Delhi; the Kuru forces being commanded by Bhíshma, and the Páṇḍavas by Dhṛishṭadyumna, son of Drupada (832; and see S'alya-parva, 1590). While the hosts stood drawn up in battle-array, Kṛishṇa, acting as Arjuna's charioteer (see p. 109), addressed him in a long philosophical discourse, which forms the celebrated episode called Bhagavad-gítá (830—1532; and see p. 32 of this volume).

It would be useless to detail all the fights between the warriors described in this book, which closes with an account of a terrific conflict between Bhíshma and Arjuna. The latter resorted to what was deemed an unfair artifice, making use of S'ikhaṇḍin, who shot Bhíshma in the breast after his bow was broken by Arjuna (5610). Arjuna then transfixed Bhíshma with innumerable arrows, so that there was not a space of two fingers' breadth on his whole body unpierced (5653). Then Bhíshma fell from his chariot; but his body could not touch the ground, surrounded as it was by countless arrows (5658). There it remained, reclining as it were on an arrowy couch (*śara-talpe śayána*). In that state consciousness returned, and the old warrior became divinely supported (5659). He had received from his father the power of fixing the time of his own death (5674), and now declared that he intended retaining life till the sun entered the summer solstice (*uttaráyaṇa*).

All the warriors on both sides ceased fighting that they might view this wonderful sight, and do homage to their dying relative (5716). As he lay on his arrowy bed, his head hanging down, he begged for a pillow; whereupon the chiefs brought all kinds of soft supports, which the hardy old soldier sternly rejected. Arjuna then made a pillow for his head with three sharp arrows, which Bhíshma quite approved (5735). Soon after this, he asked Arjuna to bring him water. Whereupon Arjuna struck the ground with an arrow, and forthwith a pure spring burst forth (5785), which so refreshed Bhíshma that he called for Duryodhana, and in a long speech begged him, before it was too late, to restore half the kingdom to the Páṇḍavas (5813). He then tried to persuade Karṇa to desert Duryodhana and join his brothers, the Páṇḍavas (5838). When, however, Karṇa refused, Bhíshma told him that his duty as a Kshatriya was to go on fighting (5854).

It is to be observed that this book does not close with the death of Bhíshma. He is supposed to retain life supernaturally, and appears again in both the S'ánti-parva and Anuśásana-parva, where, lying in a moribund state on the bed of arrows shot at him by Arjuna (*śara-talpa*), he yet had strength given him to edify Yudhishṭhira, after the conclusion of the war, with most prolix discourses on the duties of kings, &c. &c.

SEVENTH BOOK or DROṆA-PARVA.—This book is spun out most tediously, and there is much sameness in the interminable descriptions of single combats between the heroes. After the fall of Bhíshma, Karṇa advised Duryodhana to appoint his old tutor Droṇa (who was chiefly formidable from his stock of fiery arrows and magical weapons *) to the command of the army (150). This was accordingly done (173); and we have then a long narrative of battles. The king of Trigarta and his four brothers bound themselves by an oath to slay Arjuna (683); and we have an account of the destruction (782) of these conspirators (*saṃśaptaka*). Innumerable battle-scenes are then described, both single combats (see p. 26 of this volume) and general engagements or mêlées (*sankula-yuddham, tumula-yuddham*), in which the Kuru party sometimes had the advantage.

Abhimanyu (son of Arjuna by Subhadrá) was slain by the son of Duhśásana (1940). A terrific fight took place between Droṇa, Arjuna, and Kṛishṇa. Hundreds of arrows were discharged on both sides; but Arjuna at last retired from the contest, declaring that he could not contend against his old tutor (3250). Then we have an account of how Jayadratha was killed by Arjuna (6275). Yudhishṭhira had his armour pierced by Kṛitavarman (also called Hárdikya), and was obliged to retire from the combat (7395). Ghaṭotkacha (son of the Rákshasí Hiḍimbá by Bhíma) was put to flight by Aśwatthámán (7435). Afterwards occurred the great battle between Ghaṭotkacha and Karṇa, in which the former as a Rákshasa assumed various forms (7995), but was eventually slain (8104). This disaster filled the Páṇḍavas with grief (8178), but the fortunes of the day were retrieved by Dhṛishṭadyumna (son of Drupada), who fought with Droṇa, and succeeded in decapitating his lifeless body, after Droṇa had laid down his arms and saved Dhṛishṭadyumna from the enormous crime of killing a Bráhman and an Ácharya, by transporting himself to heaven in a glittering shape like the sun (8861). His translation to Brahmaloka was only witnessed by five persons (8865), and before leaving the earth he made over his divine weapons to his son Aśwatthámán. The loss of their general caused the flight of the whole Kuru army (8879).

The sage Nárada, who is introduced in this book, gives a short account of the history of Ráma (2224), which is more fully detailed in the Vana-parva (15913).

EIGHTH BOOK OR KARṆA-PARVA.—This is a much shorter book than the last, but various single combats are again described with far too much diffuseness. The grief of the Kurus at the death of Droṇa was profound (52), but they appointed Karṇa general, in his place, and renewed the combat.

A fight took place between Bhíma and Karṇa (2423), in which the latter was struck

* These *ágneyástra* were received by Droṇa from the son of Agni, who received them from Droṇa's father, Bharadwája. See Johnson's Mahá-bhárata Selections, p. 1.

down senseless, but was rescued by S'alya (2438). Karṇa, however, renewed the combat with Bhíma, and a tremendous general engagement ensued, so that the rivers flowed with blood, and the field became covered with mutilated corpses (2550. 3899). Again numbers of warriors bound themselves by oath (*sanśaptaka*) to slay Arjuna, and again were all defeated by him (2608 and 4124). An army of Mlechchhas or barbarians with thirteen hundred elephants was sent by Duryodhana to attack Arjuna, but they were all routed (4133).

The combat between Bhíma and Duhśásana is next described, in which the latter was slain, and Bhíma, remembering the insult to Draupadí, and the vow he made in consequence (see p. 103, line 15 of this volume), cut off his head, and drank his blood, on the field of battle (4235).

Then occurred the great conflict between Karṇa and Arjuna. Arjuna was wounded and stunned by an arrow thrown by Karṇa (4777), and seemed likely to be defeated had not the wheel of Karṇa's chariot come off. This obliged Karṇa to leap down, and his head was then shot off by one of Arjuna's arrows* (4798). His death struck terror into the Kuru army, which fled in dismay (4816), while Bhíma and the Páṇḍu party raised a shout of triumph, which shook heaven and earth (4824).

NINTH BOOK or S'ALYA-PARVA.—This book brings the principal details of the great battles to a conclusion. On the death of Karṇa, S'alya, king of Madra, was appointed to the command of the Kuru army, then much reduced in numbers (9 and 327). A general engagement (*sankula-yuddham*) is described, in which the Kauravas were routed (188). Kripa advised making peace (228); but Duryodhana would not hear of it (264). We have then a description of Bhíma's mace (577), and of the combat between S'alya and Bhíma with this weapon, in which both were equally matched (693; and see p. 25 of this volume). Afterwards a great battle took place between S'alya and Yudhishṭhira. S'alya was at first aided and rescued by Aśwattháman (860), but was eventually killed (919). We have then an account of an attack made on the Páṇḍavas by S'álwa, leader of a band of Mlechchhas. He was mounted on a savage elephant (1067), and the Páṇḍavas gave way before the fury of his attack (1074). Dhrishṭadyumna, however, stood firm, and meeting him, killed his elephant with a blow of his club (1089). Sátyaki then shot off his head with an

---

* This arrow is called in the text *Anjalika* (4788). The arrows used in the Mahá-bhárata are of various kinds, some having crescent-shaped heads. It may be useful to subjoin a list of words for arrow, which occur constantly in the description of battles, as follows: *śara, váṇa, ishu, śáyaka, patrin, káṇḍa, viśikha, nárácha, vipáṭha, prishatka, bhalla, tomara* (a kind of lance), *śalya* (a dart), *ishíká, śilímukha*.

arrow* (1091), and the Páṇḍavas rallying, the Kuru army was in its turn broken (1093). Again the Kuru side gained a temporary advantage, and the Páṇḍu army was thrown into confusion by a storm of arrows discharged by S'akuni (1211). After this the Kauravas suffered continual reverses; one by one the chiefs were slain or put to flight, and only Duryodhana remained on the field (1582). He rallied his scattered forces for a final charge, which led to a complete rout and general slaughter, Duryodhana, Aśwatthâman (son of Droṇa), Kṛitavarman (also called Bhoja), and Kṛipa (see note, p. 97) being the only chiefs of the Kuru army left alive†. Nothing remained of eleven whole armies (1581). Duryodhana, wounded, disheartened, and alarmed for his own safety, resolved on flight.

On foot, with nothing but his mace, he took refuge in a lake, hiding himself under the water, and then, by his magical power, solidifying and supporting it so as to form a chamber around him, and prevent others from entering‡ (1594. 1620). Here he was followed by the other three surviving Kuru heroes, who were informed of his hiding-place by Sanjaya. They called upon him to come out and renew the fight (1692), declaring that if he would join them they would still be more than a match for their enemies. Their colloquy was overheard by some hunters (1676), who gave information to the Páṇḍavas. The latter came to the lake (1742), and finding it impossible to get at Duryodhana, were recommended by Kṛishṇa to resort to stratagem (1749). Yudhishṭhira then commenced taunting Duryodhana, "Where is your manliness? where is your pride? where your valour? where your skill in arms, that you hide yourself at the bottom of a lake? Rise up and fight; perform your duty as a Kshatriya" (1774). Duryodhana answered, that it was not from fear, but fatigue, that he was lying under the water, and that he was ready to fight them all. He begged them, however, to go and take the kingdom, as he had no longer any pleasure in life, his brothers being killed. Yudhishṭhira then continued his sarcasms, till at last, thoroughly roused by his goading words (*vák-pratoda*, 1853), Duryodhana rose up out of the lake, his body streaming with blood and water (1865). It was then settled that a single combat on foot should take place between him and Bhíma with clubs.

When Balaráma heard that his two pupils (see p. 114, l. 20) were about to engage in

* The arrow was of the kind called *bhalla*, see note to the last page.

† Sanjaya was taken by Dhṛishṭadyumna, and would have been killed had not Vyása suddenly appeared and demanded that he should be dismissed unharmed (1605; and compare p. 115, l. 11 from bottom).

‡ So I interpret *astambhayat toyam máyayá* (1621) and *vishṭabhya apaḥ swa-máyayá* (1680. 1739). Duryodhana is described as lying down and sleeping at the bottom of the lake (1705).

conflict, he determined to be present, that he might ensure fair play. Before the fight, Kṛishṇa made another attempt to bring about a reconciliation. He went to Hastinápur, and had an interview with Dhṛitaráshṭra (1974), but returned *re infectâ*.

A long episode is here inserted about the *máhátmya*, or efficacy of tírthas, and especially of those on the sacred Saraswatí (2006). The story of the Moon, who was afflicted with consumption, on account of the curse of Daksha, is also told (2030), as well as the celebrated legend of Vaśishṭha and Viśwámitra (2296). Then follows the description of the great *gadá-yuddha*. The two combatants entered the lists and challenged each other, while Kṛishṇa, Balaráma, and all the other Páṇḍavas sat round as spectators. The usual portents then occurred (3135). The fight was tedious, the combatants being equally matched (see the description of a similar fight between Bhíma and Śalya at p. 25 of this volume). At last Bhíma struck Duryodhana a blow on his thighs, broke them, and felled him to the ground (3292; and see p. 28 of this volume). Then reminding him of the insult received by Draupadí, he kicked him on the head with his left foot (3313). Upon this Balaráma started up in anger, declaring that Bhíma had fought unfairly; it being a rule in club-fights that no blow should be given below the navel (3345). He was, however, calmed by Kṛishṇa, who informed him that the blow on the thighs was fated, being the consequence of a curse pronounced on Bhíma by Maitreya in former days (3357). This did not convince Balaráma, who maintained that Bhíma should ever after be called *Jihma-yodhin* (unfair-fighter), while Duryodhana should always be celebrated as *Riju-yodhin* (fair-fighter). Balaráma then returned to Dwáraká (3365—3370), and the Páṇḍavas with Kṛishṇa entered the camp of Duryodhana, and took possession of it and its treasures as victors (3492).

When Arjuna and Kṛishṇa alighted from their chariot, the ape-emblazoned banner vanished, and the chariot, filled with an internal fire, (caused by the *ágneyástra* of Droṇa [Droṇa-parva, 3227], and only prevented from bursting forth by the presence of Kṛishṇa), was suddenly reduced to ashes (3473).

The five Páṇḍavas, with Sátyaki (see note, p. 111), by the advice of Kṛishṇa (who was prescient of the coming night-attack), took up their abode outside the camp, on the bank of a river (3498), and Yudhishṭhira, afraid of the wrath of Gándhárí, (her son having been vanquished by an unfair blow,) sent Kṛishṇa to Hastinápur to soothe her (3511). Kṛishṇa did so, but foreseeing the treacherous attack about to be made by Aśwatthámán, returned suddenly (3573).

The book closes by an account of how the three surviving Kuru warriors (Aśwatthámán, Kṛipa, and Kṛitavarman), hearing of the fall of Duryodhana, hastened to the place where he was lying. There they found him weltering in his blood (3629), but still alive. He spake to them, told them not to grieve for him, and assured them that he should die happy in having done his duty as a Kshatriya. He then told Kṛipa to fetch a jar of water and to inaugurate Aśwatthâman general (3666). Duryodhana's death, however, is still delayed.

TENTH BOOK or SAUPTIKA-PARVA.—The three surviving Kuru warriors (Aśwatthâman, also called Drauṇi; Kṛitavarman, also called Bhoja; and Kṛipa, also called S'aradvata), leaving Duryodhana still lingering alive with broken thighs on the battle-field, took refuge in a forest (17). There, at night, they rested near a Nyagrodha-tree, where thousands of crows were roosting (36). Aśwatthâman, who could not sleep, saw an owl approach stealthily and destroy numbers of the sleeping crows (41). This suggested to him the idea of entering the camp of the Pâṇḍavas by night and slaughtering them while asleep (*supta* *). He communicated his project to Kṛitavarman and his uncle Kṛipa (see note, p. 97), who were both weary, and recommended deferring the attack till the morning (142). But Aśwatthâman declared that he could not rest till he had avenged his father Droṇa by killing Dhṛishṭadyumna (167; and see p. 117, l. 20). Kṛipa answered, that to slaughter sleeping men could not be right (186). But Aśwatthâman reminded him of various instances of unfair fighting on the part of the Pâṇḍavas;—how Dhṛishṭadyumna had killed Droṇa after the latter had laid down his arms (see p. 117, l. 21); how Arjuna had taken advantage of the accident to Karṇa's chariot, and so killed him (see p. 118, l. 14); how Arjuna had made use of S'ikhaṇḍin in his fight with Bhíshma, and killed him by an artifice (see p. 116, l. 9; and compare S'ánti-parva, 1362); and how Duryodhana had been unfairly struck down by Bhíma in the single-combat with maces. He then set out for the Pâṇḍu camp, followed by Kṛipa and Kṛitavarman (215). At the gate of the camp his progress was arrested by an awful figure, who is described as gigantic, glowing like the sun, dressed in a tiger's skin, with long arms, and bracelets formed of serpents. This was the deity S'iva †; and after a tremendous conflict with him, Aśwatthâman recognised the god and worshipped him (251). Suddenly a golden altar appeared surrounded by multitudes of frightful spirits and goblins (263); Aśwatthâman was appalled, and to appease Mahâdeva entered the fire on the altar, offering his own person as an oblation thereon (306). This appears to have satisfied the god, who preserved his body from harm, and informed him that, having been formerly pro-

---

* Hence the adjective *sauptika*.

† The description of S'iva in this passage is very remarkable. Hundreds and thousands of Kṛishṇas are said to be manifested from the light issuing from his person (224). Most of S'iva's names also are enumerated (252) as follows: Ugra, Sthâṇu, S'iva, Rudra, S'arva, Iśâna, Iśwara, Giriśa, Varada, Deva, Bhava, Bhâvana, S'itikaṇṭha, Aja, S'ukra, Daksha-kratu-hara, Hara, Viśwarûpa, Virûpâksha, Bahurûpa, Umâpati.

pitiated by Kṛishṇa (313), he (Śiva) had hitherto protected the family of Drupada, but that their hour was now come, and he should defend them no more. Upon that he entered the body of Aśwatthâman, which forthwith shone brilliantly, and was surrounded by attendant spirits and Rákshasas (318).

Aśwatthâman then directed Kṛipa and Kṛitavarman to stand at the camp-gate and kill any of the Páṇḍu army that attempted to escape (327). He himself made his way alone and stealthily to the tent of Dhṛishṭadyumna, who was lying there fast asleep. Him he killed by stamping on him, declaring that one who had murdered his father—a Bráhman and an Áchárya—was not worthy to die in any other way (342). Aśwatthâman then killed Uttamaujas when asleep (353), and afterwards Yudhámanyu (356), and many other warriors who had no power to resist, believing themselves to be attacked by a Rákshasa. The five sons of the Páṇḍavas by Draupadí (see their names, second note, p. 100), hearing of the death of Dhṛishṭadyumna, now attacked Aśwatthâman, and were all successively killed by him (372—378). Next he killed Śikhaṇḍin (383), the whole family of Drupada, and hundreds of others, murdering and mutilating some when half-asleep and others as they attempted to fly. Those who escaped by the gate were slain by Kṛipa and Kṛitavarman (425). Such was the carnage that the ground was covered with thousands of dead bodies (432), and Rákshasas flitted about devouring the mutilated corpses (452). After killing every one in the camp and destroying the whole Páṇḍu army (the five Páṇḍavas themselves with Sátyaki and Kṛishṇa excepted, they being stationed outside the camp, see p. 120, l. 28), Aśwatthâman joined his comrades, and they all three proceeded to the spot where Duryodhana was lying. They found him still breathing (*kinchit-práṇa*, 480), but weltering in his blood and surrounded by beasts of prey. Aśwatthâman then announced to him that he was avenged, as only seven of the Páṇḍu army were now left (viz. the five Páṇḍavas, Sátyaki, and Kṛishṇa*)—all the rest were slaughtered like cattle (531). Duryodhana hearing this, revived a little, and gathered strength to say, "Not even Bhíshma or Karṇa or Droṇa did for me what you have done, farewell! we shall meet again in heaven" (*swasti prápnuta bhadram vaḥ swarge naḥ sangamaḥ punaḥ*). He then expired; his spirit rising to heaven and his body entering the ground (536). The three Kuru chiefs, as morning dawned, returned to their own city. Thus perished the armies of both Kurus and Páṇḍavas (540).

Meanwhile the charioteer of Dhṛishṭadyumna, who had by some means escaped the slaughter, conveyed the news to the Páṇḍavas. When Yudhishṭhira heard of it, and of the death of his own son, he fell down in a swoon. They then proceeded to the camp, where the sight of their slaughtered kindred and army moved them

* To these should be added the charioteer of Dhṛishṭadyumna.

deeply. Draupadí was sent for, and was so affected at the death of her five sons, that she made Bhíma promise to take revenge on Aśwatthámán and bring her the jewel on his head. He accordingly set out with the intention of killing him (602), and was followed by his brothers and Kṛishṇa. When Aśwatthámán saw them approaching, he hurled towards them a fearful arrow (*ishíka*), called *Brahma-śiras*, which he had received from his father Droṇa, and which would have burnt up the three worlds (669) had not the Ṛishis, Nárada, and Vyása interposed. They prevented any further fighting, and settled the matter by requiring Aśwatthámán to give up the jewel on his head, which Bhíma then made over to Draupadí (748). The book ends by Kṛishṇa's explaining to Yudhishṭhira the assistance that Śiva had rendered to Aśwatthámán in his night-attack (765). Kṛishṇa also gave a curious account of the part which Brahmá wished Śiva to take in the creation of all living beings, and of the delay occasioned by a long penance performed by Śiva immersed in water (770).

ELEVENTH BOOK or STRI'-PARVA.—Dhṛitaráshṭra was so overwhelmed with grief for the death of his sons (194), that his father Vyása appeared to him and consoled him by pointing out that their fate was pre-destined, and that as mortals they could not escape death (205—211). He also declared that the Páṇḍavas were not to blame (228); that Duryodhana, though born from Gándhárí, was really a partial incarnation of Kali * (*Kaler anśa*, 223); and that he and his brothers had perished through their own fault (*átmáparádhát*).

Vidura also comforted the king with his usual sensible advice, and recommended that the *preta-káryáṇi* (funeral ceremonies) should be performed (252). Dhṛitaráshṭra then ordered carriages to be prepared, and with the women proceeded to the field of battle (269). On his way he met the three surviving Kuru chiefs, Kṛipa, Aśwatthámán, and Kṛitavarman, who informed him of their successful night-attack and destruction of the Páṇḍu army (300). Then, leaving him, these three took leave of each other and made good their escape; Kṛipa taking refuge at Hastinápur, Kṛitavarman (also called Bhoja and Hárdikya) returning to his own kingdom, and Aśwatthámán retiring to the hermitage of Vyása.

The five Páṇḍavas and Kṛishṇa now came to meet Dhṛitaráshṭra, who pretending a return of affection for them, suddenly formed the resolution of revenging himself on Bhíma for killing Duryodhana unfairly. He first embraced Yudhishṭhira very warmly, and then requested that Bhíma might come to him, his intention being to hug him like a bear and so squeeze him to death †; but Kṛishṇa, who foresaw his

* So also Śakuni is said to be an incarnation of Dwápara; *Swargárohaṇika-parva*, 166.

† Dhṛitaráshṭra, though blind, was remarkable for his strength; see note *, p. 94.

design, quietly pushed Bhíma aside, and placed an iron image of Bhíma in the blind man's arms. The old king, hoping to demolish his victim by a tremendous embrace, crushed the image to pieces, and fell to the earth covered with his own blood; then immediately repenting of his treachery, he exclaimed, "Alas! Bhíma!" but was consoled by Krishṇa, who explained that he had harmed no one except himself (325—342).

Dhṛitaráshṭra then became reconciled to the Páṇḍavas, and presented them to Gándhárí (360). She, however, would have cursed them had not Vyása suddenly appeared and prevented her (366). Yudhishṭhira then expressed his anguish for having participated in the slaughter of so many relatives, declared he was worthy of her curse, and had no desire either for life, kingdom, or riches (408). Gándhárí upon that became appeased. The Páṇḍavas next embraced and comforted their mother Pṛithá.

We have afterwards a description of the wailings of the queen Gándhárí, and the other wives and women, over the bodies of the slain heroes, as one by one they came in sight on the field of battle (427—755). Their lamentations resemble those of the females over the fallen Rákshasas, in the Yuddha-káṇḍa of the Rámáyaṇa.

In the Śráddha-parva (or upa-parva), at the end of the book, we have an account of the funeral obsequies (*śráddha*) as performed at the command of Yudhishṭhira by Dhaumya, Vidura, and others (779.)

TWELFTH BOOK or ŚÁNTI-PARVA, i.e. the book of Consolation.—This is the longest in the poem, but is chiefly episodical. After the events recorded in the last book, Vyása, Nárada, Kaṇwa, and other Ṛishis presented themselves before Yudhishṭhira and congratulated him on the conclusion of hostilities and his accession to the throne.

Yudhishṭhira answered, "The whole earth has indeed been conquered through reliance on the power of Krishṇa, by the favour of the Bráhmans, and by the might of Bhíma and Arjuna, but deep grief abides in my heart, that lust of dominion should have caused the destruction of my relatives. When I remember the slaughter of my son Abhimanyu and of Draupadí's beloved children, this victory appears to me as bad as a defeat" (13—15). He accordingly expressed his disgust with the world, and his desire to give up the kingdom gained after so much hard fighting. Upon this Vyása and the Ṛishis urged upon him his duty, as a Kshatriya, of governing his subjects (1203). Various stories are told and topics suggested for the tranquillising (*śánti*) of his troubled spirit.

Yudhishṭhira then roused himself and determined to undertake his kingly duties. He entered the city of Hastinápur in triumph, accompanied by his brothers (1386).

All the streets were decorated; and Bráhmans offered him congratulations, which he acknowledged by distributing largesses among them (1410). One Bráhman, however, was an exception. This turned out to be an impostor, a friend of Duryodhana—a Rákshasa named Chárváka—who in the disguise of a mendicant reviled him and the Bráhmans*. He was, however, soon detected; and the real Bráhmans, filled with fury and uttering imprecations, killed him on the spot.

Krishṇa then explained, that in ancient times this Rákshasa, after practising austerities, had obtained from Brahmá, as a boon, security against the attacks of all creatures; but only on one condition, viz. that he should abstain from disrespect to Bráhmans (1430—1442).

After this incident, Yudhishṭhira, seated on a golden throne (1443), was solemnly inaugurated king, and Bhíma was associated with him as heir-apparent (1475). Still restless and uneasy, and his mind filled with doubt and anxiety, Yudhishṭhira wished for advice and instruction, and Krishṇa recommended him to apply to Bhíshma (1574), who remained alive on the field of battle, reclining on his soldier's bed (*víra-śayana*: see p. 116, l. 19), and surrounded by Vyása, Nárada, and other holy sages (1591). Accordingly, Yudhishṭhira and his brothers, accompanied by Krishṇa, Kripa, and others, set out for Kurukshetra (1700), passing mutilated corpses, skulls, broken armour, and other evidences of the fearful nature of the war. This reminded Krishṇa of the slaughter caused by Paraśu-Ráma, who cleared the earth thrice seven times of the Kshatriya caste (1707). His story was accordingly narrated to Yudhishṭhira (1707—1805). Part of it will be found translated in Wilson's Vishṇu-Puráṇa, p. 401. They then approached Bhíshma lying on his couch of arrows (*śara-sanstara-śáyinam*, 1811), and Krishṇa begged him to instruct Yudhishṭhira, and calm his spirit by his sage advice (1843. 1861). Bhíshma replied that, pierced as he was with arrows, he was too weak to talk, and begged Krishṇa to excuse him (1871). Krishṇa then removed the weakness and faintness caused by his wounds, and gave him supernatural strength to speak.

The discourses and episodes which occupy the remainder of this long book are comprehended in three sections: 1. The Rája-dharmánuśásana-parva, or duties of kings. (This commences at l. 1; but the Rája-dharma, as enunciated by Bhíshma, extends only from 1995 to 4778.) 2. The Ápad-dharma-parva, or rules of conduct in adversity (4779—6455). 3. The Moksha-dharma-parva, or rules for obtaining final emancipation (6457—13943).

* See a full translation of this passage, and some valuable remarks thereon, in Dr. J. Muir's paper on Indian Materialists, Asiatic Journal, vol. XIX. part iii. p. 299. Mr. Cowell has lately written an interesting paper on the Chárvákas in the Bengal Asiatic Society's Journal.

It is to be observed, that Krishṇa, Nárada, Vyása, and other Ṛishis join in the didactic discourses contained in the Śánti-parva. At l. 1241 we have some curious rules for expiation (*práyaśchitta*), and at l. 1393 rules for what to eat and what to avoid (*bhakshyábhakshya*). Some of the precepts are either taken from or founded on Manu. For instance, compare l. 6071 with Manu II. 238. Many of the moral verses in the Hitopadeśa will be found in the Śánti-parva; and the fable of the three fishes in the Sandhi is founded on the story at l. 4889.

THIRTEENTH BOOK or ANUŚÁSANA-PARVA, i. e. the book of Precepts.—This is very like the last, and almost as long. Yudhishṭhira, looking at Bhíshma's body covered with arrows, and haunted by the remembrance of the sufferings and slaughter of his kindred, declared that his spirit was still untranquillised, in spite of the soothing discourses and stories contained in the last book. He therefore begged Bhíshma to continue instructing him, in order that, purified by precepts, his soul might be delivered in the next world from the guilt of blood (1—14).

The whole Parva is divided into two very unequal sections; of which the first, or Ánuśásanika-parva, is by far the longest, and extends to l. 7705. In this we have further discourses from Bhíshma and others on the duties of kings, liberality (*dána-dharma*, 2926—4812), rules about fasting (*upavása-vidhi*, 5133), rules about eating, &c. (5594), mixed up with tales, legends, wise axioms, moral and metaphysical disquisitions, and much really sensible, practical instruction on various social and political questions. At the end we are told that Yudhishṭhira, *prakṛitim ápannah*, restored to his usual tranquil frame of mind (7694), wished to return to Hastinápur, and undertake the government. Bhíshma permitted him to do so, but requested him to revisit him as soon as the sun had entered its northern path (*uttaráyaṇa*, 7702). Yudhishṭhira then returned to the city, accompanied by Krishṇa and the Ṛishis.

The second section is called the Swargárohaṇika-parva, and describes Bhíshma's ascension to heaven (7706—7796). Yudhishṭhira dwelt fifty days in Hastinápur, conciliating the affections of his subjects, and recompensing the wives and families of the slain heroes by gifts and largesses (7710). Then, remembering his promise, he returned to Bhíshma, accompanied by his brothers and by Krishṇa, Dhṛitaráshṭra, Vidura, Gándhárí, Pṛithá, &c.

We have then a description of the last scene in the life of Bhíshma, who had been lying for fifty-eight nights on his spiky bed (7732). Surrounded by his relatives, he bade them farewell, and asked Krishṇa's leave to depart (7742—7751). Then suddenly the arrows left his body (7761), his skull divided, and his spirit, bright as a meteor, ascended through the top of his head to the skies (7765). They covered him with garlands and perfumes, and carried him to the Ganges for the performance of the last obsequies. The goddess of the river raised herself from the water, and bewailed her son in a mournful dirge (7780), but was comforted by Kṛishṇa (7788).

FOURTEENTH BOOK or ÁSWAMEDHIKA-PARVA.—On the death of Bhíshma, Yudhishṭhira was so overcome that he fell down on the bank of the Ganges, like an elephant pierced by a hunter (2). Dhṛitaráshṭra and Kṛishṇa tried to rouse him, and the latter recommended him, as a remedy for his grief, to perform sacrifices, to fee Bráhmans, to regale gods and pitṛis with *soma*, to feast guests, &c. (22). Vyása also encouraged him to turn his mind to sacrificial acts, and in support of his advice related various stories, such as that of Marutta (65—290), and the old legend of Indra and Vṛitra (299). Then they all returned to Hastinápur; Yudhishṭhira, calmed and satisfied, assumed the government (359), and prepared for sacrificing.

Meanwhile Kṛishṇa and Arjuna took a tour together (366), and had a long conversation (407), in which the former entertained Arjuna with a variety of curious traditions, and introduced Bráhmans, Ṛishis, and Saints, who repeated legendary narratives and discoursed on mystical topics, such as those discussed before in the Bhagavad-gítá, which Arjuna had forgotten (812). Thus we have a conversation about Moksha-dharma (823), the story of Arjuna-kártavírya and Paraśu-Ráma (817), that of Alarka, &c. &c. (840). This long episode is called the Anugítá (subsequent Gítá).

They then rejoined the rest of the party at Hastinápur (1482), and Kṛishṇa after remaining there a short time set out on his return to Dwáraká, accompanied by Sátyaki. On his way he was met by a certain Muni of great sanctity, named Utanka (1544), who threatened to curse him for having permitted the slaughter of the Kuru race (1556). Kṛishṇa, however, averted the curse by explaining his own divine nature, and his identity with Brahmá, Vishṇu, Indra, and the whole universe (1576). Thereupon Utanka acknowledged the god, and requested him to exhibit himself in his divine form, which Kṛishṇa did (1597). Utanka's story and his reason for wishing to curse Kṛishṇa are then related, and his connection with the sage Gautama and Ahalyá (1625).

On his return to Dwáraká, Kṛishṇa narrated the whole history of the war to his father Vasudeva (1772). He tried to conceal from him the death of Abhimanyu, but Subhadrá found it out (1890); and to soothe their grief, Kṛishṇa told them that Abhimanyu's wife (Uttará) should bring forth a child that should rule the whole earth (1843. 1863).

We have then an account of the preparations for the Aśwamedha (1873). Vyása appeared at Hastinápur, and by his advice Yudhishṭhira did homage to Śiva and Kuvera, and obtained great treasures, golden vessels, and implements of all kinds (1922). Kṛishṇa and Sátyaki, accompanied by Balaráma, Śámba, Kṛitavarman,

Subhadrá, and the Vrishṇis, returned to Hastinápur to be present (1937). Soon afterwards was born (1943) Parikshit, the posthumous child of Abhimanyu (by Viráṭa's daughter Uttará) and the father of Janamejaya (the king to whom the Mahá-bhárata is recited). Parikshit was born dead (1944); but the corpse was taken to Kṛishṇa, who pronounced some remarkable words over it (2026—2032) and brought it to life.

The preparation for the Aśwamedha then commenced in earnest. Vyása urged it in these words,—*Yajaswa vájimedhena vidhivad dakshiṇávatá, Aśwamedho hi rájendra pávanaḥ sarvapápmanám Teneshṭwá twam vipápmá vai bhavitá nátra sanśayaḥ* (2070). Yudhishṭhira requested Vyása to consecrate him by the initiatory ceremonies (*díkshá*), and this was done accordingly at the proper time (2084. 2110. 2620). The horse, according to the usual custom (see note, p. 63 of this volume), was let loose to wander over the earth for a year, and Arjuna was appointed to guard it (2096—2105), while Bhíma and Nakula defended the city (2108). Arjuna had some trouble to defend the horse as it roamed about from one quarter of the compass to the other; and did battle, first, with the people of Trigarta (2142); then with Dhṛita-varman (2157); then with Vajradatta and his elephant (2175—2214); then with the Saindhavas (2222), to the great grief of Duhśalá, daughter of Dhṛitaráshṭra (see p. 95, l. 23 of this volume), who tried to prevent the fighting (2275—2290); then with his own son Babhru-váhana at Maṇipura (2303—2431; and see p. 101, l. 12 of this volume); then with Sahadeva's son Megha-sandhi (2436); then with Chitrángada at Daśárṇa (2471), and with the Nisháḍas and Dráviḍas in the Dakshin or South country (2476); then in the West with the son of Śakuni (2483); till at last the horse ceased from its wanderings and returned to Hastinápur (2510).

Then commenced the sacrifice. The ground was duly measured out (2521), sheds erected, posts fixed, houses for the Bráhmans built, &c. &c. (2521—2525). We have, lastly, an account of the ceremony itself and the largesses to the Bráhmans (2620—2683).

The remainder of this book is taken up with the story of the Bráhman Unchhavṛitti, related by Nakula (2172).

FIFTEENTH BOOK or *ÁŚRAMA-VÁSIKA-PARVA*.—This and the remaining books are comparatively short. The Páṇḍavas and king Dhṛitaráshṭra lived happily together for some time; Yudhishṭhira ruling the kingdom, though deference was still paid to the old blind monarch (60). The father, however, never forgave Bhíma for having killed his son; and was always meditating evil against him (61). Bhíma, also, indulged resentful feelings against Dhṛitaráshṭra, and publicly insulted him (64). At last the old king asked Yudhishṭhira's leave to escape from the troubles of life by retiring to the woods (97). Yudhishṭhira at first refused, and begged to be allowed to go himself, leaving Dhritaráshtra to rule (108). In the end, however, by the advice of Vyása (148), he gave his consent to the departure of Dhritaráshtra, who thereupon proceeded to the forest with his wife Gándhárí (428), Kuntí also (the mother of three of the Páṇḍavas) accompanying them (496). They took up their abode in a hermitage, on the banks of the Ganges (510), where Vidura and others afterwards joined them. They were also visited in their solitude by the Páṇḍu princes and Draupadí, who were solicitous about the welfare of their relatives (637). While resident in the woods, Vidura, by penance, devotion, and complete mental abstraction, obtained release from his mortal body, and union with the supreme spirit (691, 941). Then Vyása consoled Dhritaráshtra, Gándhárí, Kuntí, and the others by a sight of all the warriors killed in the war, whose ghosts he called up from the waters of the Ganges (874). After this the Páṇḍavas, with Draupadí and their followers, returned to Hastinápur (1010).

Two years passed away, when one day the sage Nárada appeared (1011), and informed Yudhishṭhira of the fate of his relatives in the forest—how they had continued to emaciate themselves by penance on the banks of the Ganges at Gangádwára; and how a forest conflagration (*dávágni*) arising, the old king and Gándhárí and Kuntí refused to escape (1029). They sat down and calmly awaited the fire, persuading themselves that by self-immolation they would secure heaven and felicity (1034). Sanjaya (Dhritaráshtra's charioteer) alone escaped, and retiring to Himavat, died there (1044).

The news of this calamity affected the Páṇḍavas deeply. They broke out into lamentations, execrating themselves, their kingdom, and their hardly-won triumph (1050). This prepares us for the final catastrophe in the seventeenth and eighteenth books.

SIXTEENTH BOOK or MAUSALA-PARVA.—In this is narrated the death of Krishṇa and Balaráma, their return to heaven (261), the submergence of Dwáraká by the sea (217), and the self-destruction of Krishṇa's family through the curse of some Bráhmans. The curse is narrated, 15—21, thus: "One day Sáraṇa and some others of the race of Vrishṇi and Andhaka saw Viśwámitra, Kaṇwa, and Nárada, rich in penance, come to Dwáraká. Influenced by destiny, they dressed up Śámba (son of Krishṇa and Jámbavatí) as a woman, and placing him in front, approached the sages, and said, 'This is the wife of the illustrious Babhru, who desires a son. Know ye, O sages, what offspring she will produce?' Then the munis, being thus addressed, and feeling themselves insulted by the trick, answered in the following manner: 'This Śámba, the son and heir of Krishṇa, will produce a terrific iron club (*musala*), for the destruction of the race of Vrishṇi and Andhaka; with which you yourselves, while indulging your wicked and cruel passions, shall exterminate your whole family, except only Balaráma and Krishṇa. As to the illustrious Balaráma, abandoning his body, he shall enter the ocean, and (the hunter) Jará (or 'old-age') shall pierce the magnanimous Kṛishṇa while reclining on the ground.'"

The working of this curse is then described, and will be found also narrated in the Vishṇu-puráṇa (Wilson, p. 606). The club was duly produced from Sámba, but was ground to powder and thrown into the sea (28). The particles of dust, according to the Puráṇa, floated to land, and became grass. A proclamation was then made, that none of the citizens of Dwáraká should thenceforth drink wine or spirits, on pain of being impaled alive (30). But Kṛishṇa did not think fit to counteract what had been predetermined by destiny (24). Fearful omens now occurred, and the sage Uddhava, foreseeing some terrible disaster, went away (67). One day, at a great assembly or festival which took place by desire of Kṛishṇa at Prabhása, the Andhakas and Yádavas (i.e. the race of Kṛishṇa) indulged in the forbidden liquor (71). Balaráma and Kṛitavarman sat drinking together near Kṛishṇa on one side, Sátyaki and others on the other (72). Then Sátyaki taunted Kṛitavarman for his treachery in assisting Aśwatthámán to kill the sleeping Páṇḍavas (74; and see p. 122, l. 17). This led to a quarrel, in which Sátyaki cut off Kṛitavarman's head. Upon that the Andhakas attacked and killed Sátyaki (88), and the quarrel became general. Fathers killed sons, and sons fathers (97). Kṛishṇa also, seeing his own son and Sátyaki dead, became infuriated, and plucked a handful of grass, which was turned to an enormous club (92). Then the others also in their fury plucked the grass or rushes (*eraká*), which turned to clubs (95), and with these they slaughtered each other; till none were left but Kṛishṇa and Balaráma. Among the slain were Kṛishṇa's sons, Sámba, Chárudeshṇa, and Pradyumna, and the latter's son Aniruddha (100). Kṛishṇa, overcome with grief and vexation, sent his charioteer Dáruka to inform the Páṇḍavas. Then, leaving Balaráma standing under a tree near a wood, in profound abstraction, Kṛishṇa went to his own father Vasudeva, and begged him to take care of all the women in Dwáraká until the arrival of Arjuna; adding, that he (Kṛishṇa) intended to devote himself to penance along with Balaráma for the rest of his life (114). On returning, however, he found Balaráma expiring; a large serpent coming out of his mouth and entering the ocean* (117). Soon afterwards, while Kṛishṇa was reclining on the ground in deep meditation, a hunter named Jará [according to the Vishṇu-puráṇa, his arrow was tipped with a piece of iron from a part of the club that had not been reduced to powder] mistook him for game, and, shooting at his foot, pierced the sole (126). Kṛishṇa then abandoned his mortal body, and returned to heaven (130).

When Arjuna heard of this calamity from Dáruka he set out for Dwáraká, and

* Balaráma is often regarded as an avatár of the great thousand-headed serpent Ananta.

great was his grief at the sight of the slaughter. He first sought out Kṛishṇa's father, Vasudeva (here called Ánakadundubhi), whom he found distracted by sorrow. Arjuna then told him of his intention to remove from Dwáraká all the old men, women, and children who were left alone (181). He next searched for the bodies of Kṛishṇa and Balaráma, caused them to be burnt, and performed the usual funeral rites (207, 208). Arjuna then lodged for the night in Kṛishṇa's house, and next morning Vasudeva died (by self-immolation, according to the Vishṇu-puráṇa, p. 613), his four wives (Devakí, Rohiṇí, Bhadrá, and Madirá) burning themselves with his body (194). Some of Kṛishṇa's wives (viz. Rukmiṇí, Gándhárí, Haimavatí, and Jámbavatí) also burnt themselves; but Satyabhámá and others retired to the woods (249). Arjuna then commenced removing all the surviving population to Indraprastha. As they departed from Dwáraká it became submerged by the ocean (217).

On their road to Indraprastha, they made a circuit and passed through the Panjáb (*Pancha-nada*, 221). Here they were attacked by a band of freebooters*, who were attracted by the sight of so many women and so much treasure defended by one warrior (224). Arjuna protected the women as well as he could; but to his astonishment found that he had lost his wonted vigour, and that even the arrows from Gáṇḍíva failed to take their usual effect. As a last resource, he was obliged to strike the robbers with the horn of his bow (238); but in spite of all his efforts, they succeeded in carrying off many of the women (239).

The remainder of the women, old men, and children were established by Arjuna, some at Mártikávata in Kurukshetra, some at Indraprastha, with Vajra (great grandson of Kṛishṇa) as their ruler (245—248).

Arjuna then went to Vyása, and related the story of his own defeat, attributing the loss of his vigour to the death of Kṛishṇa, bereaved of whom he did not wish to live (277). Vyása comforted him, declaring that it did not become him to grieve at the working of destiny (279—290).

SEVENTEENTH and EIGHTEENTH BOOKS, called MAHÁPRASTHÁNIKA-PARVA and SWARGÁROHAṆIKA-PARVA.—In these we have the fine description of the renunciation of their kingdom by the five brothers, and their journey towards Indra's heaven in mount Meru, which has been already given at p. 29 of this volume.

* *A'bhíras*, who were shepherds and herdsmen as well as marauders.

KHILA-HARIVANS'A-PARVA, i. e. the supplementary book on the history of Krishṇa and his family*. This supplement, which is a comparatively modern addition to the Mahá-bhárata, consists of no less than 16,374 verses, comprised in three subordinate parvas. The following are the principal contents of the first, or Harivanśa-parva. A description of the creation of the world and of all creatures (27). The story of Prithu (283). An account of the various Manus and Manwantaras (407) and Yugas (516). History of the solar race—birth of Vivaswat and his family (545). Story of Dhundumára (690). Birth of Gálava (728). History of Triśanku (749). Account of the birth of Sagara and others of the solar family, including Rámachandra, son of Daśaratha (797—822). The creation of the Pitṛis, with allusions to the śráddha ceremony, sacred to them, as related by Bhíshma while reclining on his bed of arrows (845; and see p. 116 of this volume). History of the lunar race—Atri, Soma, Budha (1312), Purúravas (1364). The family of Ámávasu, son of Purúravas, Gádhi (1429), Viśwámitra (1457) and his son S'unahśepha† (1471). The family of Áyus, son of Purúravas, viz. Nahusha (1476), Yayáti (1600). Line of Puru, son of Yayáti, viz. Dushmanta, husband of S'akuntalá and father of Bharata (1723), Ajamíḍha (1756), Jarásandha (1811), S'ántanu (1823), Vyása (1826), Dhṛitaráshṭra and Páṇḍu and their sons (1826). Line of Yadu, viz. Sahasrada (1843), Haihaya (1844), Kanaka, Kritavírya, Kritavarman (1850), Arjuna, son of Kritavírya, and therefore called Kártavírya (1852), Vrishṇi and Andhaka (1908), S'waphalka (1912), S'úra (1922), Vasudeva, or Ánakadundubhi ‡, and his sister Prithá (1923—1928). Vasudeva's fourteen wives; the first and best-loved of whom was Rohiṇí, mother of Balaráma (1950), and the seventh Devakí, mother of Krishṇa (1953). Krishṇa's acquisition of the jewel Syamantaka § (2068). Vishṇu's manifestation of himself, and an account of his various incarnations (2200), with his destruction of various daityas or demons (2200—3179).

* Khila means any thing which fills up a hole or vacuum; hence, 'a supplement.' This supplement has been translated into French by M. Langlois, and the translation was published by the Oriental Translation Committee.

† This agrees with the Vishṇu-puráṇa, which also makes S'unahśephas the son or adopted son of Viśwámitra (Wilson, p. 404). As the author of various Súktas, he is called in the Bráhmaṇas, the son of Ajígarta; and in the Rámáyaṇa, he is the son of Richíka; see p. 66 of this volume, note ‡.

‡ So called because drums and tabors (*ánaka*, *dundubhi*) were heard in the sky at his birth, besides the ordinary portent of a shower of flowers.

§ An account of this will be found in my English-Sanskrit Dictionary, under the word Krishṇa.

The second, or Vishṇu-parva, gives a detailed biography of Kṛishṇa. It commences with an account of the Asura Kansa (king of Mathurá and brother of Devakí), and his efforts to destroy the young Kṛishṇa, by shutting up Devakí and killing her offspring (3214). We have then all the well-known incidents in the life of Kṛishṇa, beginning with his childhood, which are also detailed in the tenth book of the Bhágavat-puráṇa, and its Hindí paraphrase, the Prem Ságar*, as well as in the fifth book of the Vishṇu-puráṇa (Wilson, p. 491).

The third, or Bhavishya-parva, commences with an account of the future condition of the world, and of the corruptions that would prevail during the Kali-yug†, especially at its close (11132). A very similar description will be found in the Vishṇu-puráṇa (Wilson, p. 622). Among other characteristics of the age, the distinctions of caste were to be destroyed (11133), the seasons were to be reversed (11141), and infidel opinions were to be every where prevalent (11176).

We have next a curious section called Paushkara (11279). In this is described the production of the lotus (*pushkara*) out of the navel of Vishṇu, while sleeping on the waters, and the development of the globe and all material objects out of the various parts of the plant (11444—11460), Brahmá himself, with four faces and a white turban, being seated in the middle of it (11470).

The latter portion of the Bhavishya-parva contains an account of the Váráha, Narasinha, and Vámana, incarnations of Vishṇu (12278, &c.), and of his journey to Kailása for the purpose of worshipping Śiva and performing penance (14393).

The book closes with a metrical summary of all three parvas (16325—16356).

---

* The details will be found in my English-Sanskrit Dictionary, under Kṛishṇa. I have not thought it worth while to repeat them here.

† The Kali-yug was supposed to commence at the death of Kṛishṇa. The events of the Mahá-bhárata must therefore have taken place during the third or Dwápara age, and those of the Rámáyaṇa at the end of the second or Tretá age. From the gambling scene in the Second Act of the Mṛichchhakaṭi, it is probable that the names of the four ages are connected with throws of dice; Tretá being the throw of three, which was the second best throw, and Dwápara the throw of two, which was a worse throw, the worst throw of all being Kali. The Hindú notion appears to have been that gambling prevailed especially in the Dwápara and Kali *yugas*. In the episode of Nala, the personified Dwápara enters into the dice, and the personified Kali into Nala himself, who is then seized with the fatal passion for play. On the subject of the four *yugas*, see Muir's 'Sanskrit Texts,' vol. I. p. 37; Weber's Ind. Stud. I. 286 and 460.

ORIENTAL WORKS

BY

MONIER WILLIAMS, M.A.,

BODEN PROFESSOR OF SANSKRIT IN THE UNIVERSITY OF OXFORD.

A PRACTICAL GRAMMAR OF THE SANSKRIT LANGUAGE, arranged with reference to the Classical Languages of Europe, for the use of English students. 2d edition, published at the Oxford University Press, 1857. *Price* 15*s*. 6*d*.

STORY OF NALA, a Sanskrit poem, with full vocabulary, and Dean Milman's translation. Published at the Oxford University Press, 1860. *Price* 15*s*.

AN ENGLISH AND SANSKRIT DICTIONARY. Published by the Court of Directors of the East India Company. (W. H. Allen, 1851.)

VIKRAMORVASI', a Sanskrit drama, published as a class-book for the East India College. (Stephen Austin, Hertford, 1849.)

S'AKUNTALA', a Sanskrit drama. The Devanágarí recension of the text, with critical notes and literal translations. (Stephen Austin, 1853.)

A FREE TRANSLATION IN ENGLISH PROSE AND VERSE OF THE SANSKRIT DRAMA S'AKUNTALA'. 3d edition. *Price* 5*s*. (Stephen Austin, 1856.)

AN EASY INTRODUCTION TO THE STUDY OF HINDÚSTÁNÍ. *Price* 2*s*. 6*d*. (Longmans, 1859.)

ORIGINAL PAPERS illustrating the history of the application of the Roman alphabet to the languages of India. (Longmans, 1859.)

BÁGH O BAHÁR, the Hindústání text, with notes, and an Introductory Essay on the application of the Roman alphabet to the languages of India. *Price* 5*s*. (Longmans, 1859.)

HINDÚSTÁNÍ PRIMER. *Price* 1*s*. 8*d*. (Longmans.)

A PRACTICAL GRAMMAR OF THE HINDÚSTÁNÍ LANGUAGE. *Price* 5*s*. (Longmans.)

A SANSKRIT MANUAL, containing the Accidence of Grammar, and Progressive Exercises for composition. *Price* 5*s*. 6*d*. (W. H. Allen and Co., 1862.)

THE STUDY OF SANSKRIT IN RELATION TO MISSIONARY WORK IN INDIA: a lecture delivered before the University of Oxford, on April 19, 1861. With notes and additions. *Price* 2*s*. (Williams and Norgate, London: J. H. and James Parker, Oxford.)

Shortly to be printed.

A DICTIONARY, SANSKRIT AND ENGLISH, in one volume.

www.ingramcontent.com/pod-product-compliance
Lightning Source LLC
Chambersburg PA
CBHW031122020726
47495CB00007B/2314
* 9 7 8 3 7 4 1 1 2 7 1 0 6 *